MW01122767

WAVERLY ESTATE
GHOST DANCE

MT Maliha

Relax. Read. Repeat.

WAVERLY ESTATE: GHOST DANCE
By MT Maliha
Published by TouchPoint Press
Brookland, AR 72417
www.touchpointpress.com

ISBN-10: 1-946920-77-0
ISBN-13: 978-1-946920-77-5

Editor: Kimberly Coghlan
Cover Design: Colbie Myles, colbiemyles.net
Front cover image: Adobe Stock, Horror ghost girl in abandoned building by bonciutoma
Background images: Provided by MT Maliha

Visit the author's website at www.mtmaliha.com/

First Edition

Printed in the United States of America.

This book is dedicated to the ghosts dwelling in our closets, those that live under our beds, and voices that need to be heard.

The names within this book have been changed to protect the perpetually haunted.

Other books by MT Maliha

The Wild Dogs of Winter
The Meek
Divorce By Murder
Lillian Shay

Connect with the author at maureen@post.com

PROLOGUE

Waverly Mansion stood atop a rocky precipice high above The Hudson River. Its fading stone and shutter-less windows looked west from behind tall elm and hemlock trees that had, for more than two hundred years, been thrashed by wind and tempestuous storms. Their exposed roots reached out like arthritic fingers toward the river and then sharply down the cliff she road alone, where they met among boulders that held the earth back, or perhaps the mansion itself, from tumbling into the brackish waters.

Brynn Waverly, avoiding too long a look as she drove up the overgrown driveway to the mansion, sighed and focused on the lovely rows of hemlocks that stood on each side and ended at the front courtyard of the estate. She forced herself up and out of her car and went straight up the steps that led to the front doors of Waverly Mansion. Stepping inside, she saw that her attorney was exactly right: the words cold, austere, and out of date came to mind.

She had inherited Waverly Estate from her father, whom she had never met. If not for the sense that she might get to know him if she took possession of it as his will intended, she would have entirely passed on the idea and donated it to the state of New York.

The great turrets and many angled roof surfaces were in good repair thanks to her father's recent remodeling, and even though the bones of the enormous forty-room mansion were judged sturdy, she disliked the idea of engaging in any major overhaul to bring it up to date. Built somewhere around 1785, the estate had seen war and birth and death. It had passed between Waverly descendants without fail, and she was next in line. No other Waverly was alive to take ownership of it.

She wandered around the first floor and found an immense room, which she assumed was the formal dining room. Sitting down on a dusty chair, she kicked her heels off. From that vantage point at the head of the long, wood table, she could easily view portraits of her ancestors that lined the walls. They bore grim expressions, and she found it rather distasteful. But the portraits, she thought, were something to deal with down the road. Miles down the road by the looks of things.

The ride from Boston had been long and the traffic bumper to bumper for most of the way. But the spring sun was shining and she needed a break from her job and her husband and her ordinary life. Laying her head down to her arms and closing her eyes, she wished that she had decided to take a hotel room instead of staying alone in the mansion. But she was promised by the family attorney that a woman who tended the gardens would be along before dark and stay the night to get her acquainted with the place. Maybe, she thought, it wouldn't be so bad.

"Hello." A young woman with long hair that hung into her face suddenly appeared beside her.

She jolted upright. "Oh! You scared the hell out of me. Are you...you're the gardener?"

The woman smiled pleasantly at her. "I garden."

"Sit! My name is Brynn. What's yours?" She thrust her hand out to the woman who just stared at it. "Oh, okay." She laughed and withdrew it.

"You can call me Lilly."

"Okay, then. Hello, Lilly. Pleased to meet you. I was just wondering about this place. Do you know anything much about its history? I'd love to hear about it."

Lilly laughed softly. "I know its entire account. Would you like to hear it?"

"Now?" she asked.

"Yes."

"Okay." Brynn laughed. "Let's hear it then." As she stared into the woman's strange green eyes and waited, she wondered if the woman was a tad crazy.

"I shall start from the beginning," Lilly said.

"That's a fine place to start." She smiled and leaned back in her chair.

"Good, but be warned, it isn't all pleasant, miss. I will tell you things about your forefathers that may cause you to wish you didn't come to this place. Or, you may even find yourself wishing you did not carry the name of Waverly."

"I'm intrigued! Go on. Tell it all." The truth was, she didn't think anything could make her feel the way Lilly described, but she was always up for a good story.

"I think I shall begin with a death."

"Lovely," Brynn said and rolled her eyes.

One

Garson Waverly died on November 12th 1858 at the age of sixty, exactly three months past the date of his birth. He was utterly alone when he left the world—without even his favored dog at his side. Some swore that he was en route to hell, and yes, he heard the talk, but he disregarded the barbs and traveled on with no regrets. Others' opinions didn't bother him, even as he lay dying because Garson Waverly had divined the perfect path that would secure a final word—*his word*. None other mattered. *Ah*, he had thought, *if only I could be alive to see it.* Though his life was ending, their trouble was just beginning.

He did not bother himself worrying that things he had done and said would be revealed. He had used a lifetime trying to conceal the very things he knew would one day be known. Upon discovering all of his secrets, chaos would reign—even if it took many years. Hopes would be dashed; fortunes won and lost, and what seemed most predictable about their silly lives would suddenly become particles of dust.

Their greed would see to the rest.

The domed ceiling above his bed bore paintings he had commissioned during one of his extended visits to the north of France. For hours before he died, he stared at the blues and greens of the landscapes in the dome, which depicted black steeds and bare-chested women with long flocks of golden hair that drifted toward unknown places across a sea. In the distance, sailboats and skiffs coasted away from shores through peculiar mists; mainsails occupied by wind, keels bashed with teal and white wave.

He spoke little during his final days, capable of only a slight gesture or a grunted command to his nurse. He accepted the rare visitor to his bedroom suites, which even rarer included visits from his son, Martin, who had taken up residence in the estate's cottage. In Garson's last hours, his expression turned to one of mournful ache, and despite his nurse's best efforts, she reasoned there'd be no coming back from where his mind had wandered. Soon, he said nothing at all.

When he was found dead, his gaze still transfixed on the dome, his eyes appeared more alive than dead for perhaps the first time in his life. Even he would have enjoyed the ultimate irony.

Garson and his wife, Hannah, were frequent visitors to a villa they owned in France. There, at his wife's urging, he commissioned the art that he transfixed upon in his last days. Garson did not find much use in art, unless he thought it would bring his massive castle-like estate additional admiration. But in the case of her newest whim, he had simply given Hannah her way. While he rarely did anything she wished, he thought it best to occasionally permit her what she asked. In exchange for what he viewed as his magnanimous gift of agreement, he might be allowed to take pleasure from her. He knew she found little to delight in him and had recently taken to sleeping in a different bedchamber.

Hannah, younger by thirty years and beautiful in an inexplicable way that some found uncomfortably startling, possessed unreadable, deep blue eyes that peered from the depths of tightly curled black hair and china-white skin. Some found it comforting that she refused to look into the eyes of those with whom she conversed, since whether viewed as witch or angel, her eyes were prisons from which there was no escape. She did not appear to be troubled or curious that she might have missed something significant or pleasurable in another's countenance. She, like her husband, never did so unless angered. Some said she had become like Garson during their seven-year marriage, and others said that he'd chosen her because she was just as he was—remote, passionless, and perhaps, as some whispered, without a soul. He had no doubt that she viewed his vast wealth as his most titillating quality, but the trade-off worked just fine for him.

Rene Bonhomme, the creator of the last thing on this earth Garson saw, begrudgingly began the paintings in May of 1854 and completed them three years later. Painted on segments of what would become the dome, Rene used oil and layered color washes to achieve the required outcome. During the last month he worked on the paintings, he added a little something more—something he thought righteous and fitting, and the process, however wrought with dangers, gave him great satisfaction to know they would eventually be committed to the medium he painted upon.

Garson was impatient for the art's arrival, which all things considered Bonhomme found amusing, and while Garson frequently sent blistering notes to Rene informing him that he would not be paid if the work was not soon completed, the artist had no inclination to respond. Garson thought it sufficient to threaten rather than simply inquire of the arts' status, and so the notes did not cause Rene to work faster—and neither did he respond in letter. Rather, he found use of the man's wife, whom Garson had left behind to oversee his work, to be a suitable substitution to any response he might have been tempted to give. Until he decided on the new addition.

When the art, which consisted of four parts, was completed to his satisfaction, it was carefully packed with gloved hands and then sailed across the Atlantic to New York City. From there, it was transported by railway and then by tandem flat beds, which were led by four muscled horses, and behind, another four horses, to slow the flat bed's descent when navigating the steep declines of The Catskill Mountains of New York State. It took more than one year for the art to travel to the Waverly Estate. Once delivered, it was masterfully set into place.

Ensconced within the carriage leading the laborious trek toward the Waverly Estate was a little man by the name of Willham Montrose. His peevish expression and tiny, grey-blue eyes set into his nearly bald head and lack of chin, distracted from the fact that he was a deeply sensitive man, albeit one with odd, and what would have been viewed in that century as, perverse predilections. Supporting his spectacled wire-rim glasses, a long and angled nose tilted hard right at its end, giving one the impression that he had sat many years behind easels, since there was no other place that he might comfortably dwell. This was a partially true assessment, for on the whim of Rene, he would scurry away to fetch food or drink or more oil paints from many towns away, without complaint or question.

Upon meeting Willham, Garson had immediately christened him *the little titmouse*, purportedly after a tiny bird that he viewed as energetic and somewhat shy. But his emphasis on the syllable *mouse* was far too emphatic to miss. Garson would never know that Willham was well read and well-traveled, simply because Garson didn't care a lick about the man except where it concerned the art he was there to complete.

Willham had been to ten countries, had studied in London, and had even spent three months in Mexico, right before The Mexican-American War.

He had befriended an Indian tribe while there, which might sound improbable, though he managed it via trickery and use of his fundamental medical knowledge, and successfully, albeit at the end of an arrow, saved the life of an elder chief's wife. He learned about their spiritual nature and was an honored guest to witness the tribe's *Ghost Dance*, a religious ceremony performed in the hopes of ending European and American aggression. Peyote-induced trances, which in his cultured estimation resembled animalistic dances fraught with howls and bare-breasted women, sometimes lasted for several days—the hallucinogenic cactus parts, playing a major role. Tempted to share their experiences during the Ghost Dance, he decided against partaking after seeing a brave thrust himself into the fire, mouth foaming. Afterward, he was sure he had made a right choice.

But traveling back to America to construct the art dome for Garson Waverly, he gained the sense that the so-called civilized master of Waverly was far more bestial than the ones he left in Texas and Mexico. Willham assembled the artwork and Willham who bore the brunt of Garson's endless needling and verbal provocations as he ordered him to speed up the completion of applying the art to the dome, and return to France. Willham wanted to return in equal portion but never once responded to the barrage of insults and demands. He rendered himself deaf and mute. No other boulevard but utter silence existed where he could realistically travel when confronted with Garson's multitude of complaints and commands. It was a method of distancing oneself from needless acts of idiocy he had learned from the Indians. Murder once crossed his mind, but he deemed homicide far too untidy, and the death of the master of Waverly Estate would require he remain many more days at the dreadful place. And then, who would pay him?

It was not as though Willham did a poor job of it all. It was not as though he malingered or gave Garson any cause to complain, but it appeared that the man was most contented when he growled or belittled others. He did not blame the lovely Hannah for her, as he called it, *conference* with his art master. No, he could plainly see that her face became illuminated by something almost otherworldly when she and Bonhomme were together, and having met the priggish, and he dare thought cruel, Mr. Waverly, he could only wonder why she insisted on returning. But such, he thought, were the whims of the rich, and such, he mused, would be his master Rene's undoing if he did not take authority over the situation.

Willham had intended to become a doctor, but his stretch at medical school in England was short-lived. He had witnessed the ongoing and mysterious deaths of the upper classes he had befriended and felt powerless to stop it. If even his professors could not find the reason why they had been stricken and in so many numbers, then how could he be of use? His posh London acquaintances often looked to him for advice regarding the deaths. But Willham, having nothing of import to contribute, used the flimsy rationalization he had titled *frustrated ineptitude* to blame for his departure. It was all a weak disguise for his accurate motive, so poor indeed, that he kept it to himself. Instead, he informed everyone he met that art was his truest passion and he would leave, return to France, and pursue it. But the truth was he had met Rene. He was all Willham could think about. He was all he *wanted* to contemplate.

At one of London's grand balls, a fine woman had become enamored of the dark-haired artist and had taken Rene for what Willham viewed as a pet. There were still slaves a-plenty for her to exploit during that time, had she thought to make use of them. But Annabella Stewart preferred the tall and sophisticated artisan to any of the remaining West Indies slaves traded to London. It was rumored that when she became bored during one of her husband's extended trips abroad, she had taken up with more than one of them, but it was an unmentionable social crime that few could out-right accuse her of, and so it simply was not discussed beyond a rare whisper.

By day, she was the dutiful wife of Colonel Roger Stewart and by night, governess of Rene. It was an open secret that Willham abhorred keeping and finally, finding the entirety intolerable to observe, he arranged a grand reveal of the couple's tryst. It had required a simple letter left for Colonel Stewart, who was, it appeared, the only one who knew nothing of the pair's rendezvous. That very night, while the lovers fumbled about with their undergarments, Rene, tearing at Lady Stewart's ballonet-like pantaloons, and she, tugging furiously at his sash, the very proper Roger Stewart burst into the lovers' borrowed quarters and exploded with rage.

The exquisite but wicked Annabella gathered herself in a flurry of lace and stocking and shoe, and as she ran toward the door, her husband lifted one meaty hand and wrenched her by the hair back into the room. As he held her there, she bent down wailing. Then, as he stared silently at Rene for what must have seemed many moments, and Rene, having had quite enough of it all, slowly gathered his articles, chuckled, placed his hat upon his head, bowed slightly to the couple, and was permitted to saunter out of the loft and out to the rainy street.

That night Willham and Rene met for a drink at a pub some miles away, and Willham, realizing he had concurrently done precisely the correct and incorrect thing for Rene, was quite certain he had entirely done the acceptable thing for himself.

Willham tilted his scraggly head toward Rene's far superior one, and asked, "Shall we go back now?"

Rene laughed and replied, "Yes, I think it's a fine idea. You will be my assistant, and I will teach you all I know about my art. We'll make a fine pair, you and I, sir. A fine pair, indeed."

But Willham was not a fair matching part, not in the way he had hoped, nor would he ever be, as long as women like Annabella stood in his way of appealing to Rene's potential sexual inclinations. In the subsequent two years that followed, he managed to send some of the artist's ladies fleeing, and others, much to Willham's relief, simply became bored and moved on. But Hannah Waverly was a different story. Could it be, he asked himself, Rene had found the woman he could not let go?

He had learned quite enough in medical school to understand methods and means of poisoning. Suggesting it to Rene required properly-placed suggestions delivered with resolute calm and his unique brand of reasoning. Killing Waverly would solve multiple woes, and he had explained it to Rene one night while they sipped brandy by the stone fire at the art studio.

At first blush, he had balked at Willham's suggestion, but as the night grew to dawn, they came to agreement. Willham would travel with the artwork, set it in place, and with the aid of newly acquired knowledge he had derived from the latest medical publications, he would add something additional to the paintings. The substance had killed scores of the London elite. It was a sneaky poison, disguised in the pigments of elegant wallpapers that were all the rage in London at the time. The vibrant and long lasting colors were glorious. Deadly. Arsenic was the ingredient that led to beauty and demise. Merely avoiding contact with the wallpaper was not enough. The flaking of color and substance was sufficient to promote the dastardly eradication of the most distasteful Garson Waverly.

The brilliant emerald greens, fortuitously insisted upon for inclusion in the paintings by Waverly himself, were achieved through application of copper arsenite. Victims were beset with pain, found it increasingly impossible to swallow, and over time, many of the most infirmed or young, succumbed to the poison. With Waverly's particular penchant for letter writing, a simple supplementation of copper arsenite to stamps would ensure success. Had Waverly been a healthier man, the flaking of arsenic from his bedchamber's ceiling would perhaps give him escape. But no, he was not all together well, and it would, the pair surmised, take little to do away with the cantankerous man who was ill of something and appeared much older than he was.

Hannah no longer occupied the bedroom, and they say that it was not frequented by a soul, save for the master of the estate. Yes, said Rene, it would achieve what had previously seemed to be unachievable. Hannah would be free and double her wealth. Rene would soon reside in the magnificent Waverly Estate, and Willham would be free to write or paint or do whatever it was he chose to do. All would be well.

Yes, replied Willham, yes to it all. But, he thought, as he made his way out the door and into the new day, Hannah would then be easily removed. Only then would it all come right for him at last. Only then would he find the happiness he so deserved and earned.

Two

Martin Waverly stood outside the door of his father's bedroom and waited for the telltale sounds of the nurse's faux weeping. His back, pressed firmly against the stone wall, his arms crossed one over the other caused him to appear as though he were waiting for a carriage that would transport him to one of many preferred taverns. But he was waiting impatiently for the nurse to open the deeply-carved wood doors that led to his father's bedroom, at which time she would announce that his father had died.

The pronouncement, he imagined, would be swift and formal—the nurse's tears merely a perfunctory requisite that would indicate something distressing had taken place, an event that would signal a soul had moved on from within the walls of Waverly Estate. But no one would care, and neither would tears be genuinely spent when Garson finally gave it up and died. Even Garson's dog appeared to understand something was about to happen to his master but had abandoned him. The handsome beast had taken up residence with Martin in the cottage as soon as Garson could no longer order that he occupy a position at his bedside. At the top of the stairs to his left, the dog, named Phillip, waited not for the dying man but for Martin.

The nurse, hoping for some portion of the estate's massive wealth, could offer little more than her obedient care and soon her tears, in the hopes that she would likely rouse from his benefactors the singular hoped-for compensation and thereby, relief. But it would have made no difference if the tears were authentic or counterfeit. If she had come into the hall and stated her glee that he had passed, Martin would have ensured that she received the equivalent sum had she not, even if he paid from his own accounts. She had rightfully earned something for her two years of being dismantled, maligned, shouted at, and otherwise abused by the man.

He looked down at his waistcoat to examine the fine material, knowing that his father would have deemed his attire 'unfortunate.' The mournful occasion would have required that he wear his greatcoat, as though it were he that was about to depart. He chuckled to himself at the thought of retreating from that grand place with his hessian boots slung across his straight, fine back, with the woman he loved in tow. He would not wait for the driver of his carriage, nor would he care to say farewell to the servants. He would simply, gleefully summon cash from the vault, stow jewelry and essentials in his pack, and ride off into the sunset, as it were. Even his father's dog would run along beside him as they made their escape. But there were no assurances that she loved him, and being a man of propriety, he never made an overt physical suggestion that would betray it.

The first stifled sob arose from behind his father's closed door. It was followed by a long sigh, the kind one might expel heavily from his lungs after the completion of an arduous journey, when home was in sight over the horizon. He turned, placed a large hand to the doorknob, and turned the brass hard to the right. Pushing the door wide, he walked past the nurse who appeared ready to summon him, directly to his father's bedside.

The man laid there, his eyes wide, staring up. His fingers, intertwined, were blue veined and swollen. He reached his hand out and shut his father's lids. It was not done out of kindness for the man, but rather that he no longer wished to see the eyes that belonged to his father. He sighed as the nurse had and turned toward her.

"I am so terribly sorry, sir, for this sad loss." She pressed her hand on his back and sighed again.

"All is well," he said, turning to face her, in a voice that he had learned from his father. It was deep and full and resonated with surety, but unlike his father's, it rung with tones of earnestness and compassion. The lines on her otherwise smooth face seemed deeper than he had recalled they had been, previous to her employment there.

"Yes, now that there is no more suffering. Poor man." She wrung her hands together and shook her head from side to side. Wisps of hair from her bun fell as she moved and revealed silver threads she had earned prematurely, due to her master's conduct. The declaration elicited a tiny laugh from Martin, but the sound that came from his fine throat was more of a snort.

"Margaret, do you assume you will not be paid for your countless difficulties with that man if you *don't* say such things?"

She slid her eyes toward him and dropped her hands to her sides before speaking. "You are so much like your blessed mother, young Martin. So much. God rest her soul."

"Yes," he said, reaching to place his hand on her shoulder. "She was fine, and gentle. And we all miss her terribly so."

"Yes, those of us who knew she mattered."

With those true words spoken and a slanted look toward the dead man, the nurse ran from the room and disappeared down the hall. He listened to the click-clack of her shoe heels until the sound stopped and he felt truly alone with his father's body. He stood over him, spine rigid, his fingers curled to make two tight fists.

"You were a putrid, appalling person. You spared love where you imagined callousness would do. You took to yourself two lovely women and destroyed one, my mother, Anne. But you have not succeeded in Hannah's regard. I do not wish you safe and easy journey to your next life, sir. I wish you to be visited by double the misery you imposed on all who had the misfortune to know you."

As if his father's intemperate soul desired one last declaration, a rogue gust of wind from the river banged hard against the shutters and rushed past the window frame to flutter the bed's coverlets. Or, as Martin later mused, his mother's spirit had joined with him in agreement.

He strode into the hall and nearly ran headlong into his father's butler, James, who had been by his father's side for nearly thirty years. Without stopping, he turned his shoulders to avoid collision, and as he continued down the hall, he said, "Your master is dead."

James watched Martin walk down the long, marbled hallway to the stairs. At the very top, before descending, Martin stopped.

"Sir?" James called down the hall.

Martin waited a moment before responding. He gripped the stair post and turned his head slightly in the direction of James. "Do send notices to his associates, and to his solicitor, but do not send gloves. I will retrieve Mrs. Waverly from wherever it is she has gone off to. We shall have one day of mourning, one evening visitation of his body, which will be set in the second parlor. We shall have the usual flowers. I will order the memorial rings. There will be no black shrouding. He will be buried in the evening."

"Yes, sir," James replied, still staring at the side of Martin's head, feeling there was something else Martin would say.

"And James…"

"Sir?"

"We will not bury him beside my mother, nor will he be buried in the center of our family plot. He will not be placed in the vault as he wished." He paused and gripped the stair post more tightly before continuing. His father was in dread fear of being buried beneath the ground, but Martin needed to inflict a final blow to his father while simultaneously allowing others to observe that he was offended by the man's existence. "None of you shall prepare his body. Call Mr. Hommingsworth from town to take care of that. He will be buried at the outskirts, near the dead oak, away from the others. His plain stone marker will read, '*Here lays Garson Waverly. Master of All. Friend to none.*'"

And with the last of it out and said and done with, he descended the grand stairway, two steps at a time, Phillip tight on his heels.

James walked slowly into his former master's bedroom and once at his side, bowed his head down. "You could have been loved."

He pulled the silken coverlet over Garson's head—the pale blue one with the red thorny roses emblazoned along the edges. Then he crept slowly toward each of the five great windows that looked out over The Hudson River. Drawing each sash closed, he stood in the darkened room for a long moment, his back turned away from Garson. He exited the room without looking at the dead man again and gently shut the door.

Martin, who was twenty years of age when his mother died, spent the following seven years of his life alternating between wishing his father dead and wishing that he was the one deceased. Fate had made the decision for him, he thought, considering his father was at that moment being prepared for visitors. Despite his best efforts to tempt fate, which he viewed as the only true god, Fate apparently had other plans for him.

He was a wild child that preferred the wilds of The Catskill Mountains and his pony to his studies or the stuffiness of the mansion. While his mother refused to tame him, his father fought mightily to rein his feral characteristics in: to break him, mold him, teach himself self-restraint via a closed fist or punishment that involved locking him into the root cellar where spiders and the pitch dark, or an occasional rat, were his only companionship—sometimes for hours, and once for more than a day. 'Find your way out,' he'd say.

Because of the cruel treatment he had received, he suffered a dread fear of closed quarters. Sometimes even a too crowded room would be enough that the fear urged him out of the room and away; a carriage was often impossible to ride within unless he peered from the windows and distracted himself. Of course, his mother frequently freed him when his father became occupied with something else. But none of it disciplined Martin's spirit. His mother was the perfect counterbalance of unconditional love and acceptance. But the pain his father inflicted, the harm it did to his way of seeing the world and people in it, was something only the warmth of a lover could temper, even if only while in her arms. He confessed that he had taken solace in many, but most were not acceptable to the society into which he was born.

He could not, would not, be shattered. As he grew older and found ways to circumvent his father's iron hand, he became more like the wild things in the forest that surrounded Waverly Estate, and less of what his father wished he would become. Even when Martin was sent aboard one of the family's grand merchant ships at the age of seventeen, he remained who his mother hoped he would be. The education gained while aboard that ship had nothing to do with learning the location of afterdeck or how to mend a boltrope. He learned of indignities the men aboard suffered; he learned to respect their bravery as equally as their bodily and psychological strength.

When a man was taken by the sea or succumbed to sickness while aboard one of the many ships, his father thought only of the dead as lost commodities. During the earlier days, it was commonplace for English shipmasters to abscond with the American sailors and force them to sail away with them. Most were never heard from again. But Garson simply waited for a British ship to come to port and convinced the sailors to defect to his.

Only the money and outcomes mattered to his father—not the illegal opium trade he participated in—and not the many dark skinned men he helped round up for trade into slavery. Not the men who were forced to eat maggot-infested salt pork or bits of molded bread, which they would dunk into their coffee and then wait for the maggots and vermin to raise to the top before scooping it out.

He sat at the base of an enormous maple tree, pencil and paper on his lap, where he had many times retreated during his youth, and tried not to think too long or hard about any of it.

The tree stood at the corner of the estate, high upon a grassy hill where the forest met The Hudson River. Before him, the stark angles of the mansion thrust itself against the impossible blue of an autumn sky. To his left, the river wandered slowly, and the late day sun glinted like shards of glass might on the water, all, framed on both banks by the oranges and yellow, the crimson, of fall leaves.

Sometimes, while taking refuge there as a boy, he would hear people calling his name. No one but his governess, Claire, ever ventured that far to seek him out, not merely through their laziness, but the area where the tree grew was something of an unstated demarcation point between the estate's one-hundred acres and a path that wandered high above the river that many thought haunted. Only Martin ever ventured there.

As soon as Claire had discovered him, he was delivered a message from his father or mother, but Claire, understanding the predicament of the child, or perhaps refusing to give Master Waverly the satisfaction of a message being delivered, never let on that she had found Martin. Of course there were the typical warnings delivered regarding his refusal to obey his father, but the most empathetic of the admonitions was that Martin should not, as Claire stated it, 'tempt the spirit' that moved to and fro along the path nearby.

Claire was a good soul, possessed of warmth and a bright smile that even the austere confines of the estate mansion could not force away or diminish. Sitting at the tree base that evening, he thought how he still missed her and wished he had realized how important it might have been for him to know something more about her than the obvious. Her wiry red hair and skinny bones, when recalled, still made him smile.

One day when he had just turned thirteen, his father terminated her employment. He was away at boarding school at the time and was not afforded so much as a simple goodbye. Her services were no longer needed, she was packed off, and he never saw her again. But Claire left a note, and within the confines of his ability to recollect the exact wording, he repeated it often when things were too hard to make sense of. It went something like, *'you are nearly a man, Master Martin, and now taller than your father and smarter by far. You no longer need me. Go where you must and go with joy toward all things, forsaking not your spirit, betraying not the hearts of those whom you love and love you.'*

With the last of the light that shone that evening, he completed the inscription that would be engraved on the funeral rings. It read, *Forsake not your spirit.* The commemorative rings were frequently given at funerals by the wealthy and upper classes after a family member had died. Normally, the rings would be inscribed with sayings such as *prepare for death*, or, *death conquers all.* But Martin was not a man of superfluous convention, and neither did he feel the need to make the man's death something more than it was. He used the custom as another means to express what he felt he needed to say. He smiled, imagining the faces of those that would receive the rings. Chuckling, he shrugged. Anyone that knew his father would understand, but if not? What difference would it make? He had succeeded in becoming and remaining the man his mother hoped he would be. The rest of them, they could go straight to blazes.

He was pleased that the interior of the house would not be creped in black, serene at the knowledge the preacher would say a few words at the gravesite and then be on his way. The custom of gathering after the burial had been declined, and no gloves were sent to relate the death had occurred- since the gloomy funeral practice was nothing more than yet another ritual he did not feel his father deserved.

18

Martin heard Hannah's carriage traveling the pitted lane that led to the mansion before he could see it. His stomach clenched once, twice, and he shoved the paper into his pocket and snapped the pencil in half before tossing it away. At first he walked swiftly, but then his legs, as though they had other plans, sped to a gallop toward the front of the cobbled drive where he finally stopped, out of breath, his heart racing. The very sight of her caused his blood to do such things, and when she emerged, as beautiful and wraithlike as always, he took a few deep breaths as though he willed his lungs to inhale the loveliness and possess it as his own.

Walking slowly toward the carriage, he reached his hand out as he approached, thinking to help her gather her long deep blue dress from the carriage. The color, he assumed, was a compromise she had made in lieu of mourning black. He stopped. His legs as though mired in quicksand, felt the earth try to suck him down.

"Good evening, Master Waverly," Rene said as he exited the carriage, his hand extended out. "I'm sorry to hear...I was in New York City last night when I was given word and traveled all day to be here. The kind Mrs. Waverly sent the carriage to the ferry post to greet us." His hand hung in the air waiting for Martin's, but instead, Martin nodded his head down and gave one quick look toward Hannah and then to Willham, who exited slowly from the other side of the carriage. Hannah did not dare meet Martin's gaze.

"It was not unexpected." Martin walked away leaving Hannah to call on the servant to retrieve whatever it was that needed retrieving.

He had thought it was all over because she had promised it was. He had thought it was done and ended, as finished and cold as his father was, who was laid out in his best garments in the great hall. But by appearances, it seemed not.

W illham sat beneath one of the forty towering hemlock trees that lined the path from Martin's cottage to the mansion. They stood in militaristically ordered style. Nothing about Waverly Estate felt welcoming.

He let his eyes wander from the tips of the treetops to the mansion itself, along the fanciful turrets that spired up from its jagged roofs and many chimneys, then down along the asymmetrical outlines of its many cut edges carved out of granite, limestone, and boulder. Ivy crowded the many windows and crept up toward the towering widow's walk that he assumed offered magnificent views of The Catskill Mountains and mighty Hudson River. It was an odd fusion of gothic architecture and something else he could not quite recall the name of, but the entirety gave the mansion a look of austerity and order. He had not failed to feel a rush of impending gloom as he entered the mansion from beneath the double great arches and through the front doors. Or maybe he simply knew too much about its inhabitants to see it any other way.

While he had worked there to assemble the art for Garson, he would have had time to examine the entire mansion many times over, but was not permitted to do so. He had been confined to the master bedroom to do his work, and each day, precisely at 10:00am, he was escorted through a side door that led into the kitchen, then up a back staircase where he walked a dozen or so steps to the bedroom doors. Then, at exactly 5:00pm, James, the butler, retrieved him, and he was walked back out the way he had come in. He packed his own food, his own drink, since none were supplied to him. When finished for the day, he walked off the grounds and to the Turning Arch Inn where he was provided quarters. It generally took him 20 minutes to walk to and from his labor each day, but Garson did not provide him with a horse or carriage, no matter the weather. It always took him longer to arrive than to reach his quarters, which was something he attributed to his dislike for having to be there at all.

After his arrival that day, he had a quick look-around inside the mansion while the servants gathered his and Rene's belongings. He stumbled first upon the great dining room where at its east wall a massive stone and marble fireplace stood. The fire within it crackled as one would suppose fires do, but to his ears, he swore it sounded more akin to a malevolent hiss. Spiraled beams of wood thrust up to the ceiling from the fireplace's base, and each, intricately carved out and etched with the Waverly name, in all probability cost more to create and install than his entire home back in France.

The north and south facing walls were entirely made of glass: heavily leaded windows from floor to ceiling, each as wide as they were long. At the west end of the room, where the sun split the last of the evening light across the stone floors, three sets of eyebrow windows boasted brightly-colored stained-glass panels that caused him to feel that he stood within the heart of a kaleidoscope.

The ceiling was vaulted and held by massive arched wood beams and came to rest at the top of the walls where portraits of frowning men and women gazed somberly down upon him. A long table sat in the very center of the room, bounded by sixty red velvet chairs with tall wood backs, and above it hung, unlit though still sparkling, crystal chandeliers. He was interrupted by Martin's entrance into the room, before he could closely examine the portraits as he had intended.

"Willham." Martin crossed the room and stopped just inches from the tips of his shoes. It caused Willham to rock slightly on his heels.

"Good to see you, sir, even under these unpleasant circumstances." He extended his small hand to Martin, who took it briefly and quickly released it, as though he had found something disagreeable there.

"Yes, unpleasant. I was wondering when you planned to leave. When *both* of you intend to leave." Martin, who was larger by nearly a foot than Willham, blocked out the last of the daylight. But Willham did not need to see the man's expression to know why he asked. He idly noted flecks of the kaleidoscope colors glinting in Martin's black hair.

"It's yet to be decided, but I supposed that is entirely up to you now, isn't it?" Willham ventured a small smile that no doubt Martin did not return.

"Sir, you are not my quest, but I am free to state that you have no place here, nor your master, Rene. So perhaps you can consider that when, if, you are asked to stay on past the burial."

"I see."

"You appear to be fascinated by this gloomy room. There. See that?" Martin gestured toward the left of the fireplace. The man's abrupt change of topic sent Willham slightly off kilter.

"The…the wall, sir?"

Martin snickered. "No. Every space is occupied by those blasted portraits, but that one wall? There's nothing there. Why? That is the place where my mother's portrait once hung. The day she died, it was removed by my father. She died by drowning although she was an excellent swimmer. Hannah's was commissioned but never hung. And there, to the north wall. See him there? That was my uncle. Samuel. See the stairs there? You passed them as you came into this room."

Willham nodded his head and turned his eyes to view the spiral staircase that seemed to ascend to infinity. "Yes."

"Samuel died at the bottom there. Actually, he fell. From the very top. Or perhaps he was pushed. And there, to his left, see that one? The woman with golden hair was his wife, Lillian. She met a similar fate. Her unflappable mare was said to have thrown her. Lillian's neck was broken. Her beautiful mare was put down the next day although the creature had nary a mark on her beautiful bay hide."

"I see. It's all rather, rather…"

"Yes, yes. And there, on the other wall, my Aunt Christianna. Dead, too. At the age of thirty-one. Found here, right here, sir, where you are standing." Martin pointed at Willham's shoes.

Willham cleared his throat and took a step back. "Pity…"

"Yes, it was. She was taken with a fit one night after an argument with my father. Her husband? Left. Or should I say gone, a day after that. Their two children, my cousins, were sent to boarding school, yet when their instruction there was completed, they did not return home. Lost, they said, in the forest that ran as border around the school."

Martin strode off toward the eyebrow windows and Willham followed.

"Sir, I really, I sincerely don't understand why you-"

"Shut up." Martin's voice was harsh and low, and he grabbed Willham by his skinny arm, to turn him toward the wall. "That one? The one with no face?"

Willham gasped. "My lord, why-"

"Because someone scratched it out, that is why. He was my grandfather. I was named for him. No one ever discovered – or was told- who committed the defacement, but neither was any of us permitted to take it down or have it repaired. He died whilst carrying his case from his carriage after returning from a trip."

"Was he old? Did his heart fail him?"

Martin laughed unpleasantly. "No. He was not aged, and neither was he ill. They say he had slipped beneath the arches of the entryway on a perfectly pleasant and dry summer afternoon. But not a single bump or broken bone was found."

"Are you telling me that these fine people were murdered, sir?"

"I'm telling you that this is not a place for a guest that makes the choice to stay longer than advised. It is not a place for anyone. I'm telling you that nothing good comes to or from this place, and while the murderer is perhaps there, lied out in the second parlor, unpleasantness is visited on those who linger too long at Waverly Estate, and some malevolent things cannot depart this life."

Martin turned sharply and walked from the room leaving Willham to stare the way he had gone, his mouth agape. As he made way to leave, he could have sworn he heard a voice whisper. It came from near the fireplace where the missing portrait once hung. He swore until his dying day that the voice whispered, *'Too many shadows'*.

THREE

Hannah was stationed near her husband's head, wearing the obligatory black dress she had conceded she must wear. She sat erect with her hands folded together and rested them on her lap. If not for the light grey lace that adorned the bottom of her long dress or the opaque color of her skin, she would have been nearly invisible. A starched collar emerged from the base of her long neck and then to her ears, which did not bear earrings. She appeared more like a specter than typical, and something in her expression told Martin she was cognizant of that fact and approved.

The second parlor, as Martin had instructed would not be creped in black, had generally seen little use, save for those hours he would sit beside his mother on the piano bench and she played for him or he took instruction from her. Occasionally he would see her there, sitting quietly by the fire all alone. But she appeared restful, and even at a young age, he understood how rare those moments were for her and did not wish to disturb her private reverie.

It was a small room, probably the smallest of all rooms within the mansion, and its walls, rather than decorated with dark scenes and portraits of relatives that his father preferred for the rest of the house, instead bore lovely paintings of serene places he dreamed one day he might visit, and some of his mother's own stitch work. The windows looked out toward her gardens, and while certainly there was plenty of help to tend to garden chores, his mother had refused it. Instead, she spent many hours in the sun, the rain, pruning, planting, weeding- creating magnificent borders of every variety of flower that could tolerate the harsh Catskill Mountain climate. Her complexion, despite exposing it to the elements, appeared flawless and delicate. Sometimes he found himself comparing it to the petals of the blushed-pink roses she tended.

Conducting his father's visiting time in that room meant many things to Martin. But mostly he did it for his mother. It provided a rare opportunity for him to betray his father by ignoring his last wishes. He hoped, somehow, his mother could see him at that moment in time, a man grown tall and handsome and wiser; a man that understood what she had endured, and as a small token of that understanding, even as it came too late for it to matter, it might signal a little gift had been repaid to her.

Martin took his place beside Hannah. The dog hovered near the entryway and waited, at Martin's command. She did not acknowledge Martin, and neither did she object when he stepped on the bottom of her dress. She tilted her eyes downward, and he detected one corner of her pale mouth lift up when he moved his boot away to reveal a shoe print had been left. She seemed amused. Things that roused a giggle from her never appeared congruent with events or a place in time; rather, they were oddly placed smirks or smiles or looks of bemusement—inharmonious reactions that indicated she had a secret thought or desire that she would not share.

"How are you, Hannah?" he asked, not looking at her but leaning slightly to his right to address her.

"How do you think?" she responded, in a barely audible whisper.

"Will you continue to ignore me?"

"Not now, Martin."

"As you wish."

He spotted a Mr. and Mrs. Bryant Monroe, a pair of unconvincing weepers who had come all the way from Albany. Monroe, Garson's accountant, was a surly fellow with black eyes and heavy brow. Years before, Martin had judged the quality of the man's voice to be similar to, and slightly more annoying than, that of the old meat grinder cook used, and when he spoke, sprays of spittle flew uncontrollably from his mouth and upon whomever was unfortunate enough to be standing nearby. Monroe caught his eye, and Martin excused himself to Hannah. As he walked away, he heard her sigh. It was a bored sort of exhalation that caused him to wince.

Mr. Monroe, after hurriedly expressing his condolences, immediately launched into a full-throated condemnation regarding the funeral arrangements, which was punctuated by the usual spittle storm and communicated his horror concerning the method and direction with which Garson would be removed from the home.

"Martin, it is not- appropriate- that your father should be carried down steps when he is removed to the cemetery. Is there no death door to pass through? It is highly improper to allow him to exit through the same door the living pass through!"

"Mr. Monroe, we have no death door, as my great grandfather built this estate and did not carry superstition with him from England, and neither did he conform to new America's ways when he erected the estate. Additionally, I must inform you, so that there is no fussing later, it does not matter if the pallbearers carry him head first or feet first, when he finally exits the front door. I don't think he will notice."

Mrs. Monroe gasped and clutched at her throat as though she had swallowed too large a piece of meat. "But it's not proper! Have you no sense of dignity?" Her voice quivered.

"I do not intend to offend anyone, dear lady. I simply have no use for the majority of customs imposed upon us by long dead forefathers and superstitious ninnies. Please do excuse me."

As he turned to retake his chair beside Hannah, he heard Mrs. Monroe gasp, and it was followed by her husband attempting to calm her. He wanted to laugh, but at that moment, he spotted Rene, who had taken his seat. It was bad form, more than improper, but rather than engage either of them, he ignored it and walked to the side of the room where the great piano sat. Phillip got up and took his place beside him.

The piano had been silent since his mother had died, but he thought sometimes at night he could still hear the keys sound out in solitary notes, no more than a few at a time, before it would fall quiet again. Servants had believed the same, but he brushed it off as the superstitious leanings of the less informed and his own overwrought imagination. Yet, a few months into the mid-night musical soundings, and after having exhausted all means to disprove the validity of it, he moved from the mansion and into the cottage. He could have avoided his father if he had so desired, but obvious disdain for him served handily as the justification for taking up in the cottage.

If the keys continued to sound when no one was in the room to play them, he did not know. He did not ask, and the servants knew better than to speak of it to him. But sometimes when the moon was gone and no stars held place in the sky, he would look from his tiny paned windows and toward the house, believing he saw someone moving across the room and sitting at the instrument. On one such night he had bolted from his quarters, run the entire length of the drive, and thrust open the large doors, leaving them agape as he careened down the hall and into the room, but found no one there. That night he had placed an amour in front of the window, so he would never be tempted to look again.

Martin shot a glance toward Rene and Hannah. Though they were conversing, neither looked at the other, but it was clear they were occupied in a mutually engaging conversation. Behind them stood stuffy little Willham. The remaining hair at the top of his head stood out at strange angles, much like, Martin thought, a baby bird's fledging scruff. He did not speak with them, but it was evident that he minded every word spoken.

Profoundly and mercifully silenced, his father laid at the head of the room between two towered candles, obviously unable to articulate just what he thought about the odd gathering. People passed by his mahogany coffin as though they were viewing an artifact at a dusty museum. There was some dabbing of the eyes, some muffled sniffles. But generally, by all appearances, those who attended viewed the sitting as a social necessity, and perhaps, he snickered out loud, they feared the riches and position of the family to such a degree that to be absent from the spectacle might cost them something in the future.

The Waverly family was considered *old money*, and with that came a set of responsibilities as well as benefits. Their wealth had been made from China trade and inter-coastal shipping, but some whispered that illegally gotten slave trade gains were stingily held in accounts around the world and secreted within numerous side businesses. Martin, when old enough to understand, wanted no part of what he considered the coarser side of the business.

The family shipping company, of course titled *Waverly Shipping,* boasted twelve ships and various by-land carriers, and was said to be one of the most lucrative in the world. While Martin had no care for any of it, aside from the forced necessity of performing rudimentary tasks for the sake of those that depended on the family for their income. His own businesses were flourishing, thanks to holdings he had amassed in recent years that had been gathered using his charm and intelligence, and yes, sometimes his name.

He assumed the bulk, if not all, of the estate would go to Hannah, and whatever hatred the man had for him until his dying day would be proved by some paltry sum and properties he was always certain he would become beneficiary of. But none of it mattered. None of it. And as he walked to the door to greet Pastor O'Mara, he knew that the last segment of the day's torment would soon be over. The man would be buried near the dead tree, the bogus weepers would be on their way, and Martin would set about making his life what he always intended it to be. A happy life. A good life.

"Martin, my son," the pastor said as he took Martin's hand and gave it a gentle shake. His stony expression did not relay any empathy, nor did his voice possess a soothing tone one might imagine fitting at such an occasion. "It is time."

Pastor O'Mara was a master of perfect comportment and duty and donned in his black suit and too shiny shoes that peeked out from his overlong trousers—the stereotype was complete.

"Thank you," was all Martin could summon.

"Shall we then?"

Martin nodded and cleared his throat.

He went first to Hannah, as was expected of him, and paid no mind to either man that stood flank. He reached his hand to her, she took it, and he gently helped her to her feet. Leading her away toward the doors, all mourners followed behind, save for six pallbearers, who gingerly closed the lid and lifted Garson Waverly's coffin up from the planked perch.

Martin and Hannah stood at the top of eight steps that led down to the arches where the carriage, adorned in black crepe, waited. He had forgotten to mention he did not want it bedecked in that fashion, but he told himself that soon none of it would matter. Behind him, the others hung back as the coffin was slowly, carefully, maneuvered down the stairs. Hannah, who had been standing stoically at Martin's side, shivered. She gripped Martin's muscular arm and leaned closely into him.

The smell of her breath as it lingered in the frosted air was sweet and familiar, and he was beleaguered by the need to wrap himself around her. Despite it, he said, "Are you quivering with the cold or excitement, my dear step mother?"

"Would you really have me answer?" she replied evenly and stepped down toward the carriage. Her voice, part ice and portions of fire, the description dependent upon one's particular prejudices, caused him to feel hatred and want, in equal parts.

"When this is done, we will meet Rockingham, father's attorney, in the library," he whispered just loud enough for only her to hear.

"Yes."

"Your Rene will be pleased when it's done. I'm sure." He wanted to laugh, but there wasn't anything particularly amusing about it, if he were to set aside the sarcasm.

"I'll take care of you, darling step son. Don't fret about starving." Shoving her black handkerchief to her mouth, she concealed a grin.

"You can keep this old place. I will never fight you for it. It's haunted, in its way, and you, my dear, are part of the wickedness that floats the halls at night—and I dare say by day."

He helped her climb into the back of a carriage that was stationed to the rear of his father's, and eased in beside her. Phillip leapt up and deposited himself at his new master's feet.

"My god, that dog. I wish he'd go away and not return...I could easily arrange that. And as for you, Martin, you're such a fool," she said, as she settled her dress about herself. Free to talk as the horses' hooves concealed their tête-à-tête, she added, "I did love him, you know. I did. But he was most disagreeable, and even on a good day, he would never allow himself to love you or anyone. Don't blame me for that. Don't blame me for being younger than he was and for wanting to feel something in this dreadful world besides sadness."

"Martyrdom does not suit you well." He yanked a bit of fabric of her dress that had wedged beneath his toned thigh and shoved it away.

"There would have been talk, if you and I—"

"Since when did that ever matter to you, Hannah?"

"There would have been repercussions. For the business."

Martin laughed, and patted her firmly on the knee. "You know well that the business would and will survive, unless of course you permit that blackguard to have his hand in it."

"He isn't what you think, Martin. He's very kind to me. He has an artist's sensibility, that's all. Something you wouldn't understand a thing about despite your mother's—"

"Don't," he said through his fine, gritted teeth. "Don't bring her up. Unless you want…"

"Want what, Martin? This conversation is becoming tedious, and now you threaten me?" She moved as far as she could to the opposite side of the carriage and looked out toward the rolling hills that had become covered in a dismal fog.

They said nothing more until the carriage lurched to a stop beneath the wrought iron arches of the cemetery that bore the letter W. He didn't bother to stop her body from pitching forward as the brakes were engaged. Her hands jutted out just before her face would have hit the metal of the carriage's interior.

"This is all meaningless, Hannah. In a short while, you'll have what you want, and so shall I." He swung the door open and it bounced against the side of the carriage as he got out with Phillip as always at his side in an instant. Slinging his legs away, he yanked his long black coat about himself and strode off toward his father's carriage, leaving her to fend for herself. One quick look over his shoulder assured him that she wouldn't find need to do so for long, as Rene took hold of her waist and deposited her down to the mossy ground.

The forty or so mourners that had made the short ride to the family cemetery, followed silently behind Garson Waverly's coffin as it made its way to the burial spot. Above, the tops of giant hickory and elm trees seemed swallowed by the fog, and below their feet, the spongy moss intruded on bulging roots and some of the headstones around them. At the front of the pitiable procession, Pastor O'Mara walked, bible pulled closely to his chest, blonde hair matted to his balding head, dampened down by the foggy night.

Stopping at the newly dug hole beside the dead tree, Martin detected whispers of surprise coming from those around him. Some murmurs became louder voices of dissent, and a woman could be heard trying to silence them.

"It is how it should be!" Martin, surprised at the volume and resolute tone to his voice, stationed himself to the left of the tree and leaned against it.

"This is wrong, sir, wrong!" Barnaby Crispell, a distant cousin to Garson walked toward Martin. 'Wrong!"

"The only thing wrong about his final resting place is that he is being buried here in the same ground as so many fine relations."

"What would your mother think?" the man gasped.

"My mother, dear sir, would heartily approve. Now kindly stop wasting the good pastor's time, and let's get on with this chore." He waved his hand toward Pastor O'Mara and then folded his arms across his wide chest.

Pastor O'Mara, unsure of how to proceed, looked to Martin who nodded that he should continue, and the man cleared his throat and began to read.

"Grant that our brother Garson may sleep here in peace until You awaken him to glory, for You are the resurrection and the life. Then Garson will see You face to face and in Your light will *see* light and know the splendor of God, for You live and reign forever and ever...Amen." The pastor clapped his book shut and bowed his head to the sound of multiple 'amens'.

Martin watched as the men lowered his father down into the cold earth where he had specifically demanded he not be placed and feared the most to be interred. A thud, a small cry from someone who stood behind, and then a sprinkling of flower petals, delivered by one of his female cousins, ended the charade.

As the earth covered the beautiful mahogany wood, Martin's gaze shifted toward the river and the shore beyond, feeling liberated for the first time in many years, and ready for whatever might come next.

"Well, that's done." Hannah stood behind him and tugged on his sleeve. "Shall we?" She motioned her head toward the waiting carriage. The horses clapped their hooves into the ground, and blasts of steam floated from their nostrils.

"No. You go on. I think I could do with a walk home. Take Phillip with you."

He removed a lantern from the side of the carriage, lit it, and walked off toward the small path that ran parallel between the pitted road and the river—the one from which he had been many times warned to stay away.

"It's foolish!" she called after him. "You could slip and break your neck!"

He stopped, looked over his shoulder, and said, "Perhaps. And I will be yet another story to tell when portraits in the dining room are under examination by unwanted guests and afterward to yet to be born descendants."

"That is decidedly not funny, Martin." He could hear something like concern in her voice, but he moved away toward the wood line and disappeared into the gathering fog.

M iriam, the house manager had taken a liking to Martin the moment she first saw him as a small boy. Hannah claimed Miriam for duties as her personal chambermaid. Hannah's previous chambermaid, Shelly, whom Hannah had accused of lacking 'fortitude,' resigned her post after a hellish morning when Hannah threw objects at her person and shouted foul words so obscene that Shelly fled from the house, never to return. Miriam found nothing redeemable in Hannah's character. Had she possessed any moral kindness whatsoever, Miriam might have tolerated her. She agreed to do Hannah's bidding to keep Mrs. Waverly in sight and out of Martin's line of attack, which seemed the only benevolent thing a woman in her position could do for the beleaguered man.

"Mrs., you left him out there alone? In all of that?" Miriam asked in an accusatory tone and jerked her head toward the windows of Hannah's rooms.

"For goodness sake, Miriam, he's a full grown man and quite able to take care of himself. He'll be along presently. Now go get my bath drawn, and stop all this hand wringing. It's decidedly a waste of time, and I need your help. Go on." She waved her hand at Miriam and waited until the older woman, her cheeks brighter red than usual, trudged out of the bedroom. But the woman returned in a moment.

"Don't you know about that path, Mrs.? If there is anything more haunted than this old place, it would be that path. Haven't you heard of—"

"I've heard, and I take none of it seriously. They are merely stories told to stupid children and perpetuated by the ignorant lower classes. Now go do as I say, or I will send you out there to look for him. Alone. *Go*."

artin reached the crest of the last hill before the mansion and stopped. To his left, the river flowed from Albany and south to New York City. From that vantage point, he could make out the severe lines of the place that would no longer feel like a prison. Yet why did he resist going home? He was a solitary sort of man who learned at necessities' lap to prefer his own company. Or perhaps he favored the company of fauna and wild flora that existed in relative peace amidst the acres of land surrounding the estate. Or maybe when alone, he was not held prisoner to the whims of the household or the woman he tried not to love. His once wild heart had lately been threatened with awareness that he was contracting a growing ambivalence toward everyone he knew. His situation created a terrible purgatory that he feared would permit neither great highs nor lows. If not for those moments, all of life was a flat line with indistinct beginnings, which could easily be forgotten, begetting a future not worthy of who his mother had hoped he would become.

Light glowed from some of the windows, and in the distance, a foghorn groaned a word of warning. He listened to it, muffled against mist and the silence of the forest's trees. It was as though the world had become still, expectant, and he closed his eyes to feel the calm seep deeply into his very tired bones.

He willed himself to consider favored memories: a slow drift of thought and reminiscence, effortless recollections of things. Moments that contained visions such as the gently quavering fluff of an East Indian bird feather joined atop a hat worn by a lady he had once made love to while visiting New York City. The day his mother touched his face and smiled while she piled white roses from her garden into the basket he held. The melodious sound of raindrops against the roof of his dormitory bedroom. The smell of Claire's hair after she had washed it in the rain bucket. The first morning he awoke on the open prairies of the New West, as the entire earth and sky melded together in orange and gold and subtle pale blues, the likes of which he would have thought could only be imagined. The—

"Sir."

Startled, he felt his limbs jerk to attention before his mind caught up to the idea that he was not alone. He swung around, and before him stood a young woman with long wheat colored hair, and she smiled.

"Good *lord*, woman! Creeping on a person that way!" He held his hand to his chest and let out a long breath he had not realized he had arrested.

"Pardon me, sir. I do apologize, but it seems unlikely that I should meet someone along the path this time of night. It hasn't happened in many years." She smiled again, and when she did, he considered that she might become one of the recollections he would add to the fine thoughts from his life.

"Quite alright, I suppose. But I didn't hear you come up the path. How long have you been walking behind me?"

"Behind you?" She laughed, and the sound it made was like a song.

"Weren't you?" He wanted to laugh, too.

"It doesn't matter, really. I'll be on my way. I just thought I should announce myself, since this is no night for abrupt meetings. Although I dare say I gave you a fright despite my best intentions." She turned to walk away but did not head toward the path. Rather, she took steps towards the dark forest.

"Wait. Should you be going that way? You have no light, lady, and how will you find your way, to...to...where are you going?" He reached his arm out, palm side up. He never knew for sure why he had, but he left it there, and she took a step back.

"I'll be quite alright, sir. Quite alright." She took more steps backward, not turning away from him, and he swung his arm toward the mansion, his head following.

"See? My home. Why don't you come with me down there and—" She was gone when he turned back to face her, but he finished his sentence anyway in a whispered voice. "To get warm."

He watched for any sign that she might come back, listened intently for any wayward rustle of leaf or her beautiful voice, but it was not to be.

He called out to her, but nothing was returned. Shrugging off his bewilderment, he continued down the path toward home. Once there, he entered the doors of the mansion and went directly to the library where, no doubt, his father's solicitor and Hannah would be bothered at his tardy arrival.

"At last!" Hannah said in her most practiced huff. "We thought you had forgotten us and—what's wrong with you?" She stood and walked toward him, her hand reaching for his handsome face. For some inexplicable reason, at that very moment, he realized that he did not love her. He backed away.

"I apologize, Hannah. Mr. Rockingham. I was—detained." He moved in a wide arc around Hannah and sat next to the fire. "Where is Phillip?"

"James sent him straight away to the cottage. He seemed in a terrible state, what with your departure. The confounded animal barked for an hour after you."

Rockingham cleared his throat, shuffled a stack of papers before him that he had laid on Garson's desk, and said, "Never mind it. Let's press on, shall we?" Rockingham stood nearly as tall as Martin, but his weak posture and bowed shoulders did not give him the appearance of height or strength. To the contrary, his physical appearance, from balding head to gaunt cheekbones, gave the notion that he was sickly, and much older than his sixty years. He cleared his throat again. It was a most disagreeable habit that he employed as an odd break between thought and word when he was distressed or when he readied to deliver distasteful news.

"Let's be done with this, Mr. Rockingham. I am exhausted." Hannah wiped her hand across her forehead with a dramatic flourish and, as was her way, looked at the wall rather than meet the man's eyes.

The solicitor shuffled the papers once more before sitting back in his chair. One side of his mouth crooked up. "Let's begin. It's been a dreadful stretch for you both, and I'm sure we could all appreciate a conclusion to this day."

"Agreed." Martin leaned back into the chair and closed his eyes, thinking of the beautiful girl on the path. He smiled and did not listen to the solicitor, and neither did he bother to be concerned that they noticed.

"Martin, this pertains to you, and you *do* need to pay mind, young man. Martin!"

Martin jerked his eyes open and mumbled something about being sorry. Then he sat up and leaned forward to amuse the man. Hannah pressed her hands on the desk and wore a look of expectancy shared by children about to be served dessert.

"Mrs. Waverly. Do you prefer I read to the parts you have been waiting patiently for during this past hour or—"

"Read it, just read it," she replied, testily.

"Very well. I'll go past the legal terms and get to the point then, as it is written."

Martin yawned and leaned back again as Rockingham continued.

"'I, Garson William Waverly, being of sound memory and mind, do hereby bequeath the following: To my faithful servant James, I leave the black stallion known by the name of Arabia, whom he loved and cared for all its days, all it's tackle and assorted miscellanies, and saddles; $1,000.00; my gold cuff links. To the remainder of the servants, I leave $800.00 to each and one book from my rare collection. To each of my cousins, I leave $1.00. They will understand why. To my business associate James Forney I leave—"

Hannah threw her hands up in the air and said, "Rockingham, please, dispense with this and get to—"

"You?" Martin laughed aloud and tossed himself back into the chair. Hannah made her trademark huffing noise and dropped her arms across the chair sides.

Rockingham cleared his throat. "Very well. 'To my dear wife Hannah Anderson Waverly, I leave...I leave...' Mrs. Waverly, perhaps we might... Perhaps we need—"

"Continue!" she said loudly, banging her arms so violently against the arms of the chair that one previously tight curl from her dark head came undone from the tight chignon and bounced on her shoulders. Rockingham cleared his throat and nodded vigorously in cautious agreement.

"'To my dear wife, Hannah Anderson Waverly, I leave her precisely what she came into our marriage with. $4,000.00. Her clothing. Assorted female accessories and one of her maids. If the maid will tolerate same...'"

"What?" She uttered in a gruff whisper, leaning forward again and grabbing the papers from the desk. Martin, who never sought joy in anyone's discomfort, could not help but explode in laughter, and he leapt from the chair.

"So then he leaves nothing to her and to his associate he leaves it all?" Martin walked toward Hannah and grabbed the papers from her hand. Rockingham said nothing.

"What?" Hannah repeated in a whisper that ascended exponentially toward a shriek as she continued to repeat the word until Martin thought she had finally lost her mind.

"Rockingham, this says—"

"Yes, sir, you are the beneficiary of all his Earthly belongings, business dealings, holdings, and every property he holds—including Waverly Mansion, surrounding buildings, both cottages on the north along the river, land holdings across the globe, ships—all of it, with the exception of one small dwelling known as Blythe House that lies in the forest near the border of Waverly land. It shall be titled to a person whose name will be revealed in separate document."

Hannah rose from the chair as though she had been stung by hornets and ran from the room. The black hems of her dress hissed as they trailed behind her against the floors. Martin did not pursue. He sat down heavily as though pulled into the cushions by unseen hands.

"Why?" Martin asked, gently laying the papers down again.

"Because you are his son," Rockingham said plainly. "Because you are his only legal heir, and his wife was never true to him. I must go but will send on papers for you to sign in some days. I'm sorry, son, for all of it. You might consider selling off some of the cottages. Perhaps you consider tearing down Blythe House as well, since it has fallen into disuse all these many years. But let's leave that trouble for another time. Good night, Martin."

He did not move from the chair as Rockingham saw himself out. He was not sure whether he was displeased Hannah had been denied or glad it was so. But Garson Waverly had the last laugh.

In the papers, Garson advised Martin to take no pity on his disinherited wife, and neither should he feel guilt at removing her as promptly as possible from the property. If she refused, Garson continued, Martin should seek the legal help of Mr. Rockingham to achieve the same.

Martin stood and looked about the room. Thousands of books lined the shelves in addition to exquisitely priced furnishings, lamps, and assorted memorabilia. Marble eyes of the taxidermy boars, deer, and fox stared down at him. Files in the hundreds, jammed into drawers and the desk harbored complex mysteries. He knew little about the day-to-day operations of the companies, and now it had fallen to him and only him. His partner would retire and stay on as an advisor until Martin sorted it all out. This was not a thing from which he could flee. Men and women, families depended on him taking up the reins and doing so with diligent care.

Years had been spent ever so miserably, wasted on hating his father and believing he might champion Hannah. But now? Making his way through the disorder was over. His trade partnerships, borrowed from what his father no longer found use for, would somehow need to be incorporated. Would he stay? Hand it all over to Hannah or...he did not know.

He opened a draw at his father's desk, removed the key that belonged to the master bedroom chambers and went straight away up the stairs and to the bedroom so that he might lock the door, which he intended to keep bolted forever more. Once accomplished, without a single look into the room as the lock clicked closed, he deposited the key into his breast pocket. Retreating to the cottage, he hoped to avoid being subjected to the shrill of Hannah's voice that pierced the halls as she screamed at the help. Perhaps, he thought, he might sleep and find that the entire day had been a gloomy dream, but upon a new awakening, what day would he arise to?

Once inside the relative safety of the cottage, he removed the key from his pocket and searched for a place where it might never be found. Perhaps, he thought as he considered the perfect location, he might forget where it was as well. He walked to the small desk that he had bought while in England one year, the one with the simple lines and five drawers contained within, and pulling the metal handle of the very bottom one, he slid it open and removed some files it had contained. Then, removing the shelf that concealed the false bottom, he turned the key around between his fingers before unceremoniously dropping it into the bottom of the drawer. Refitting the shelf, he then locked the drawer of the desk, walked toward the white settee, and turned it on its side. Pulling a bit of fabric from the corner underneath, he pushed the desk key into the guts of it, re-secured the fabric, and flipped the furniture back into place. He sat heavily into it.

Phillip sat at his feet but was just as restless as Martin. The dog's fine head twisted left and right over its large back, taking wary glances at the windows behind him that faced the far hill toward the river.

"Quiet now, boy. It's done, all done. Tomorrow we start again. Lie easy, fellow; better days will come." He patted the beast's head, lay back on the settee, and closed his eyes.

The woman with long wheat hair sat on the hilltop and stared down at Waverly Mansion. One by one, all the lights dimmed, save for a single lamp lit within the cottage.

She stood, and moved slowly down the path toward it.

How could this be?" Rene asked, his voice rising with each word. He stood in the shadowy corner of the courtyard, away from prying eyes.

"Do watch your tone, Rene. And recall I told you that my husband lied as easily as men breathe. I have far more than he claims I came into the marriage with, and I intend to reclaim every crumb."

"Do you understand what I have done? *Committed*? Given up? For you?" His voice rose once again, and Hannah took a few steps closer. A crunching of snow caused them to stop speaking, but hearing nothing more, they continued.

"Alas, your proclamations of enduring love were wagered against your assumptions of wealth claimed by default, yes?" Her eyes threatened to slap him, strike him hard with her open hand against his angular face, but she clenched her hands together and stepped back.

"A lie is a lie, madam, and no matter what you state to be true, at this juncture, I believe none of your utterances, and on those grounds, perhaps it is time to take leave and return to France."

"Do as you wish. But know this. If you depart, I will tell the authorities about what you and your little shadow have done to my husband. Oh yes, I know, Rene. Goodnight, sir. If you leave, I'll expect you to take your sodomite with you!"

His hand went up and viciously slapped her delicate cheek, which caused her to fall back against the side of the stone wall. She did not reach to where he had cruelly struck her nor did she cry out. Instead, she righted herself and shifted her garments back into place. She did not return the deed but instead reciprocated it with a terrible smile that set his bones to ice.

He watched her walk away. Though he should have been plagued by remorse, since he had never before struck a woman, he realized he had made a mistake—one he would somehow, someday, pay handsomely for if he did not stop it.

"Rene." Willham appeared from the darkness. The night was previously so still that the single whispered utterance tugged at what was left of his wits.

"What is it, Willham?" Rene continued to look the way she had gone and rubbed his hand against his pant leg, as though trying to eliminate the sullied thing he had just done.

"I heard. I heard all of it," he whispered, turning toward a small noise he heard coming from behind. "Will we let this happen to us?" he asked, knowing what the response would be. His voice, lowered down past a whisper, continued on. "After all we have done to insure that we—"

"No," Rene replied, at last turning to face him. "No, we shall not. You have the ability and the—shall I say—tools, to turn this right again. We shall not let them undo what I have given my all to obtain. It is rightfully mine, since I dare say—"

"Ours!" Willham interjected, and he reflexively ducked down as the volume of his voice rose.

"Of course it is 'ours.' And do these loathsome people deserve what they merely covet but do not value? I say not."

Another sound came from behind. Both nodded their heads in agreement that they should discontinue their discussion in the open. If someone had heard them, it could all go wrong. Separating, they walked away: Willham to the courtyard and Rene toward the house.

FOUR

"Try to understand, sir. The trade situation with Japan is not yet finalized." Rockingham did not like the expansionist design that Martin presented him with, although he had listened and tried.

"But this will mean open trade for us. Be damned England and her—"

"You shouldn't speak that way, Martin!" Rockingham looked nervously around his office as though someone might overhear.

"My father dealt in the opium trade for more years than I will care to recount. I see only opportunity; the prospect of better profit that is *clean* profit, sir. Not gained on the backs of slaves and opium inebriates."

Martin had entirely disliked his father's source and content of trade, and as the political and moral conflict began between the states regarding slavery, he knew it was time to step away and establish the companies as he saw fit. He imagined it as a merciful business—one that benefited all nations, all people, no matter their skin color, no matter on which side of the ocean they dwelled.

"Yes, yes, yes, of course, but there is a time and place for things. You've stated your intent to build ships—ships that can outrun British ships, which surely will increase trade. Sir, you have a fine idea, but—what you are proposing isn't well thought out, and I'm certain if you just let a little time pass between your father's death and settling the affairs, you might see things more clearly."

"It's been a month, Rockingham, and I have thought of this well before his passing. We shall both consider all aspects of this notion and meet again in one month. By then, the trade pacts will be settled, I hear. Come to Waverly and see me then. I've spent far too many days in this city, lord, and feel the need to go home."

"So, it's better now? For you and—"

Martin stood and gathered his papers and tall hat. "She will be gone when I return. Or so she has sworn. I thought it best to go 'round this matter gently or suffer more of her crying jags, which only serve to blacken her eyes and irritate the staff."

"And you, Martin? Have you moved back from the cottage yet?"

"No. Perhaps when I return, if she is gone, but for now, the significance of working diligently toward beginning our coal trade with Japan is paramount. The rest can wait. We may soon be granted the right to own properties there. We can certainly find ourselves ahead of the trade hostilities if we put the rest aside for the moment. And with the forests along The Hudson becoming scant since builders plundered for their ship building, I believe that now is the time for metal and steel and iron."

"Indeed, sir. I'm simply taking observations on your behalf, as I wish you nothing but good." Rockingham stood and walked around the desk to Martin. He laid his hand on Martin's shoulder and smiled. "And if I might say, perhaps it's well past your time to take a wife?"

Martin laughed and patted the man's hand. "Truly, my concern lies more with the notion that a wife might take *me*. And besides, I have no time to dilly with women and sort out the gold seekers from the more, shall we say…virtuous."

"I fear that the time is fast approaching when the businesses will fold. Don't you hear of their struggles? Let us pray that the great Waverly Shipping and her assets do not suffer as well. Travel safely, and in one month, I will see you at Waverly. Take care, son. And do try and have yourself a Happy Christmas."

❦ Hello? Is someone there?"

Willham, stopping before he reached the first step of the stairway that led to the guestroom, held his lantern high, moving it right, left, and then turned toward the front doorway again. The sound he heard was solitary and had gently toned. Just once.

The house was quiet, save for the clack of the clock near where he stood alone in the entryway of Waverly Estate. He slowly placed the light down on the round table that bore flowers in an enormous crystal vase and walked in a tight circle around it.

"Hello?"

The snow that had threatened all day became a reality. Through the windows near the door he saw his carriage sitting idle, the grey horse bobbing its head, impatiently waiting for the stable boy to fetch him and bring him into the warmth of his stall.

Again, he heard it: a soft tone and then silence. He lifted the lantern and moved slowly toward the second parlor to his right, where a month before, Garson Waverly had been placed on display. Dying flame and embers from the fireplace gently flicked light against the far wall of the parlor, and he walked through the door, although his heartbeat, troubling itself beneath his heavy winter coat, warned him to do otherwise.

Once within the confines of the room, he again lifted the lantern high above his head. Moving it this way and that, he paused, noting a wine goblet left on a table near the mantle. He walked to it, lifted it, and noted that it was half-empty. As he placed it down the tone jingled again, and he nearly dropped the lantern as he swung around.

"Hello, I say!" he said firmly, but just above a whisper. "Come from your hiding place this once!" But nothing moved within his sight but the tree limbs shifting outside the window, heavy with snow.

With no response forthcoming, he slowly backed out of the room, not taking his eyes from the corner where the now long-deceased Anne Waverly's piano stood.

"Someone is here. I know it. But you have not frightened me, and I will not give you your way in that! Good evening!" he said loudly. Once at the doorway, he bolted toward the stairs, the lantern swinging back and forth in his sweating hand as his legs carried him fast away from the phantom, his great black coat flagging behind.

With one foot on the first step up, the single pinging tone became many discordant banging notes upon the piano keys that chased him

43

further and further up the stairs. Up two flights he ran, and when finally at his door, he plunged himself within it and slammed the heavy wooden door shut against the terror.

"What manner! What manner!!" he yelled, unable to find a word to complete his thought. He swung around and around again, turning the light this way and that to examine the room he knew would not afford him any sleep that night.

Down the hall, they whispered to each other. Having heard the piano playing and then Willham's hysterical climb of the stairs and slamming of door, they paused for a moment, curiously waiting to hear if there would be something more. But when it became silent again, they continued speaking.

"I know what you have done," whispered the first.

"Yes. I assumed that when you came barging through my door and accosted me."

"You have nothing to fear. The old man's death was a favor to me. But now I require something in return. I require half of what you shall procure from the will."

"Yes, yes, I assumed you would demand something like that."

"Or, if you prefer, I tell him all about your trickery and murderous deed. You shall be drug off and imprisoned and then what good will that serve? None, I declare, none. But if you wish to have it all, I can arrange something for you." The voice was filled with mockery and self-amusement.

"Indeed? Well then. I shall make plans," the voice replied, laughing.

"Martin will return in two days' time. I saw the telegraph on the entryway table today."

"As did I. Let's not make more waste of time. What a lovely New Year we shall have once we—"

"Agreed."

Leaving through the newly discovered exit, he smiled.

"Did you hear it again last night? The demented hammering of piano keys?" Miriam leaned in toward James so as not to be overheard by the kitchen staff that had begun to prepare the Christmas Eve meal for their master, Martin. She slung a wet rag over her shoulder and turned her back to them all, as she poured tea for Hannah.

"Shush, woman! If any soul in this place claims to not have heard it, I'd give them my last penny. It would be all lies."

"Ah, you and I. We're just servants here, and that wild cat up in her room is demanding her tea whilst the rest of us fight off fright and sleepless nights! Wouldn't you think she'd be the least concerned at what we heard?"

James smiled wryly. "You presume she was home to have heard it, Miriam."

"Ah, indeed. Indeed."

"Hedge-creeper she is, despite her title and snobbery."

"James! Calling her such a thing—and in ear shot of the staff!"

James laughed. "She would make her money any way she chose and probably has. Convention and decency are foreign words to that...*woman*. She may very well have been at her vocation last night. That's why she is the only one in this place with her nerves intact." He waved his hand in the air and pretended to tidy up something on a side table.

"Why Master Martin has had us decorate the second parlor for Christmas confounds me. The room is bewitched! How long will it be until the specter makes use of the entire house, if Martin continues to make her feel so welcomed?"

"You assume a woman plays the keys? Ah, I know not. But we must not speak of it to him. None of it. You know well how he—"

"Yes, yes. But he promises the New Year will bring better things to us all."

She looked over her shoulder, assured that the staff was all busily engaged in their chores, reached over her head to the shelving, and took down a rather dusty bottle of port. She grabbed two small glasses, opened the bottle, and spilled two gulps each into the glasses.

"To you and me and Master Martin. And the ghost of Waverly Estate."

They pretended to clink their glasses, gave one more wary look about themselves, and then swigged the contents down.

"I'd best bring the tea to Her Majesty before she brings god's thunder down on this beleaguered house."

Rene, still ensconced in his bed, pulled the coverlet tightly over his ears and closed his eyes. He willed himself to recall happier days, when painting was his only vice and his only true love. He wondered if all of his plans would turn to naught and if Willham had finally dug them both so deeply into an untidy ball that they would never unwind themselves from a plan gone too far.

Had Willham feigned a ghostly occurrence in the hopes of further jangling nerves? He shook the idea off and concluded that Willham did not have the imaginative fortitude to concoct such a capricious affair. His talents were more direct in nature, and to simply endeavor to perpetrate a three AM scare would not be a technique that he would even consider. He knew that Willham appreciated only beginnings and ends—things that happened in the middle? He had no use for them. He was not one to manufacture circumstances or manipulate others so that they did his will. Rather, he thought of himself as the sole master of any fate and accordingly set to whatever task it may require.

He thought of the portraits in the great dining room, and the tales Willham had imparted to him regarding them. What a dreadful history— but one that could create the belief that anything was possible in The House of Waverly. Anything. Anything...as long as it engaged matching fates to those that frowned from the walls—as long as the conclusions were similarly appalling.

He sat upright as he heard a servant scurrying down the hall and calling out, "Master is home! Master is home!" Doors opened and shut, and he heard someone running down the long hall toward the stair.

He got up and walked to the leaded window that looked out over the snow-covered lane that led to the house. The rows of hemlocks bowed heavily under the weight of wet snow, and the sun forced itself through the clouds. The jingle of bells fastened to the carriage were more irritant than pleasing, as he was sure they had been intended to be, and he watched as the carriage came to a slow stop. Martin emerged.

His hair had grown longer than when they had first met, and his shoulders seemed broader somehow. Perhaps since the burdens of being the son of Garson had lifted, a burgeoning vitality to the already viral man had been granted. Rene watched as he reached into the carriage and brought out brightly-colored boxes, all with tidy and festive bows attached. He wondered if Martin had thought to bring something back for Hannah. But why would he, should he care?

Martin turned toward the first servant who had come to greet him, and he smiled down upon her face. Juggling the boxes of varying sizes, he slipped one into her hands. She curtsied and said something to him. He said something in turn that obviously pleased her because as she turned and ran back to the front doors, her face beamed. Martin watched her go and turned his head to say something to his coachman but then suddenly changed his focus to the window where Rene stood. The smile on Martin's face dissolved, and they stared at each other for a long moment before James came out to take the gifts from his arms and Martin turned away.

Where is Miriam?" Martin stood in the hallway outside of the servants' quarters and frowned at James.

"She's—she's gone, sir. I'm afraid to say. Left last night and did not say where she would go."

"For what reason?" Martin was fond of the woman, and he confessed she frequently stood as a buffer between him and Hannah.

"Sir, she...she had a fright, and then there was a trouble between her and Mrs. Waverly."

Martin leaned against the wall and dragged his hands through his thick black hair. "Come. Sit with me near the fire." He walked to the kitchen fireplace and pushed aside bowls filled with potatoes that were set on the mantle. James sat beside him on the slate ledge but dared not look into his face, since he very well knew where the conversation would lead them, even though Martin did not.

"Sir, I fear you will not like any of it."

"James, I already do not. Tell me all of it. What happened? What did Hannah do to frighten her? She is the most imperturbable woman I know."

James took a deep breath and began. "No, sir, Hannah did not frighten her. She is well accustomed to the lady's, shall we call it, irritability. It was the second parlor, sir. The parlor. The ghost in the parlor!"

Martin sighed, rubbed his face, which clearly needed a shave, and sighed again. "That rubbish again. Have we not decided to make an end to those tales? You are a reasonable fellow, James, and surely, you can attest to the fact that phantoms are not prowling the darkened corners, nor have they scared our Miriam away. Perhaps it was some mistake. Perhaps—"

"Pardon me, sir but have you not heard it yourself? The tinkering about on the piano keys late at night?"

"Must we insist on this, James?"

"We cannot disprove it, sir, and therefore, it can be said that it *could* be true."

"Fine reasoning, James. However, for the sake of the care we all have for Miriam and my need to know the facts so that I might dispute them and end this nonsense once and for all, please do continue."

"The piano keys played. As they frequently have. That night, they went on longer than ever before. Instead of one tone, there were multiple chords struck, all as though the keys themselves had become possessed with some unseen fury that mocked poor Willham as he went to climb the entry stairs to his room. And as he escaped the scoundrel or ghoul and fled, I dare say to preserve his very existence, the keys stuttered wildly, a madwoman or man hammering upon them until Willham reached his chambers and slammed the door shut. The whole house heard it, sir; there was no escaping the terrible cacophony of crash and bash of keys! And I confess, much to my own shame, I did not go to see for myself what had happened but know very well that it was the same as before. The same phantom, as it were!"

"Go on. We must finish this." Martin shook his head, trying to dislodge both the tale and the thought that he was not in any position to say it could not be true since he, himself, had fled because of it.

"Very well, sir. Miriam, being the braver of us, I am humiliated to tell you, walked the servants' hall and knocked upon each door. Every servant was accounted for, sir, as was Rene and of course poor Willham. I saw Rene myself, sir, as he came in and went straight away to his chambers."

"And where was Mrs. Waverly when this began?"

"That I cannot say, sir, not for sure, but when the key bashing reached its height, I heard her door slam shut as I peered from the kitchen toward the stairs, and yet, the last of the notes had not yet rung out."

"What of the stable workers, James?"

"They were in their quarters at the barn, and I know this as true because both boys ran out from the courtyard and into the kitchen to see what the troubling was all about. And sir, having heard the commotion, they ran back out!"

"This is entirely not possible, James. Someone did this thing and caused Miriam to flee."

"Well, not entirely correct, sir. She was as staggered that next day as we all were. Well, not all, sir, if I may correct myself. Mrs. Waverly appeared quite unaffected by the ruckus. Miriam and I wondered if perhaps she found it amusing to frighten Willham and so we reasoned she was not affected because she herself was the one who committed the deed. But then I recalled I heard the hard shutting of her door and realized that all others had been accounted for, and it had to have been her door and therefore, sir, she who closed it."

"I still name this foolery. We shall get to the bottom of that. But now tell me what transpired between Miriam and Hannah?"

"Ah, sir, it was nearly as bad as the phantom piano playing. I dare say worse. Mrs. Waverly was particularly unkind to Miriam the entire time you were in New York. Each day it grew worse, and then finally Hannah said some dreadful, revolting things to her and called her names that no woman would to another, or deeply shame themselves. Then Miriam, I suppose tired of it all, ran down the stairs, and Hannah close behind her, threw things at Miriam as she fled. A shoe, a book, and the vase on the second floor landing, which sir, I am sorry to inform you is broken beyond repair. And with that, Miriam turned toward Hannah and reversed course and lunged up the stairs at Hannah, who ran in a fright, screaming, she was, but running away and then took refuge in her room and bolted the door. But Miriam told her what she thought of her right through that door! It was all so...you know sir."

"Hmm!" Martin laughed. "And where is Mrs. Waverly now?"

"I think she is in the library. Little Theresa brought her a tea not a half hour ago."

"Poor Theresa. We shall remedy this, James. Now."

Martin took long strides out of the kitchen, into the entryway, past the second parlor, and down the hall, and James trotted behind him. Martin stopped suddenly just before he was about to enter the library and James bashed into his back.

"Sorry, sir."

Martin frowned, steadied his anger for fear of what he might do to Hannah when he saw her, and walked calmly into the room.

Hannah sat near the fire with a book in her lap and tilted her eyes ever so slightly as he walked in. "I presume you have come to ask me about Miriam." She dipped her eyes back down to the book.

"No, I know what happened. I'm here to deliver an ultimatum to you."

Hannah slowly closed the book and shifted around to look toward Martin where he stood near the doorway. "I do so love to spar with you. Go on then; tell me what manner of gauntlet you will throw down for me this day. I'm glad for it. I'm bored."

"You will leave Waverly today."

"Or what?" She laughed.

"Or you will live in Miriam's old room, and when I fetch her from wherever she has gone to, she will reside in yours."

"You cannot force this, Martin. You're behaving exceedingly so— unhinged...and childish, as usual. Siding with the servants? My word. Go away and do whatever it is that occupies you these days and let me alone with my reading." She flicked her hand in his direction and opened the book again.

"No," he answered flatly. "That's not to be. Get up woman and collect your things. Move them to Miriam's or, as I prefer, move them entirely out of this house."

Hannah sighed, as though bored, and nestled back into the chair. She turned a page, and sighed again.

"Mrs. Waverly, if I might, I—"

She tossed the book down and stood. "Are you addressing me, James? Did I ask you to speak, you wretched, twisted, excuse for a man!" She clenched her hands into tight fists and pounded them against her legs. Her face turned red, and James backed away. But Martin did not.

"You are done here, Hannah. Done." He stalked toward her, head down, and when he came to stand beside her, she lifted her chin in defiance.

"What? What is the taunt now, Martin? Did you intend to strike me?" She smiled.

"No."

In one motion he collected Hannah in his arms, tossed her like a sack of wheat over his shoulder, and marched away with her dangling there, thrashing at his sides, his head, as they went. He went back down the hall, where many of the servants had gathered to observe the tumult, past the second parlor, and through the kitchen and then straight to Miriam's old room. He kicked the partially open door wide until it banged upon its hinges and nearly flung Hannah inside. He slammed the door shut and called James to retrieve a set of keys that had not been used in more than 80 years but still hung by the fire.

Martin held the doorknob tightly while James did as was asked, and once Martin had the keys, he turned them in the door lock, shutting Hannah inside.

"No one will release Mrs. Waverly," he ordered as he turned to address the servants who had followed them into the kitchen. "No one. Should I discover that any of you have opened that door for any reason at all, you will *all* be dismissed and set out on Christmas Day, which I remind you is tomorrow, and you will be out in the cold and snow with nothing on your backs but the clothes you wear!"

He had shouted at a volume he had not used in many years, but it was necessary in order for him to be heard above the foul words she screamed from behind the closed door. No lady would whisper much less bellow the things she uttered!

The servants nodded in agreement, furiously, one might say, and there could be heard a burst of giggling from Theresa, the newest and youngest of the staff.

"Now get back to—to—whatever you were all doing, and someone fetch me tea, blast it all!"

He lurched away and disappeared out the front door but returned a moment later, to the sight of the servants still standing where he left them as though they had become frozen to the floor. Hannah, continuing to hurl a barrage of profanities, repeatedly kicked the locked door.

He tore at his hair and screamed, "And! And! Happy Christmas!"

Sarcasm dripped from his words. His arms flagged in the air, and then he stalked back out the front door.

"Shall we bring him his Christmas Eve dinner then?" Theresa asked, wringing her tiny hands.

"Oh, shut it," James snarled and walked out of the room via the side door to the courtyard, without bothering to pull on his coat.

With that, Theresa burst into tears and sobbed, to the backdrop of the howls emanating from Hannah's new quarters.

Martin spent Christmas Eve alone in the cottage, forcing into his stomach the delectable fare cook had prepared and delivered to the cottage door. He expressed his regrets for not sitting in the dining hall where the staff had made a fine show of brightly colored linens and fresh garland strung along the walls and above the doors in the hopes of cheering him. They had even decked out an additional Christmas tree and set it near his chair in the dining room, although there had always been just one customarily situated in the library. Each was so fond of their new master and wanted nothing more than to know that they had earned his kindness. But it was for naught.

He feigned a headache, but in truth, he could not imagine sitting at the lonesome table and digesting food, no matter how sumptuous it was, while listening to the howls that Hannah continued to inflict on the entire household.

But about nine that evening, he could bare neither the solitude nor guilt for a moment more, and with a reluctant heart, he pulled his great black coat about himself and walked the hemlock-lined path to the mansion.

As he made his way slowly along the drive, Phillip at his side, he thought about Rene and Willham who were ensconced within his estate's walls but stated their intention of leaving the day after Christmas. They had been wise to make themselves scarce. He pondered the state of his dim-witted heart and engaged in relentless self-rebuke. How, he wondered, could he have thought he loved a woman such as Hannah? Perhaps it was not love at all, he reasoned, but a twisted thing borne out of hatred for his father. He was deeply pleased that he had never pushed her too far in his regard, or she might have given him his way, and there would be a completely new set of woes to untangle.

'*Remember to thank God for prayers left unanswered*' his mother often said. But he could not in good conscience leave Hannah imprisoned in a dingy room on Christmas Eve, no matter her transgressions, and he would free her that night.

But first, he intended to draw all the servants together and sit with them in his library, where he would hand each of them a fine sum of money, the gifts he had bought them while in New York City, and tell them that they must invite their families to celebrate Christmas Day with them at Waverly Estate.

The moment he entered the great hall at the entrance, he was struck by the silence that greeted him. It caused a great sadness to rise through him, and he felt shame. He walked to the kitchen where they were all sitting, enjoying the food cook had prepared. They stood, but he waved them to sit.

"I was going to speak with you in my library, but, here you all are together. So I shall make it easier for us all. You must bring your families here tomorrow to enjoy Christmas Day. There will be no more long faces to darken this already too dark place. And here…for you. Small tokens of my appreciation." He withdrew from his coat ten envelopes each tied carefully in red ribbon. "Spend it as you wish. Be careless with it, and make sure whatever you choose to do with it, you choose it because it makes you feel happy." He handed each of them an envelope and watched as not one of them moved to remove the bows to examine the contents. "As you wish." He laughed. "But if you go to my library, you will find gifts for all of you with your names attached to each. Please go and fetch them and bring them to the parlor where you might share in your opening of them. Hmm?" They did not move. "Go!" He laughed, and Theresa was the first to set straight for her gift, screeching her chair as she went. The others, save for James, followed.

"This is quite kind of you, sir." James fondled the envelope and laid it down to the table. "You've made a happy house tonight. I dare say I have never seen it so. It's been many years…"

"It's long due, James. We both know that."

"I have something for you, sir. Something I've been saving for such a night. Will you come fetch it with me? It's just in my room."

Martin followed him down the hall and up the short stairs to the servants' quarters and stopped at the room where Hannah was locked within. He paused to listen but heard not a single sound.

"Has she been quiet all evening?" he asked, and James smiled with one side of his mouth.

"No, she was going on for a long while until suddenly the commotion ended, and I thank God for that." He laughed.

James stopped at his door and turned to face Martin. "Sir, please excuse the sight of this. When my blessed Caroline was alive, she surely did make neat of things and always brought in fresh flowers to cheer the place, but…"

"Ah, James…no, don't worry yourself over—" He stopped speaking as they entered the room. "I haven't been in this room in what is it now, James? Twenty years? I have fond memories. Oh…" He walked to James's chest of drawers and lifted a frame that contained two photographs.

"Yes. I don't speak of them very much. Some days there is no point to it. But I miss them. Surely you know that."

"Ah, this is—this is Amelia. Your daughter. She played piano with my mother some evenings after she finished her work. She looks rather like—no. That can't be, so never mind it. And this is Caroline, your wife. A lovelier woman there never was, indeed. It was dreadful that she was taken by the lung disease."

"Yes, but who does Amelia remind you of, sir? Tell." He took the photographs from Martin and stared into the eyes of his wife and daughter.

"A young woman I saw on the path along the river, the night we buried my father."

A troubled expression overtook James' face, and he gently set the frame back atop the dresser. "I see," he said, as he turned away from it. "She was very fond of you as I recall it, always defending you to your father and…well…it is long past, but sad, how when Caroline left us, Amelia blamed your family for her mother's demise. But Amelia was not well. In her spirit. Was she…" He grabbed Martin's arm and gently wagged at it. "Forgive me, sir, for speaking thus, but she was wrong. She was very wrong. We mustn't speak of it again. And it is Christmas! And I brought you here to give you something, yes?" He smiled, and walked across the tiny room to a very old trunk that creaked on its hinges when he pulled it open. "Here. I've saved this for you. At your mother's wish. She asked that I wait, and so I did. Here, sir. Merry Christmas."

Martin reached his hand out and took the small box from James, but before he could discover its contents, they turned their heads toward the doorway as a shuffling sound met their ears. They waited, it passed, and Martin sat on a chair beside a woodstove and gently, slowly, opened the lid.

"It is a pin as you can see. A lovely diamond and sapphire pin. See? It's shaped like a dragonfly, and before her, it belonged to your grandmother and her mother before. Yes, it's very old, and Anne intended to give it to you when you married. For your bride. But one day before she died, it would not have been more than perhaps a month before, sir, she came to me and asked that I keep it safely for you—that I must give it to you at your marriage. But seeing how you appear intent on being without wife, I thought this a good time to give it to you."

Martin sat with the beautiful pin in his hand and set it in his palm. He looked long at it, watching as the light from the stove caused the stones to shimmer and glitter.

"I don't know what to say, James. Thank you. Thank you for being present in my life tonight and for so many nights preceding. You are not my servant, James, and you must call me Martin because you are my family."

"You, sir—Martin—you have always, in my heart, been like a son to me though circumstances prevented me from expressing it."

"Ah! Enough sentimentality, James! Let's go free the wild woman and hope she behaves."

James turned away, wiped a solitary tear from his eye, and nodded his head. "Yes, it is Christmas after all. A time of miracles."

Martin laughed and patted James on the back as they walked the hall to free Hannah.

"Are you ready to come out, Hannah?" Martin asked as he rapped lightly on the door.

"Go away, you beast," she said, and sniffled once then twice, no doubt for effect.

"Very well then. You shall sit in there all night by yourself and pout."

"Hmmph," was the reply.

But she was not alone.

FIVE

He had fallen asleep in the large chair beside the fire in his library, after the servants had all opened their gifts; they were so gleeful that they had burst into off-key renditions of favored Christmas songs.

He awoke to the sound of laughter, and he must have been slumbering for some time because there was nothing but ember within the stone fireplace. A strange sensation quickly replaced the shiver he felt. Was it happiness? He thought so. Perhaps. Maybe. It had been so long.

Dragging his hands through the tangles of his hair, he smiled. He listened to children running the halls of the mansion. Playing! Shouting! Singing! He smiled. Christmas Day.

Emerging from the library, a tiny child of perhaps five years of age ran headlong into his legs and bounced off, to land on her bottom. He bent down, picked her up, and looking into her face, he surmised that she could not have been anyone else's daughter but cook's.

"I believe this child belongs to you?" He smiled and handed the very blonde little girl back to her mother.

"Thank you, sir! And a Very happy Christmas to you!"

"And to you, cook Sharon!"

He spent the day pleasantly in the company of people he discovered were more than their titles and far more than their functions within the household.

Beatrice, the rotund upstairs maid, had two grown children and her husband had run off with the loosest woman in town. Terrance, the groundskeeper, was the son of an Indian woman and Dutch merchant but did not seem the least bit interested in discussing any of it.

Daniel, one of the stable boys, had fallen helplessly in love with Theresa, apparently overnight. He was massively built with arms that seemed coiled to strike and a ruddy complexion that gave hints to the amount of time spent outdoors. A former servant had suggested him for the position of stable hand He was accepted into Waverly Estate's employ after his father, Samuel, had been killed aboard one of the Waverly Shipping's steamboats, which exploded off the coast of the Carolinas when the ship's boiler exploded. Martin attempted to explain why there had been so many similar explosions of steamboats in recent years and enlightened the young man regarding Congress' passing of the Steamboat Act of May 30, 1852, which would enforce better inspection of the ships. He realized it was a law too late in coming to undo his father's fate but could think of nothing else to offer. Daniel seemed unwilling to discuss his father or his terrible death, so Martin moved toward Stephen, the older of the two stable workers.

Stephen had his hopes set on becoming a physician, if he could only find a way to attend medical school. Martin had resolved to help the young man succeed.

They ate. They drank. For that one day, they were merry; they were family. They were, dare he say it...happy.

Despite Martin's insistence that Hannah leave her temporary room, she continued to refuse. Sometime around midnight that Christmas evening, Willham and Rene climbed into a carriage and it drove away down the snowy lane. If they intended to leave and return, or had left before planned, Martin did not care. Every moment they were not present was a moment he felt he had reclaimed his home.

"Will you be moving back in, sir—Martin?" James smiled as he walked into the second parlor and stood near Martin who sat in a chair near the Christmas tree.

"I think so. Perhaps in a day or so. Do you know if our house guests have left for good?"

"I'm afraid not. They told someone, I forget who, that they needed to attend to something in town. But on Christmas Night? Ah! I don't know. Won't we be happier when they are gone!"

"I thought they might have tried to insinuate themselves into our merriment today. But alas, all was calm and bright." He smiled. "I suppose a little charity might have been kind on my part, but they have been prickly thorns from the start. Why are you still prowling about tonight? It's rather late."

"Ah, Martin, I confess that I had a little too much Christmas cheer and find it hard to sleep. And you?"

Martin shrugged. "I suppose after hearing this old place so filled with joy and good will, the thought of returning to the cottage is, well, not particularly appealing."

"I've made your old room ready, Martin. I thought perhaps you'd grant us all the pleasure of your time here. The fire is burning, the shades are pulled, and old Phillip's bed is beside yours. Go. Sleep. Tomorrow is soon enough to worry. Tonight? Dream happy dreams, Martin. I'll leave you to it. Goodnight."

Martin watched him walk away and knew that beginnings sometimes had to start in the middle of things, and nothing was meant to be perfect, but most things could be made right.

It was near dawn when Martin awoke to the sound of terrible screaming. Phillip lifted his head and made a low rumbling noise that came from deep within his chest.

"Shhh, old man. All is well. It seems Mrs. Waverly wants out. But she can wait another while. If it becomes too much of a bother to those sleeping nearby, someone will fetch us. Sleep again, my friend. We'll deal with her later." He had taken to speaking to the beast in complete sentences that Phillip sometimes appeared to comprehend. The dog lay back down, grumbling, and Martin buried his head beneath the pillows to block out the shrieks. "God in heaven make her stop. Make her stop. Make her stop." And just like that, the prayer was answered.

James found Hannah cowering on her side in a quivering heap, her head wedged in the corner of the room she had insisted on staying in, her legs drawn up to her stomach. He tried to lift her, but being a man of some sixty-five years and arms no longer capable of lifting more than a sack, he managed to sit her up and shouted to Theresa that she must fetch Martin from his bed.

"What is it, Theresa?" Martin sat straight up as she ran into his bedroom and from the doorway, in a high-pitched voice, stuttered and cried out. It had something to do with Hannah, and witchery, and James. Not waiting to get the details, the inferences quite enough, he sprung from bed and bolted down the stairs.

"Martin!" James stood guard outside the bedroom door, and Martin needed to part his way through the servants that had gathered in the very narrow servant's hall to get inside. "I found her this way. Look."

Martin, taken aback to see her squatted down and rocking to and fro, called out to her. "Hannah. What is it? Are you ill?" He couldn't help the notion from rearing up that he had some hand in causing whatever ailed her. Hannah would not reply. She continued to rock herself back and forth, her arms crossed protectively around her trembling body. "Someone…" he ordered over his shoulder, "get Daniel, and have him ride fast into town and bring Doctor Matthews. Now!" He lifted her ever so gently up and crossed from the kitchen to the second parlor where he placed her softly down on the divan near the Christmas tree.

"No, no, no no!" she wailed repeatedly. "No!" She tossed her body from the divan and began to crawl away like a crippled child, but Martin lifted her once again and attempted to place her back onto the cushions. She flailed at his body and used her nails to scratch at his face. He pushed her down, but she was so filled with terror, or sickness, or something of both that he found it necessary to take her from the parlor at once, and he climbed the stairs, two at a time, to the bedroom she had some years ago claimed as her own.

"What is it, Hannah? What's happened? Please. Tell me; do tell me." He smoothed her hair back, but she recoiled. Then her eyes flew open, wide, as though something landed upon his shoulder that caused her immense terror to behold. She shrieked.

"I'll sit with her, sir. Don't mind it. I'll bring her a basin and wash her face and hands with cool water. Leave us be." Theresa, thankfully, had suddenly proven herself more than a silly child. Martin backed slowly away, afraid that even a sudden motion might be enough to cause the terrible shrieks to begin again.

He closed the door and stood outside of it, as a vile mixture of confusion and dread choked his throat closed. What in the world could have happened to her? What in heaven's name had she met with?

"Martin, this is confounding. I heard her at dawn, and as you wished, I left it be, and then suddenly the calling out, the screaming stopped again, as before, and I thought all was right. But then when I rose to make you coffee, I heard something like whimpering coming from within the room, and having not heard anything quite like that since, well, since Amelia...I burst in and found her nearly as you saw her. What has happened, Martin? What is this?" His eyes were terror-filled, and sad, and bore an awful reminder of what had happened to his lovely daughter Amelia when she had lost her mind. He pushed hard at the remembrance, hoping to force its departure, but who could easily jettison a memory of their only daughter swinging from the barn rafters, rope tied to their neck?

"I don't know, James. We'll hope Doctor Matthews can sort this out and then, I guess, I don't know, I guess we'll...wait." And then something occurred to him, and he asked, "Where is Willham? Rene?"

"I'm not certain they have come back from town after having left late last night. I'll knock on their doors and…" He turned sharply on his heels and ran down the hall where he banged heavily on the doors. But no one answered his insistent calls.

She's had some kind of shock, Martin." Doctor Matthews spoke in a hush. "Do you have any idea what may have precipitated this?" Martin, readied to confess what he had done, was spared when James responded. "Nothing. She slept, and then we found her in this state this morning."

"I've given her something to calm her nerves and taken the liberty of calling on Margaret to care for her. She was a good nurse to your father. Perhaps she will do the same with Hannah. Send for me again, should you need me. For now, we can do nothing. It's a pity to see so much despair at Christmas, and so close to her husband's death. Perhaps the grief was too much for her and it broke her spirit. I'm sorry, Martin."

What, Martin wondered, could he possibly do with Hannah now? James patted him on the shoulder and shook his head.

"I'm sorry for this trouble, Martin. But please don't take it to yourself. Something strange and powerful is surely at work here; that a sturdy woman such as she is broken…and in this…this…state."

Martin walked past the bed where Hannah laid sleeping, leaned his hands to the windowsill, and looked out. The new sun had broken through the snow clouds and cast a peculiar pink light to the snow.

"It's witchcraft at work here, Master Martin." Theresa stood behind him, her hands wrapped around her neck. "It's the spirits come to—"

Martin spun around.

"Stop that!" James yelled and was tempted to give the girl the back of his hand but thought better of it. "Go and sit with her, child. Go."

Theresa shook her head. "Please, Master Martin, don't make me do what he says. She told me strange things indeed when I washed her, and now I fear her, sir, so please don't make me do it. Please, sir, please."

"What did she say?" Martin gripped her gently by the shoulders.

"She said, 'I won't leave but rolled along behind the creped carriage, and you shall all follow behind me to the grave!' And I said, 'No, Mrs.! This is a bad spell, 'tis all, you wait and see!' And then her eyes fixed to mine and she said, 'You and your kind are safe, but the Waverlys will never be.' And then she called out a name to me. She said, 'Amelia! Amelia!' But I said, 'No, my name is Theresa, Mrs., and you know that well.' But she said the name again and then became very still before her poor body began shaking all over again."

"Go to your room and rest, Theresa. There is no need for you to sit with her now. Go."

Theresa bolted past them and ran down the stairs, crying as she went.

Martin looked to James' face and it was white as the snow out the doors.

"James, let's discuss this in the hall." He looked toward Hannah, whose back was to him, her breaths slow and easy. He partially closed the door and continued once in the hall. "Perhaps she is feigning this sickness. Or some other manner of ill. Perhaps she knows about your daughter and—"

"I don't know. I don't care to know. But whether she is victim to witchery as Theresa claims or is playing a sinister game, I cannot and will not, engage with her again. Pardon me, please. I need to see to my duties." He walked away, and Martin wished he could, too.

He reentered the room, giving a look toward Hannah again, walked back to the window, and leaned his unshaven face against the cold pane. Theresa and Daniel stood together talking, the young girl's hands plastered to her cheeks. Then Daniel suddenly drew her to his chest and pressed her head into it. He smoothed her curly ash hair back and rocked her as one would a child. Martin felt a wave of remorse, and the pain of wasted time spilled over him. How he longed for someone's arms to take refuge in! He moved away to sit in a chair near Hannah's bed, preferring to occupy the space than be tortured further by the sight of the young lovers.

It was not for her that he sat guard. No. It was long past the time that he could care in that way. Rather, he sat there for his own compensation because simply, it was the humane thing to do.

She mumbled something about graves and a woman or girl by the name of Martha, and he thought the name struck a familiar chord, but he could not recall if it belonged to a favored aunt or a child she had once known. But none of it bore substance to the problems that faced him, and he leaned back, closed his eyes, and forced himself to think of finer things.

 Sir."

Martin jolted awake and sat up, disoriented, his mind still entertaining a dream from which he had been interrupted. "Margaret?"

"Sir, yes. I'm here for the lady, sir. Go get yourself something to eat. It's well past five in the evening. Nothing will be served if you too turn up sick." She pressed a caring hand to his arm, and he nodded.

"You've been told about her? All of it?" he asked, making slowly for the door.

"Indeed. Every detail. More than I needed to know, as you can imagine, since it was told to me by James and Theresa, and then of course by the others. Oh, how they went on with rubbish about spirits and pianos and Mrs. Waverly howling!"

He nodded his head. "Pleased you would come back to this place, Margaret. I am ever so grateful to you, and you will be rewarded for your kindness. I'll tell Theresa to bring you food and a steady flow of tea."

"Pish posh. Go on now. I'll call on you if needed." She turned away from him and leaned over Hannah to place a cool rag to her forehead.

In the kitchen, James helped cook prepare something for Martin's supper. They went wordlessly about their chore and were so involved in their own quiet contemplation that they scarcely heard Martin as he sat down at the servants' table.

"Ah, good. You need to eat," James said, and cook immediately presented him with a steaming bowl of venison stew. The very sight of it turned his stomach and he pushed it away. "Something wrong with it?" James peered into the bowl.

"No, no. I'm just not hungry. I need to go riding and clear my head." He made no apologies and instead went to the hall to collect his coat and riding boots and walked around the courtyard toward the stable.

The light had begun to dim, and he, for a moment, thought his ride would be ill-advised, but his intent was to gently travel the boundaries of the property, nothing more, then return, he hoped, with an appetite for the stew.

Upon entering the stable, he caught sight of Theresa and Daniel entwined in a lover's embrace and cleared his throat to warn his approach. Theresa ran for the stable door, hitching her skirt up as she passed by him.

"Master Martin. I do regret this, but I want to marry her. And all is very proper."

"And she agreed to this?" Martin wanted to smile but refrained.

"Indeed she has, sir, and we hope to stay on here and work for you."

"Of course. Now get my Morab. She needs a ride."

"The Morab? Sir, she's been skittish of late. Perhaps you should take—"

"No, I want the Morab. Now, please."

Daniel hurried to do as he was told.

The horse was a Morab named Isabella, and first bred in The Americas in the 1800's. She was to be part of the breeding stock his father brought to Waverly Estate some years before, but Martin and Isabella had taken a fondness for each other and had become his favorite pleasure riding horse.

She was a lovely chestnut with white boots, intelligent eyes, and a long sturdy neck paired with a muscular body and sturdy back that could support Martin who stood at 6'4 and was muscular in his own right. The Arabian and Morgan cross was a gentle and calm beast, and if he had children, he thought wistfully, he would have entrusted them to her.

"It's dark, sir; please be careful. You never know what may be creeping about." Daniel patted the horse's lovely neck and stared up at Martin.

Martin said nothing as he led Isabella out into the courtyard. He mounted her, and at a slow walk guided her out along the long drive. He did not push her forward, but rather, they both seemed to enjoy the cold air and silence, save for their breaths and crunch of her hooves touching the crusted snow. They made their way along the rows of hemlock trees and at the end of the drive headed west toward the river. Then they stopped.

Against the starlit sky, the silhouette of an owl passed overhead and descended to gather its meal; the sound of its great wings, parting air as it went, seemed magnified by the utter silence. In the distance, he discerned the giant limbs of the maple tree near the path, but rather than climb the hill, he pulled the reigns around and headed toward home. Renewed, he thought about stew for himself and some lovely oats for Isabella. All would be well. He was sure of it in that moment, and he managed a smile.

Halfway down the drive, something to their right stirred. Isabella hesitated and perked her ears toward the direction. It was a soft noise, perhaps a small creature burrowing in for the night. He pulled her gently up and their heads turned toward the sound. As he had surmised, a small brown rabbit hopped from the hedge and crossed their paths. Isabella snorted and bobbed her head. But they did not see the soundless shadow that passed behind as it wandered toward the hill.

"Ah, we have caught some manner of jitters, my friend. Let's go and…" He did not finish his sentence as screams interrupted their rare moment of peace. "Oh…no. It's coming from the house." He did not need to encourage the horse to gallop toward the shrieks, and they set off at a dead run.

Without fully pulling the horse up as they arrived near the front doors, he swung his body from her, landing close to the staff that stood in the courtyard, huddled together. With the exception of Margaret and Daniel, all were present. "What's happened?" he asked as he strode toward the arches that led to the doors. James trailed behind.

"It's Rene, sir. Rene is dead!" James replied, his voice labored as he tried to keep up with Martin.

"Dead? By what? Where is he?" He stopped at the door before going in.

"I don't know, Martin. We don't know! We smelled a terrible stench, and hunting it down, we found the source to be Miriam's old room where Hannah had been, and upon further investigation, poor Theresa, thinking perhaps Hannah had left food to rot, peeped under the bed, and there he was! Rene! Dead, I tell you, Martin. Very dead. Crammed beneath the bed skirts with his mouth agape and—"

A million thoughts twisted this way and that through his mind, and he could neither stop them from pouring in, nor could he force them to continue in an orderly way. He just stood there, one foot on the threshold and one out, his eyes fixed on James.

"Has someone fetched the authorities?"

"Yes, Martin. Daniel has ridden out. Not two minutes ago."

"I came from there and saw no one on the drive." He turned around and saw that the servants had turned toward him, Theresa, clinging to cook as both women cried, and the rest staring numbly at him. The thought that he had not seen Daniel as he galloped along the drive brushed aside, he continued. "James, bring them into the dining room, and do not allow them to leave there. Have Stephen fetch Isabella and bed her down. Direct him to come in when done."

"What has happened, Martin, what…and why again?" It was a rhetorical question, and Martin, shaking his head, ran in and up the stairs. His instinct always was to check on Hannah before he did anything else.

Margaret stood beside Hannah's empty bed, her face ashen, and her arms dangling limply at her sides. Her eyes were wide, terror filled, and tears streamed down her cheeks. The teacup that Theresa had brought to her was empty, the china broken on the floor near the window.

"Where is she!" he cried out, but no reply came. Margaret stood statue-like, save for the quick shaking of her head. "Did she leave?" Still, she said nothing. "Margaret! Take a hold of your senses this instant, and answer me!"

Finally, without taking her eyes from Martin's, slowly, very slowly, she lifted her left arm, and one finger rose to point toward the windows.

He rushed to them and saw that they were closed.

"She came in through there, sir. She came in, and when I woke, I thought I was dreaming. She lifted the lady up and went. Like that. Just like that. Floating through them."

Another had lost her mind, and although he doubted it would be a permanent condition, he set her on the edge of the bed and ran down the stairs toward the body of Rene Bonhomme.

It was as James told it. Rene, still wedged beneath the bed, mouth opened wide as if he had used his last breath to spend on a scream, was dead. Very dead, indeed.

Dried grey spittle puddled near his pale face. The positioning of his body, arms twisted impossibly around his body, legs, bent one over the other, head turned so far askew that one more inch would have meant his chin had turned 'round to the back of his neck. He could not have accomplished this himself. No. Someone had to have forced him beneath the bed, and whether alive or dead when done, the manner in which he'd become so horribly discombobulated was something that made the hair on Martin's arms stand erect.

"Martin." James stood at the door and motioned for Martin to come from the room. He stood, but his legs, feeling unsteady, caused him to pause at the doorway. He gripped the doorframes with both hands. "This is a monstrous thing. Monstrous. Margaret and Hannah, sir?"

"Margaret is—adrift in...something. She's in Hannah's room. And as for Hannah? Hannah is gone."

"Gone? What do you mean, gone?" James grabbed Martin's sleeve and led him toward the kitchen.

"Gone. As in vanished. As in no longer in her room. Are the staff all in the dining room?"

"Yes."

"Then you and I will search every corner of this cursed house until we find Hannah. You begin down here. I will take to the second floor. Go." He shoved James' shoulder and stalked off toward the stairs.

M r. Barberry, who served as the area's police officer, after having interviewed at great length each servant and Martin himself, repetitively tapped his fingers on the dining table.

Martin, finding it immeasurably irritating, scowled. "Mr. Barberry, do cease that unseemly noise!"

"Right. Apologies. There's nothing more I can do here. It seems, to summarize days of trials and tribulations, that Mrs. Waverly has disappeared in a peculiar manner—if you don't mind me understating the account, and Rene Bonhomme is quite dead. Murdered, of course, and no one saw a thing. No one knows anything in this place of yours, Mr. Waverly, and each of you vouch for the others' whereabouts during the times stated, save for Margaret the nurse being devoid of an alibi and mildly witless at present. She claims that Mrs. Waverly, guided by a woman, flew out through closed windows, or now as amended, through a wall near the window," he recounted and stopped long enough to smirk before continuing. "So truly, the suspect, as we might call him or her, is wandering your halls or has left to parts unknown. The man not accounted for is one Mr. ah…blasted and confounded, what is the gentleman's name. Ah yes. A Willham Montrose, who was last seen riding off in a carriage with the deceased, before he became regrettably deceased of course, on Christmas near midnight, and not afterward. The previous occupant of the room where the unfortunate was found, a Mrs. Miriam Mandalay, has not been heard from since her departure after a squabble with Mrs. Waverly. So I'm sure you can join me in saying this is all very odd, and something is missing from the retelling of the story. Some manner of hoodwinkery is afoot, sir. A man was murdered somewhere in these many rooms, stuffed like pork back under a bed on the servants floor, left dead for perhaps a day or more, and no one heard a thing."

"Sir, are you insinuating that we have, any of us, lied to you?" Martin leaned toward the man and frowned.

"Mr. Waverly, there are things called lies of omission. They are punishable if found out. So I strongly suggest that you use whatever sway you enjoy with your servants—or beat the truth out of them. The men have come to fetch the body, and our examiner miles from here in Albany will examine the remains. Our force, while small, shall continue our investigations until the murderous brute is discovered and locked away. As for your Mrs. Waverly, we have joined with you and the others in a thorough search of both house and grounds, and having not found a single hair pin from her head, I can confidently presume she has gone, most likely on her own accord and without the aid of sprites or ghoulish apparitions— and possibly with Mr. Montrose. I expect you will tell me if either of them returns. Doctor Matthews has clearly said that he cannot be certain whether Mrs. Waverly was feigning illness or was truly unwell since no medical device available can discern such a thing. And that is that. I'll come around again. Good day, Mr. Waverly. But wait, before I go…do tell how you came by those scratches on your brow."

Martin, having forgotten that Hannah had dug her nails into his face, reached up and touched the four reddened welts that marred his cheeks and forehead. "Oh. I was walking in the dark, looking for Hannah and was scratched by the evergreen near the garden trellises."

"Hmm. I see. One cannot be too careful when wandering about in the dark."

Martin was not all that convinced that Barberry believed the explanation but was grateful that the man turned to leave without saying a thing more.

As James led Mr. Barberry to the doors, Martin laid his head down onto his arms and took a deep breath. If any of the servants told the policeman that he had locked Hannah in the room where Rene was found—if any of them had told of her screams and protestations, surely, he concluded, he would be sitting not in the familiarity of his home, but in a filthy jail. All things, of course, considered. He would not have been jailed for being unkind to his stepmother, short of murdering her, and the entirety could have been construed as a family squabble, messy though it was. Eyes would have been cast to some other person who may have had a hand in the murderous deed. But it was no secret that he viewed Rene as an irksome interloper in his house, one that stood between him and an elusively peaceful existence. Or perhaps they would take a leap and think he had murdered the man because of Hanna's infidelity against his father. Whichever way he looked at it, he came 'round to the same conclusion. He was fortunate to have servants that loved him. Or maybe, he thought with a jolt of awareness, they were simply protecting each other.

Somehow, he concluded, what saved him from further inquiry into his personal affairs, was the strange disappearance of Hannah and the rather odd, Willham Montrose, since their absence cast a shadow of guilt upon one or both. He prayed they would stay missing. He prayed it mightily, much to his chagrin.

He got up slowly, almost painfully, the last few days having taken their toll, and climbed the stairs to his rooms where he hoped to sit alone, unmolested, with his dog. But passing by the room where Hannah was last seen, he felt compelled to peer in. He gently pushed open the door. Margaret sat in the chair by the window, staring out into the dark, with her back to him. Her left arm hung from the side of the chair, and he saw just a hint of her tight bun as he quietly pulled the door shut. Continuing on, he opened the door to what had been Rene's room and walked about it hoping to find some trace of anything the policeman could have overlooked. There was a small fortnighter bag, which in itself seemed odd considering how long he remained at Waverly, a book-sized sketchpad, some drawing pencils, and a black coat hanging across a chair.

Opening the drawers, he saw nothing of consequence and neither did the pad hold any clue. Checking the inside and outside pockets of his coat, he found only a small bit of paper that appeared to have been ripped from a larger piece. Barberry could have easily overlooked it. The words written upon it simply said, *'Chandler at noon'*. He made a note of it, replaced it, and continued.

He repeated the same process as he riffled through Willham's belongings, but it appeared he had either taken the majority away with him or did not have much with him to begin with when he arrived at Waverly. If he had gone for good, why didn't he collect what remained of his belongings?

The windows along the hall proved draftier than he would have liked, and he reminded himself that they needed repair. In fact, they had become so loosed from the jam and sill that the curtains moved with the draft, or so he presumed.

Passing three more rooms to the right and left, he stopped as he eyed his father's door at the very end of the hall. He walked toward it and sighed heavily. Had The Waverly Curse taken a detour and would now give no quarter to visitors, too? He leaned his head against the door, his shoulders dropping, as his hands touched the ornate wood. The motion pushed the door ajar, and with a start, he stepped back and sucked in a deep breath of air.

He had locked it, of course he had, and no one had a key. He reached out and pushed the door open until it was wide, and he stepped in. No one was there. Nothing appeared disturbed. He shut the door lightly, walked back down the hall and up the stairs where he went straight to bed, forcing himself to refuse any thought of it all until morning, but he remained sleepless.

The house was still when he woke the next morning near dawn. He walked down the halls and stairs, Phillip in tow. Headed for the kitchen and then the second parlor where he thought he would have a tea and read before the house woke, Theresa greeted him in the kitchen, and she smiled dimly at him.

"Good morning, sir. May I make your tea?" He nodded his head, and she set the water to boil.

"Thank you for staying here, Theresa. I know it cannot be easy, all things considered. I'm grateful to Daniel for recommending you."

"I'd never leave my Daniel behind. And I rather like it here, sir." She said the last of it almost as a polite afterthought.

"Do you? Forgive me for thinking that an odd statement, all things considered. But thank you. I'll wait in the second parlor for the tea." He got up, wearily, and walked into the hall.

"Very well, sir," she said, turning toward the kettle. "Afterward, as we discussed yesterday morning, I need to go to town. To see to that bit of fabric I saw hanging in Mrs. Cooper's mercantile window. The one with blue bonnie flowers and…" She stopped—he had already gone.

From behind the deep blue curtains that had been drawn for the night, a lovely light glowed as he walked in. He frequently sat long in the room, gazing out across his mother's garden that had, that week, become covered in snow. To some it might have appeared dreary, but to him, it was still full of life. The form and arches were still present through the year; the fine evergreens and bows of the juniper ripe with blue-green stems; the holly, pocked with gloriously bright red berries; bows, laden with powdery snow.

Pulling the curtain wide away from the window that gave him the best sight of it all, he stopped and stared. A startled voice within urged that he drop the heavy drapery and leave the room entirely, but he did not. There, beneath barren trellises, her back to him, a woman stood in shin-deep snow, her long wheat hair not bound up but free to her waist. Her olive green coat lightly flapped in the breeze.

At first sight, the word, *untamed*, floated into his mind.

"Sir, your tea." He spun around and seeing Theresa, strode the two steps toward her, reached out his hand, and grabbed her tightly by her arm, causing the tea to spill over and cup crash to the floor. So taken aback was she that she did not say a word. She stared at his face.

"Theresa, look!" He pointed toward the window and the woman in the snow.

"Sir?"

"The woman!" he shouted, looking back out the panes. But the lady was gone.

"Sir, I don't—"

"Never mind it, then," he said, and let go of her arm. He ran to the doors, and Theresa, more than confused and perhaps a bit frightened by it all, knelt to retrieve the broken cup from the parlor floor.

He thought perhaps he had been beset by the hallucinations that of late had been visited on the house, but as he entered near the garden, he saw the woman walking away along the space beneath arched evergreen hedges that led from the garden toward the hill and path.

As if she knew he had followed, she stopped, still not turning around, and said, "My name is Meredith Hamilton."

He rushed toward her and turned her 'round. "What are you doing here?"

"Looking at your mother's garden." She smiled.

"That I saw, madam, but do tell why. And from where have you come?" Her eyes, bright blue like that morning winter sky, shone a light he had never before observed in another's countenance.

"I am half-sister to Amelia, daughter of Caroline, or as James would have it, bastard child. Alternatively, as your father would say, I am the fairest of all his secrets."

"But—you can't mean our Caroline and James, or…"

"They are the same."

"But I was not told that you…why are you here? Your arrival is sudden, your statement abrupt!"

"Martin, if you understood who my father is, then perhaps you would not be so surprised to hear that I've been a well-kept secret. Until now. I suppose sometimes long-held secrets reveal themselves in what might seem a hasty fashion, but to the teller, they are long overdue, and one might feel compelled to blurt it all out. Quickly. To get it over with." She spoke unemotionally and without a solitary ounce of shame or regret. Rather, she seemed quite at home on the grounds and with the telling of her secret as though she knew every corner and hedgerow, and even familiar with Martin, and he remarked on it.

"You appear to understand how I view the remarkable nature of your unexpected appearance here as well as you know the grounds. Yet, my lady, you are very much a stranger to me, and I ask that you please come in and sit with me a while. So I might understand."

He held his hand out to her, and she took it, easily, as more evidence of a mystifying familiarity that he found both comforting and strange. Her small hand was soft but firm, and she slid it across his arm as he walked her away.

"Martin, the things I will tell you might rattle your otherwise organized presumptions regarding your life. It is your own, of course, and what you know about it should not be tampered with, if you are quite satisfied with what you feel you know. But if you will promise to hear me out, sir, you'll come away better for it all."

He stopped, looked down upon her earnest face that was not as fair as most ladies he had known. Rather, it had seen sun and wind, and her eyes, soft and ever so unearthly pale blue, told him that this was not a woman of a sitting parlor or a woman that had seen nothing of the world. No, this woman knew magic things; her eyes had seen places and people that he, as a young man, had only read of or dreamed.

"Lady, I fear only those things that refuse discovery, either by ignorance or design, since knowledge is not a fearsome thing, unless misused. I shall not exploit what you reveal, lady, never for sport or my own self-aggrandizement."

"You are exactly as your father described, Martin, exactly, and I shall take great comfort from that. And, I believe, in you."

Six

Miriam set her bags down at the front doors of the estate. Having taken Christmas with her sister in Albany after her abrupt departure, she had not intended to return to Waverly. Doubts crowded her decision to continue her employment at Waverly Estate, and she stood staring at the closed-door feeling seized with misgivings that left her with a terrible sense of foreboding. Had she made the right decision? She pushed it aside, opened the doors with effort, and walked in.

James, who had deciphered where she had run to after her skirmish with Hannah, had, at Martin's emphatic approval, sent a letter to her stating that she was missed and needed—that she must return at once. Miriam had no doubt that they would miss her, since no other understood the day-to-day functions and needs of the house as she did. But the sense of urgency she felt seep through the letter caused her great concern for Martin. Rather than respond to the request that she return, she simply packed her bags and took the next coach out of Albany. As if in too quick a time, she found herself back in Waverly Estate.

"Miriam!" James, ever the gentleman and not one to cross a proper margin, grasped her by her meaty arms, stared into her eyes, and shook her twice before tightly embracing her.

"James!"

"Pardon me, Miriam. I forgot myself." He released Miriam, but still, his eyes lingered on hers. "You're looking well! Come in. Come in. It's good to see you."

"I was told what happened here. By the coachman. He seemed eager to hear a telling of what I knew, but I disappointed." She followed James into the kitchen and sat down, wiping her brow with a hankie she had stowed inside her blouse.

"Ah, yes, so dreadful. I'll tell you all the gruesome details while we drink our tea. But first I need to tell you that Martin has been stowed in the cottage for hours. And still, as we speak! He was last seen running toward the gardens before ensconcing himself within his rooms."

"Do tell!"

"Theresa claims he saw a woman in the garden as she was about to serve him tea, but she did not see the lady, nor have any of us. I was told that he wandered the garden beneath the trellises and paused there, speaking to someone that could not be seen, due to, I think, the hedgerow."

"And you have no guess who this lady might be?"

"Not a stitch about her. But I'm sure we will know by and by."

"No doubt." Her eyes turned toward the doorway that led to the servants' hall and remained there as someone softly closed a door. "How is Theresa getting on?" she asked, still trained on the hallway.

"She's busily making herself needed, Miriam. If you get my meaning. She's an odd duck, I must say."

"Yes," answered Miriam, looking back to James. "I must have a word with her."

James nodded his head and related the events that led to the dreadful fate of Rene Bonhomme.

Theresa, it seems, was meant to hear every word that James and Miriam spoke. She sat at the edge of her little bed listening but was concerned that her decision to stay and find out as much as she could about Martin's guest was not the best idea. She needed to get to town, and it could not wait much longer. But to exit, she would need to pass by Miriam and James to be on her way. There would be questions asked of her, and by the sound of it, the woman would have more to say than time would allow her. So she lay back on her bed and stared at the cracks on the ceiling that fanned out in spider web form; she pondered the odd clash of want and need, daydreamed about what her life would be when it was all done...what her life should have always been. In time, she fell asleep. It was a fitful slumber, filled with visions of death and screams. But there was Daniel, his broad shoulders, his deep green eyes staring at her, making the worst of the nightmares somehow worthwhile.

M eredith sat upon Martin's settee, and nearby, Martin reclined in a high-back chair with long, padded arms. He stared into her lovely face for two hours and could not get his mind around what she had said no matter how he tried. Maybe, he mused, because he didn't want to. Or perhaps, he smiled to himself, as long as he continued to ask her to speak, the longer he would feel happy. Content. She was not frightened off by the tales he told her regarding Waverly's most recent history. Rather, it seemed to pique an interest in her—one that aroused her already inquisitive mind.

"I understand how it all must sound to you, Martin, but being a Naturalist isn't such a rare thing. Perhaps you haven't heard of Jane Colden. She worked her trade in this area of Ulster County. She was a fine woman, and I took up after her. She loved to read and had a special inclination for natural history. She was not a parlor mouse, Martin. She went out and catalogued plants and all manner of natural things, as I have done, following in her footsteps, literally, at times. But I suppose you wonder how a bastard child could make something of herself. Perhaps that's the real curiosity?"

"Meredith, could we please stop talking around this thing? I have gone gently toward it, not wanting to seem a brute, but considering your, shall we say, penchant for saying what you are thinking, good manners and gentle words be damned, I confess to being a little perplexed. Come out with it woman, please. How did you afford to be schooled? How do you know my father? And what in heaven's name were you doing in my mother's garden?" He dug his fingers into the arm of the chair, and she didn't fail to notice.

"The garden is lovely, and sometimes I had walked down to it when no one was there, just to look. But as for the rest, I suppose I hesitate telling it, although it is rather late for procrastination since being caught like a burglar on your property." There. She had done it again—smiled, and the questions and answers didn't matter; the room was empty of all save for her and that enchanting wildness that clung to her breath, her eyes, her hair, her—

"Please." His shoulder slumped down, and he waited.

"Then I will give it to you all at once. I will skip detail for now unless requested. Bear with me, please, Martin. This is the first time I have ever been permitted to tell a dot of it…A great American astronomer, her name is Maria Mitchell, said, '*People have to learn sometimes not how much the heart, but how much the head, can bear.*'"

"There are days when I think neither can take more of the same. But don't be afraid. We share in the curiosity in how the telling of it will end." He smiled weakly at her, hoping to encourage them both.

"That's a weedy smile, sir. But I'll go on. My parents adopted me. I was just a babe of two days. James had, during the two years before my birth, taken to the drink and foolery with the maids. Yes, I see your expression, but it is true. Caroline sought solace, which is a nice word to describe what came of her seeking it, from Pastor O'Mara, whose wife had taken ill and died suddenly on a lovely summer day. Caroline, having a new babe to rear in the confines of Waverly Estate, even if she managed to keep my parentage a secret, would have been nearly impossible. Her work here and the difficulty of dealing with a drunkard husband caused her to make the poor decision that brought me to the world and her own death. She died giving birth to me. And then, well, here I am."

"They said it was a lung disease that took her. But wait. Are you telling me that Pastor O'Mara is your true father?"

"Indeed. But to this day, he does not know where I had gone to. Your father loved Caroline, and understanding that he wasn't given to anything sentimental, still considered her something like a dear sister to him. So he took me as a babe and carried me off to Boston where he found a couple who had wanted of a child even in their late years. Your father cared for me, sent money to me, and provided me with schooling and all a child could need when my adoptive parents could do no more. They were older then, perhaps nearing sixty when they took me for their own. Late in life, one would think, and perhaps it is so, but they were wonderful and loved me well. I would continue to receive his assistance as long as I did not make myself known, and he requested it for the sake of all concerned, so I abided by his wishes, and I never said a word. As for James, he did not know she had born me. Neither does he know to this day that when she went away, it was not because she was ill, but because she was with child. He only knows what your father told him—and the good doctor. Back then James was too inebriated most of the time to have sought Caroline out. He never once tried to visit her."

"Then why are you here?"

"Because in Garson's last days he managed to write me a letter—I shall show it to you, if you care to read it some time. He wrote me many letters. I have boxes of them and cherish each, even now. He told me he would leave me Blythe House. And many times when you were away, he would tell me to stay there, and we had many pleasant times in that old house together. So, Martin, I know you well. Better perhaps than if I had met you because his telling of you caused me to understand you. And I confess sometimes I watched you from a distance, heard your voice, saw you ride your lovely mare across the fields. And that evening at your father's burial, I stood solitary taking every care not to be seen or heard so that I could watch as he was laid down to rest. Shocked, too, I must confess, at the location of his grave."

"You speak of him as a friend, a loving, kind man, which you found no fault in. He is buried in the place he earned by his deeds. And as you speak of him, I cannot help but think we aren't conversing about the same man."

She smiled. It was a gentle smile, and she leaned slightly forward. Her long hair swept forward across her shoulders, and she lowered her head. "That is the thing about life, isn't it, Martin? We can only know what we know. We each see the same moon, but from different angles, it may appear cloudless or bright like a sun in the sky."

"He's done terrible things."

"Have you done all good?"

"I have never, lady, *ever*, done things on level to his transgressions, his sins, his brutality of spirit and word. Never. And if I should find myself falling down that terrible chasm of ill-will and dark spirit, I think I could not breathe for the ache it would create within me."

"I am not totally ignorant to the things he has done. I am not totally without sympathy for you and his harsh treatment of you. Perhaps he did not know how to love you or anyone he felt demanded something from him. Perhaps because I didn't know I required him for a solitary thing, he was at ease to provide me with all he had given."

"Meredith, I shall keep your secrets safely here." He patted his chest near his heart. "I will not lie. I think, after hearing you speak of him, that he let you know the parts of himself that were most agreeable. I do not know why. But what shall we say about you to those who already express inquisitiveness?"

"They see me as a spirit—a lost soul wandering the path between the estate and Blythe House. Perhaps we can tell them it is true." She laughed, and the sweet sound caused Phillip to rise and resituate his body at her feet.

"That wouldn't be a good solution, lady. I intend to see to it that you make yourself at home here, to come and go as you choose. You are my favored guest and I hope companion. And no, you shall no longer be a secret."

"You're very kind to me. I enjoy my solitary days. But perhaps we can go strolling one day. And bring your lovely Phillip." She patted him on the head. If dogs could smile, Phillip did.

"I must go. I left poor Theresa in a terrible hurry after she has been so good to me since her arrival. She fancied a bit of fabric from town, and I think I'll ride in and purchase it for her, as a gift."

"How lovely. And kind. Your father was right. You are both."

"We shall tell them all that you are the sister of a friend I knew in school. They need not know more."

"Very well. Thank you, Martin. For this chat. Thank you for being who I knew you would be."

"Just mind yourself with them—the staff, I mean. I suggest you do not make yourself available to them due to the things I have told you about the estate and the terrible death. Go easy, and all will be well. "

"But it already is."

She smiled, and like the ghostly figure he thought her to be not that long ago until he could feel her breath and touch her arm, she drifted up and out of the settee, slipped on her coat, and glided out the door.

Saugerties was a tiny village, first settled under a different name in the 1600's. During the early 1800's, it quickly grew to include a giant paper mill and iron works that employed many offspring of the farmers who first made the village their home—and migrants who labored to create cold-rolling processes used to smelt the iron. The iron works company could not have known that in a few short years, it would be used to manufacture cannon banning and bracing used in The Civil War.

The town was known for its industrial innovations. The double-puddling, hoop-making, and cold-rolling processes used to smelt iron were developed at Ulster Iron Works. Papermaking was revolutionized with the invention of the endless web papermaking machine. Despite Saugerties' growth, and maybe in part because of it, it managed to retain a charm that was endlessly attractive to young women such as Theresa. Young women spent many free days wandering its lanes and dusty Main Street to purchase trinkets and baubles with their pay...and in the hopes of being seen by an eligible young man.

Martin pulled Isabella up, dismounted in front of Mrs. Cooper's Mercantile, and wrapped the horse's reigns about a hitching post. He smiled. The day was cold but lovely, and he was thinking that a surprise gift of the fabric Theresa had mentioned would manage to somehow thank her for all she had done.

Mrs. Cooper was a robust figure with beefy arms and sun-creased face. Her hair, tucked tightly in a bun high atop her head, could not contain the wiry aspects that looked as though each strand of hair was attempting a frantic escape. Her husband, long since passed on, had left her just the house she resided in at the edge of town, one horse, *worthless as day is long,* as she would say, a cow, some chickens that seemed intent on becoming the favored dinner meal for coyotes, and not much more. But she had tucked away some money when she could with pennies left from trips to town where she would buy meal or dinner necessities, and before she knew it, she had enough to rent the store from a neighbor.

As he entered, the tinkling of a small bell over the door rang, summoning her at once from a backroom. She smiled at Martin.

"Mr. Waverly! Pleasant to see you this winter day. What can I do for you? We have new carpet all the way from The Carolinas. There, see them?

Lovely, aren't they? We have books for young readers, finely bound, and a tea and saucer set that surely would delight a favored lady acquaintance or relation." Mrs. Cooper was an overly ambitious saleswoman, but Martin liked that about her.

"Actually, I was looking for some fabric. I believe it is blue or…let me think…it bore blue bonnie flowers."

Mrs. Cooper twisted her mouth up to one side and squinted. "Let me think…hmmm…no, sir, we have nothing like that."

"Then it was sold?"

"Hmm. No. I haven't made a purchase of any fabric since last spring when I managed to get to New York City to buy some."

"But I was told, specifically, that it hung here. In your window."

"Perhaps it was in another shop? The only other to carry fabric is the shop down the hill near the watering post named *Fine Lady*. But I was there not a day ago, and Mr. and Mrs. Thornton had none. I know because I was prepared to make a new dress for my niece but was disappointed."

"Odd," Martin said, more to himself than to Mrs. Cooper.

"Who, may I inquire, has told you it was here?"

"Theresa Mulvane, a newly hired maid in my employ."

"Good gracious to heavens, sir, what possessed you to take her on?" Mrs. Cooper's expression read that she had swallowed something entirely unpleasant and attempted to hack it up. "She frequents Turning Arch Inn. 'Cross the way near the iron works. Lately, as it were, sir. And I saw her there with my own eyes just an hour ago, as she snuck in like a creeping snipe, her head down, and she spoke to no one as she went in. Then not five minutes later, she wandered out, followed moments later by a man I hear has stayed at your estate. He carried a bundle and made straight the way she had gone. Odd fellow. Willham, I think his name is?"

"Are you quite certain about all of it? The fabric and Theresa and Willham?"

"Indeed I am, sir. Theresa is well known in common circles as a bit of a…how shall I say this nicely…hornswoggler. You know, sir, a cheat and liar."

Martin shook his head hard left, right, and then again as though trying to dislodge the distasteful news. Mrs. Cooper, like any man or woman, had faults, but she was not a gossipmonger, and she did not, would not, could not, lie.

"Thank you, Mrs. Cooper. I am thusly advised. Please wrap and send those tea cups and saucers to me at your earliest convenience." He laid more than they were worth on the counter and walked out of the mercantile and to his horse, climbed atop her, and rode her hard toward the edge of town and Turning Arch Inn.

Willham stood beneath a low awning in front of the pub across the street and dared not move until he saw Martin making a dash down the muddy road. It was only then that he moved in the other direction, his head down, his face hidden by his worn hat, and disappeared into the twilight.

Where have you been, girl?" Miriam accosted Theresa as she came into the kitchen from the courtyard and gripped her tightly by the arms. "This is not your day off and—"

"Mr. Waverly knows I was going to town, Miriam." She yanked her arm away and twirled around. "You left here, and I took it all to myself to do your share around here. So you'd best not to be trying me," she said defiantly.

"No one said a thing to me about that, and you best get to your chores or you'll find yourself another place of employment. And then when you're done, you come back and find me, you hear me, girl? We have things to talk about." Miriam turned her back on Theresa, and over her shoulder she tossed her arm up, dismissively waving her away. "Blasted girl," Miriam mumbled under her breath, not caring if she was heard.

But Theresa did not make it any further than the courtyard where she had turned toward the stables to see Daniel. Martin, dismounting, strode toward her, and she froze in place, waiting. His face read that he had something on his mind—something she felt very certain would not be to her favor.

"Theresa. We need to talk," he said as he grabbed her arm and led her toward the far end of the courtyard where they could not be overheard. "Sit there. Now." He shoved her toward a bench where the holly grew in great mounds on either side. She did not protest and sat down. The bright green of the ivy caused her skin to look even more sallow than usual. "How do you know Willham Montrose? And there had better not be a lie involved in your answer." He stood over her, blocking the little bit of light that remained in the sky. She began to cry, but he was not inclined to care. He merely crossed his arms and waited as she ran her face along the sleeve of her grey wool coat.

"From here, sir." She sniffled, staring unblinkingly up into his face.

"I know that. *Specifically*, what is your association with him?"

"He is rather smart, sir, and regales me with his humorous and interesting stories. That is all, sir."

"I don't believe you."

"But sir, I…"

"Theresa, this is your only opportunity to tell me what the devil is taking place between the two of you, if you wish to stay in my employ."

She lowered her head. Not being of a very bright mind, although clever in her way, she fumbled for something to say that might appease him. "Well…I saw something, sir. I hesitate to say even now but…I saw him the night that Mr. Bonhomme was murdered. He had exited Mrs. Waverly's quarters—or rather, Miriam's old quarters."

"That is not possible. I have the only key. He could not have entered to then leave."

"But it's true, sir, all very true, and when he left, I ran off to my room. But I became very curious," she continued, beginning to feel comfortable in her tale and twirled a lock of hair around her finger as she spoke. "Curious indeed, and I asked him about it, thinking perhaps, since he has medical knowledge he might have been tending to Mrs. Waverly."

"And?"

"Well, he had nothing to say to that. I had not known he had returned from town until then, and he is much like a shadow, sir, is he not? Coming and going like a rat creeps along the edges of walls." She knew Martin did not have an ounce of like for the man, and so she carefully spooned out her words, indirectly showing that she had no care for Willham, either.

"Why did you see him at the inn today, Theresa?"

"Because he asked me to do so, sir, but then when I knocked upon his door, he did not answer."

"And why did you refuse to tell that you had seen him coming from Mrs. Waverly's temporary quarters? Are you so dense a girl that you could not reason the possible importance of this when asked specifically about what you had seen?" She began to cry again. "Stop that. Immediately!"

"I- I was quite afraid of him, sir."

"Nonsense! If you were so frightened, then why did you go to see him alone today?"

"I- I- felt I had to appease him, sir, on the chance that having seen him depart Mrs. Waverly's room might mean something ill for me."

Martin made no move from the position he held above her and shook his head. "There are a multitude of lies here, and I shall find out what they are and why—including why you invented a story about the fabric you wanted, which I went as a kindness to fetch for you today, but alas, dear girl, it doesn't exist there, nor has it."

"Do you not believe the notion that sprites and ghouls are about, sir?"

"What on this earth does that have to do with anything we are discussing?"

"Have you never heard of Margaret and Kate Fox? They lived not far from here. They directly communicated with spirits, and, sir, I think we should find a person similar who can do the same for you and this haunted place—someone who can speak to the spirits and then cause them to leave. Maybe they can tell you something about Mrs. Waverly's disappearance."

"Have you lost your mind? We are not discussing the gibberish you and the servants maintain occur in the household; we are talking about Willham and…"

"But, sir! He is held bewitched by his choosing and summons ghosts and demons at his will, and to defend against the things he has wrought and no doubt intends to further inflict on us all, we must get to the core of the problem, and as I see it, sir, the problem here is Willham alone."

Martin grasped his head with both hands. "Get out of my home, Theresa. You have precisely one hour to collect whatever it is you came to us with and leave. I swear by all things holy that if I see you again on my properties, I will haul you off myself and— Just get out!"

She watched him as he grabbed the horse's reins and made his way to the stable. Theresa was not feeling the slightest bit troubled. A self-satisfied smile crept slowly across her face.

SEVEN

"She's gone, and I'm glad for it." Miriam rubbed hard at the brass candlestick and then set it down. "There was something peculiar about that child, despite her best efforts to appear otherwise."

James nodded his head. "True. This household will be more peaceful now that she has been tossed out. Poor Martin. Taking blows at every turn."

They sat together silently polishing the brass until it shone for the better part of an hour. It was well past midnight when they heard the scratching noise but could not decipher from where it had come.

"Rats." Miriam snarled after having paused to listen and then continued with her work.

"I'll call on the lad from town and have him do whatever it is he does to rid us of them."

"They're louder than I have heard them; can you agree?"

"Yes. It seems to be coming from the servant's hall." James placed the polish and rag down on the table and stood.

"How can any of us sleep tonight what with that dreadful sound? Not to mention I have a dread of the vile creatures." She lit a tall, white candle, rose as well, and they walked toward the sound. "Who could love a creature such as them? No one," She offered in a whisper.

The house, quiet at that late hour, amplified every creak and shift of old wood and stone within the estate. They followed the scratch-scratch and rustling down the hall, where a single lamp was lit upon the dark walls.

"There, James. There." She pointed her finger at the door of Theresa's vacant room.

"Let us see. Perhaps she didn't leave at all? But I did see her go out, myself." He hesitated slightly before turning the knob that complained as he slowly pressed the door open.

"Nothing," Miriam said, as she walked to the center of the room. "She's taken everything. Including the coverlet for the bed! That little….But that sound! It remains. There, near the cloak door. The scratching comes again." She walked cautiously toward it, thinking perhaps a rat had become ensconced within the cloak closet. Summoning her bravery, she edged closer across the uneven wood floors and reached for the doorknob. James grabbed her arm.

"Perhaps we should leave this for the lad to see to. If we open the door, we might set it free, and then it will run amok."

"Yes, maybe you're right. Let's leave this place. It sends chills about my body."

He released her arm, and they left the room to the sound of the incessant scratching and rustling that set their nerves ajar.

"You know, Miriam, I heard a similar sound last night, but it was up near Mr. Waverly's room in the walls of the hall between the windows and stone."

"Then he must have heard it but said nothing."

"No, not that Mr. Waverly—I refer to Garson Waverly's room. I had set to lighting the lamps on the walls and heard it then. I thought perhaps it was wind in the turrets or tower. But now that I hear it tonight, I realize it is the same sort of clambering sound." He gently shut the door.

"I dread the first site of the roofs as I approach this place. And as for the tower, no one that has ever visited it dares to again." She blew the candle out and set it down on the table. "Even Martin refuses to go there."

"I've been there once in all my years here, Miriam. There is nothing there now but remnants stowed by Martin's grandfather when he often took to sitting aloft to view The Hudson and their ships coming in. One time I climbed there to secure a loose board near the window. I could have sworn I heard a whimpering sound, like that of a woman's, but alas, having turned around toward the sound nothing was there at all. As you know, the winds along the river are mighty, lady, so dismissing it at once, I left and have not returned. I confess there is something chilling in that place that has nothing to do with the loose boards or windows. It prevents me from caring to go there again. Isn't it peculiar that we can blame almost anything on something that seems most convenient to believe?"

"Ah, James, yes. But I went there long ago to help the men from town access the roof, which needed repair. I heard a similar sound as we entered the walk, and I made straight away out of the room. Gracious! How they did their work in record pace, grabbed at their pay, which I had in my hand, declined a warm meal, and set out into the evening so quickly that I thought they were chased."

"The telling of it gives me the scares. I think we best get some sleep, Miriam. There is nothing that can't keep till the morning, and I confess that sleep is the only escape from the knocks and creaks and odd whisper-like winds that assail this place."

Martin sat at his desk waiting for the solicitor, Rockingham, to arrive. He had found so little time to do the tasks needed in order to present a more developed plan on the business' future going forward. He promised, but it didn't happen. There was the murder, of course, and Miriam's departure and Hannah's disappearance. And of course the appearance of Meredith, who had taken so much of his time. Although he had not so much as caught a glimpse of her since their unexpected meeting, she had occupied many of his waking moments just the same.

The saucers and teacups had arrived from Mrs. Cooper's mercantile, and she had wrapped them in such a lovely manner with pink bows and velvety paper, that he realized she must have recognized that they were meant for a lady friend. He hoped that Meredith would come to visit so that he might present them to her, but a few days had past, and there'd been no sign that she had intended to come. Resolved to deliver them himself, he gazed out the windows toward the far hill, imagining her wandering the forest around Blythe House, examining plants and perhaps taking samples back with her to catalog. He tore himself from the images that played 'round in his mind and shuffled the papers on his desk, but she would not leave his thoughts.

"My dear, Martin." Rockingham walked through the doors of Martin's office, hand extended, as he approached him. "Tell me all is well now that some time has passed away from the unpleasantness." He appeared more stooped than the last time Martin had seen him, and there was something awry in his eyes, but he dismissed it as the result of the long carriage ride to Waverly Estate.

"As well as can be expected. Please, sit there by the fire." Martin motioned toward one of the matching dark green velvet chairs near the hearth and waited for Rockingham to sit before taking a place beside him. "I'd like to say that I've been working day and night on the new plans but, alas, sir, I have not."

Rockingham waved a hand at him, dismissing the defense. "It's quite understandable. I thought that I would visit just the same, realizing that perhaps you hadn't gotten far with the charts and tables and so forth. It's good to sit with you, Martin. It is long past due."

"I supposed you would understand and thought perhaps it would have been better if I had sent you a note informing you of the delay, but I think I did not, as I feel the same way. And there are other matters."

"Yes? What matters?" Rockingham's dark blue eyes looked flat, despite the light from the fire's flames. Martin could not help but wonder why. Perhaps he was ill?

"I've thought long about the will, of course, and how could it be otherwise, since the contents were rather unexpected, shocking, I may say, and it is in part why I wanted to speak with you. I shall simply get to the point. Do you feel the least slighted that you managed nothing of consequence from all the years you worked for my father?"

Rockingham did not reply right off. He stared into the fire and then ran a finger across the glass of brandy he was holding. He took a sip. "I was somewhat taken aback that I received my usual fee and as executor that portion of fee as well, as is customary, but nothing more—But, Martin, you mustn't think me greedy or bearing you or your father any ill will, since it is true that your father paid me well while alive. But I thought we were friends, since I did many things that were—shall we call it—not always above board, and had I thought otherwise I may not have done things he asked. I assumed our relationship as more than business bound. Again, I thought we were friends." He did not look toward Martin as he spoke, and noting it, Martin could not decipher whether he was embarrassed to relate what he had—or if there was something else.

"I would like to make repair. Offer you something."

"Yes?" Rockingham looked slowly, almost carefully at Martin before looking away again toward the fire.

"I would like to give you a handy sum and of course give your salary a raise. Perhaps you would accept my offer to assume ownership of one of the cottages described in the will, and use it as you see fit. It looks as though the city has not done much good for your, dare I say, pale complexion. Wouldn't the Catskill's air do you some good now and then?"

"I see. It is rather generous of you. May I, without, I hope, sounding boorish or less than appreciative, ask what amount of monies you may be considering?" Still, he did not look toward Martin.

"Well, I have written it all down here for you to see. If it seems an insult, we shall discuss it. Honestly, I didn't know what might be appropriate and will leave it for you to say yea or nay." Martin removed a paper from his breast pocket and handed it to Rockingham. He watched as Rockingham read the numbers, taking longer than the reading of it would have required. It bolstered his suspicion that something was amiss. Rockingham at last gently, slowly, folded the paper and handed it back to him.

"I shall accept, Martin, and thank you kindly and profusely. But may I again risk being boorish and request that I be shown my bedroom for the night? I am feeling rather...unwell."

"I thought perhaps you were below par. Is it something serious or are you just weary?"

"Weary, Martin, very weary."

"Miriam has set your bedroom on the second floor. The fire is warm, and all necessaries have been laid out for you. I'll fetch her now."

Rockingham watched as Martin rose quickly from his chair and walked into the hall, calling Miriam's name. He shut his eyes and dug his bony knuckles into them, rubbing at his lids until Miriam's appearance at the door to the library caused him to stop.

"Good evening, sir. Mr. Waverly has imparted that you are quite tired and wish to retire. If you please, I will take you to your quarters. Cook has made you something to eat and some tea." She didn't wait for his agreement but disappeared again into the hall.

"Blast it. Blast it all," he said aloud and slowly walked the way she had gone but stopped as he neared the hall. A shadow no bigger than a young girl, and as slender, flitted from the second parlor across the hall mere feet from him and disappeared into the dark corner near the stair. He took a deep breath, steadied himself, and very tiredly climbed the stairs, not looking back.

He's in his rooms, sir, and declined breakfast," Miriam said as Martin entered the kitchen and sat down. She smiled.

"What is it? Why are you smiling?" he asked. He placed his elbows to the table and propped his head into his hands. He had not had the restful sleep he had wished for, and dawn had come too quickly.

"Ah, sir, it has always been this way, even when you were quite young. When something troubled you, you would find your way in here and wait, sometimes for a biscuit and sometimes merely for me to start a right chat with you." She reached for a plate, deposited a bit of teacake onto it, and slid it toward him. He smiled.

"Did Rockingham seem himself, Miriam?"

"No, he did not. He seemed peevish."

"Yes? I didn't note that. I thought him pale and tired. That's all." He bit into the cake and sighed. "Good. Thank you." She nodded her head.

"He wanted to know if his room is the one that Rene Bonhomme had resided in and whether or not his remains had been returned to France. Upon responding yes to the first and I did not know to the second, he became quite agitated, sir, and told me to leave. So of course, I did."

"Hmm! How unlike him. Curious why he inquired. But today will be better for all, Miriam."

"Sir, you state the same every time a storm has come."

"Do I? Well perhaps I am guilty of—what is that confounded noise?" He stopped chewing and rose. "That dreadful gnawing and scratching sound?"

"Ah, rats, sir. *Rats*. James and I supposed it to be rodents and have called for the lad from town to right it as before. I wanted to ask you first, but you were otherwise engaged and so I took it on myself."

"And yet it continues?" He walked down the hall but stopped abruptly outside of Theresa's old room. "Fetch me a lantern, Miriam. The commotion sounds to be coming from inside here."

She ran off to get the light and upon returning said, "The lad set out traps and bait but only a few field mice have been snagged, and it continues. Maddening, isn't it?"

"Quite." He opened the door and walked in.

"It's coming from the closet, sir. James and I did not wish to enter to see, but the lad did and said nothing was about but set the traps. See?" She opened the closet door and stepped aside.

Martin moved the candle toward the opening of the dark closet and pulled his mouth down hard. "It smells dreadful in there. Perhaps a rodent died." He walked into the closet and shone the light left and right and then up. He saw an empty trap, many webs from busy spiders and a forgotten slipper, but nothing more. "Let's get the buggers moving." He rapped firmly on the wall, once, then twice. "Blasted things," he sneered. "How do you find sleep with this infernal noise?" He again banged on the wall with his closed fist, then on the back wall and then ceiling. His hand rose to give it yet another thump, but he stopped, his fist paused in air. "Did you hear that?"

"No, sir, what did you—"

Martin rapped on the back of the closet once more, and in turn, a rap returned. He rapped twice more. And twice more the raps echoed back. "What in heaven's name?"

Miriam gasped. "Rats do not rap nor do they answer a person's! Sir!"

"Find Daniel and James at once and tell them to bring back hammers and chisels. I will get my…"

He did not finish his sentence as she flew from the room and down the hall, screaming for the men as she went.

Martin retreated to his library where he retrieved his colt revolver from the locked top drawer of the desk. Running back to the closet, he stood as if on guard and waited for the men. "Who is it?" he asked of the being behind the moldy wall. "What manner are you?" His voice, authoritative and demanding, elicited a rap against the closet wall that sounded further away than the previous taps. He stepped back. Not waiting for James or Daniel to come to his aid, he reared back and began kicking fiercely at the closet wall until objects hung in the musty room fell from their nails, bashing to the ground.

The near dawn ruckus, causing such a fright among the servants that they soon were gathered outside the door, teetered and whispered and continued as Martin beat on the walls.

"Stephen!" Martin called over his shoulder, "Where is Daniel?" Daniel, the broader and stronger of both the stable hands, could surely have broken the wall with his bare hands.

"I do not know, sir. What is the trouble here?" Stephen stepped forward and flinched as Martin raised his boot to strike another blow at the wall.

"Find something to pull the wood from the walls, and a chisel, or anything of use to break this in."

Stephen disappeared out the door and returned a moment later with a hammer. Handing it to Martin, Stephen gave a quick look about the room, and seeing a poker standing in the corner near the woodstove, he grasped it and began smashing it against the walls.

"What is it, sir?" Stephen asked, hammering violently despite not knowing why he did.

"Something or someone is behind this wall, and we shall not stop until we know who or what it is!"

Beatrice clutched her hands against her mouth and cried until Miriam, returning, pushed the weeping girl out of the room and into the hall.

"Get back, I tell you!" she screamed at them all, and cook, followed by the others save for James who had entered, ran back to the kitchen.

"That's the man, Stephen! Swing!"

A wood slat, weakened, splintered as did the next and next and next until Martin grabbed the last long plank and yanked at it with all his might, freeing it from the nails and boards. He stood amidst the shattered wood, the broken decorations that had hung on the walls, the bits of stone and dust and glass. Then, he gasped.

"Sir…" Seeing what Martin had, James stepped forward and crouched down. "Is this not Mrs. Waverly's hankie? See there, it bears the initials HW!" He pointed toward it, unwilling to lift it up.

Martin bent down and, reaching through the open space, retrieved it. He crumpled it into his palm and bent his head down. "How could this have found its way inside a wall? How? Kick aside the jumble and let us go further in, Stephen. But you, James, go to the outside at the adjoining wall and see what is there."

Stone by stone, beam by beam, they tore at the wall until before them a small passageway appeared. Martin, hands bloodied, and Stephen, sodden from exertion, dropped their tools. Without hesitation, Martin knelt down at the entrance.

"Hand me the lantern, Stephen." Martin's lungs burned from effort, and he snatched the lantern away from Stephen's hands. The passage, less than three feet wide and perhaps five feet tall, roused in him an old foe…the fear he had felt when his father had too often locked him in the root cellar so many years before. But yet he pushed on, ignoring the wildness of his heart as it beat against his chest. They slowly, carefully, crawled in.

"Martin!" James, imparting what he saw from the outside, knelt on the floor and called to him. "There is nothing we can tell from the courtyard, sir, what with the stone and beams. Please do come out of there, Martin, please. Let a smaller man go in your stead."

But Martin, intent on following the passage wherever it might lead, moved on with Stephen closely behind.

A few yards in, he stopped to take hold of himself. The fear of being contained within the unfamiliar space baffled his will. Setting the lamp down to gather himself, the light flickered and dimmed with the motion. A deep dread gripped at his throat and provoked the sensation that he might suffocate if he did not back out and forget the entire thing; let someone else do it; let someone else brave the margins of walls that had become comprised of stone, sodden with moisture and slick to the touch. A rank odor wafted toward him. He bowed his head, not to say a prayer, but to stop the feeling that he might gag on fear of the things within the walls that he could neither see nor anticipate. But he continued.

"Hannah!" he called out, his voice sounding foreign to his own ears. "Hannah, are you in here?" He waited for a response, but none came.

"Mr. Waverly, sir, shouldn't we back out and…" Stephen, suffering a similar dread of the unknown, was disappointed with the simple reply.

"No." They pressed on.

The floor of the route that they carefully made their way along was cramped, and dust filled the edges of the walls where they met floor. Above, spiders came into view as the light shone just a mere two feet before them. Dangling down to their hair and face, they were unable to swat them away. The creatures descended from atop Martin's sweating head to his neck and then down his sleeves. A mouse extended its tiny grey face from between two large stones, and Martin kicked it away. It squealed as it retreated and disappeared from the light.

"Stephen."

"Sir."

"Can you feel that? A draft."

"Yes. And I can smell something odd, can you?"

"Yes, it's the damp. But let's not stop," he said, out of breath, the banging of his heart speaking disagreement between word and will. They paused after they had crawled a few feet more, and Martin put the lamp carefully down before him. He reached his arms to either side of the passage. "Wood. On both sides. Squared. And then stone again."

"Can you rip at it, sir?" Stephen's breaths were hard and fast, and he hoped the answer would be no if it meant another moment in that place.

Martin gave a sturdy tug to the left side, and without more effort, it released. A light streamed into the space along with a blast of cold air. He twisted his head away from the brightness and rubbed at his gritted eyes.

"Look. The garden. We're under the hedgerows." He exited the passageway and crawled beneath them along a space that was so short and narrow that he had to proceed on his stomach. At the end of its edge, he shoved away vines that had draped across the space, and he dragged himself up and out.

"The second parlor windows." Stephen pointed. "We're not more than twelve feet from them."

"We're going back to find what lies behind the other wood slats."

He ignored Stephen's protests and thrust himself beneath the vines and under the hedgerows, instructing Stephen to pull the vines back down as he followed along. Martin, upon reentering the passageway, grasped the lantern and went straight to the second set of wood slates. Crouching again, he shook both sides of the wood that had been fastened loosely together by nails, and it easily fell away. He tossed it aside. Peering into the space, he sighed. "It's the dining room." He crawled out and stood at the south wall beneath the portraits of his glowering relations.

"It seems, sir, we have more than your typical rodent. We are beset with human vermin." Stephen wiped the cobwebs from his hair and frowned.

"Indeed. And by their nature, they surely have constructed more than one way in and out."

"What shall we do, sir?" Stephen wiped the dust from his face with the back of his arm.

"We tear this god forsaken place apart until we find every last one of them."

Don't go into the tunnel, Martin. Please, I implore you, stay out of the tunnel. Some things should not be known."

He jolted up right from his sleep and looked around his shadowy bedroom. Her voice seemed to come from everywhere at once. He called to her again, but the only sound he heard was the steady tick of a mantel clock and the wind that, earlier in the evening, began with abandon.

"Meredith?"

His body ached from the previous day's efforts. Having found two more passages, he and Stephen had sealed them both. One started in the foyer within a closet used for storing flower vases, and the other had entered and exited from the north and south wall of his father's office.

His eyes scanned the room. In the left corner of his bedroom, eerie light cast from the fire played against the wall where a map of the seven seas hung framed within maple borders. To his right, two oversized chairs mirrored each other. Between them stood an oak table upon which his uneaten dinner sat. The poster bed's ornate wood bedposts rose up and were met by curtains of deep sea green and draped lazily down its sides. Before him stood a huge stone fireplace with mantel ornaments adorning the tops, trinkets and remembrances he had brought back with him from foreign places, and brass candlesticks at each end.

He rose slowly and paced about the room, noting that the clock read five AM. Sighing, he retrieved his night robe from the white padded bench at the foot of the bed and roughly dragged his arms through it before opening the door and going to the stairs. But he stopped there, listening, and silenced a fussing Phillip with a wave of his hand as the dog appeared at his side. Again, he heard something—a soft shuffle perhaps or the wind playing against the many great eaves. No. It was footfalls, he was sure of it, and as he proceeded down the stairs without a candle or lantern to light his way, he paused at the second landing and peered over the edge to the spaces below.

The floor of the foyer was cast deeply in shadow, and the grandfather clock methodically ticked out time. The vase containing great bows of holy berry and evergreen that stood on the table near the entranceway created images of gnarled arms and fingers across the stone walls. All was still, save for the little shadowy form that moved leisurely, directly below his sight.

She was there. He saw her. He was certain of it. The sweep of her hair, the gentle way that she seemed to glide about without effort or care of gravity or surface upon which she walked; then, horribly, beautifully, one singly gentle stroke of piano key played.

He ran down the stairs, the dog just ahead, and determined to face whatever or whoever played the keys, he swung his body over the last of the stair railing. Toe to toe with a shadowy form that was neither dark nor light, nor cool or warm to his touch as he moved to clasp the shadow's figure between his large hands, it seemed to evaporate just as smoke might as it wafts away.

Not knowing whether it best to flee or chase or stand and wait, the keys played once more. That being the decider, he tore toward the second parlor and to the piano in the corner where Miriam stood, her mouth agape, her eyes wider than seemed possible. She, upon seeing him, fell hard to the floor, the candle tumbling down and extinguishing itself on the floor.

"Miriam!" He lifted her considerable body and set her gently to the settee. "Miriam…"

She opened her eyes, and they locked onto his. "Mr. Waverly. Now do you believe? Do you?"

"What are you doing in here?

"I heard a voice—no, two—and got up to see who it was that wandered the house this early morn and saw not a person but that *thing*, her hair long and light and her face, oh, Martin, her face, transparent like a fantasy and eyes bluer than blue. Oh, I don't know. I do believe I've struck my head on the floor. Help me get up please, sir, I need to."

"Stay right here. Phillip, stay," he said, and left her alone in the dark with the dog, intending to chase after the mirage, or woman, or sprite, or unpleasant person that put the scare to them both that early morning.

But an hour of searching did nothing more than awaken the entire household. Upon returning to the second parlor, he found the dog had vanished and dear Miriam lay terribly still on the settee. Very cold, she was, and very dead, he thought, as he touched her. The contact of his broad hand on her meaty waist caused her to roll to her back. No, it was not Miriam at all, but Beatrice, the maid. Her mouth, wide, her eyes open and round like a frightened animal's—and around her throat, his white linen cravat had been tied in a knot.

Miriam, upon re-entering the room, let out a terrible shriek and stumbled away from the appalling site before being caught up in James' arms and led away.

EiGHt

arberry sat across from Martin in the same chair he had occupied during his investigation into Rene's death.

"Perhaps you struck her, Mr. Waverly. Actually, that's how I'm coming around to see it. Maybe it was accidental or maybe it was a byproduct of some angry fit. That was a question posed to you, sir, since I do not intend to appear accusatory without all the facts. The article of clothing about her neck is puzzling. The marks around her throat were minimal comparative to the large bump at the back of her head. Perhaps it was used to subdue her. But that the neckwear belongs to you gives me some...how shall I call it...concern. Your knuckles and your hands, sir, can you explain that?"

Martin shook his head slowly from side to side, not looking at the policeman.

"No sign of Mrs. Waverly. Or Willham. Or Theresa. Or Daniel. And now you tell of secret passages, waifs floating about your house, and articles of dress having belonged to Mrs. Waverly ensconced within hidden walls. I heard your tales of scratching and things awry, but it seems that you are central to all this, to these ...unfortunate sets of circumstance."

Martin raised his eyes up and asked, "Are you accusing me of murdering Beatrice? Or causing the disappearances of these people—and my damned dog? Are you telling me that I have fabricated these intricate sets of events for some unholy purpose? Have I also built hidden passages, sir? Have I forced my solicitor Rockingham to vouch for my sanity and moderate temperament? Good lord, man." He lowered his head again and wished it all away.

Rockingham, who had been sitting quietly at Martin's elbow, cleared his throat. "He is making great efforts to restore this estate to its former position, sir, and the morality that once existed here. He is caring toward his staff as though they are family to him, Mr. Barberry. He is of good conscience, and without reservation, I can attest to his overall solid reputation and character. He is beyond repute! If you have beleaguered this good man, this *grieving* man, with your subtle accusations and blatant antagonism for no reason at all, then it is time for you to leave. Or, conversely, sir, please do accuse him outright and arrest him." Rockingham rapped his knuckles against the top of the table and then leaned back.

"Gentlemen, please. Let us not become so irritable." Barberry leaned back, too, and withdrew a pipe from his dark coat. Lighting it with a flourish, he continued. "If I thought for certain Mr. Waverly has done someone ill, he would not be sitting here. He would be towed away and sent straight to jail. But no, he *is* sitting here, and I, sir, am simply doing my best to ferret out necessary facts, if I aim to solve these crimes, and I certainly do intend to. You can count on that. " As he finished his sentence, the wails coming from Beatrice's sister caused them to turn toward the hall.

The sister, seeing Martin within the room, turned sharply toward him and glared in his direction. "You! You are to blame for this! You and your cursed house and all who dwell within it! May God not spare you! May He make all your days' torture and famine and ill-health!"

If not for one of the policemen that escorted her outside, Martin was sure that she would have run at him, clawed him with her nails, struck him, hurled more epitaphs...but at that moment, he felt he would have deserved it all.

He rose, and his chair screeched noisily against the floor. He slid it back into place and turned away. "I shall be in my rooms, if needed. Good night, gentlemen."

He climbed the stairs, ignoring James who walked with him as he ascended. Then he shut the door to his room against the man's earnest offers of aid. But he did not want to hear words of comfort or understanding that he would be forced to acknowledge and express appreciation for. He wanted to leave them all to their own devices—leave them all to gossip and surmise and chatter. Mostly, he wanted to wait for Rockingham to retire and Barberry to ride away in his coach.

An hour later, assured that the stillness of the house meant he would not be seen, he lifted the latch on his wood chest and removed the tea set that he had purchased for Meredith. He pulled on his boots and his double-breasted waistcoat, the red one with fox fur on the inside, and dragged a black cape across his shoulders. His black gloves, lined in the same fur as his coat, bore buttons at the wrists. It would do. Checking his face in the mirror near the door, he noted an immediate need for a shave but dropped his deerstalker hat atop his head and made for the door, gift in tow.

The night was warmer than most that early winter, and he relished the idea of a short ride atop Isabella, who whinnied to him as he approached. Assured that neither Daniel, who had been missing since Theresa's dismissal, nor Stephen were in ear shot, he saddled his horse and swung himself up. Riding along the snow-covered edges of the drive so that the horse's hooves on the cobblestone would not give them away, he sped the pace once clear of the courtyard and headed up the hill toward Blythe House.

As he neared the top of the hill where the roof of Blythe House could be seen, a wild gust of wind bore down on him, and Isabella, seemingly startled by the sudden burst of icy air, stopped her climb and took two steps back.

"What is it, girl?" Martin gently urged her forward, but she took a few more steps back. Her head thrust up and down, and she pawed at the icy snow beneath her hooves. Unable to move her forward, and Martin, being the sort of rider that would not press her forward with crop, he dismounted and stood at her head. "There now, girl. There, there. What's the trouble?" He stroked her side and leaned his face close to her muscled throat. She snorted in reply. "Let's walk you along then, what do you say?" He moved away and tugged lightly on her reins, but she continued to refuse. She had never before disregarded his authority. He thought perhaps she had come up lame. A quick check of her flanks and hooves found nothing amiss, save for some internal bother that he could not interpret. "Enough of this foolishness," he said, his voice rising as he tugged on her reins. But it caused her to rear up, and he stumbled back, falling into the deep snow. Before he could gather himself, she bolted away, and he, still sitting upon the cold ground, watched as she galloped away back down the hill toward the mansion.

By the yellow light of the full moon, he continued to follow her frenzied dash until he saw her silhouette come to a sliding halt at the front of the courtyard.

"Confounded...And she's made away with the gift." He stood, and feeling assured Isabella would make her way to the barn, he brushed the snow from his coat and breaches, took a deep breath, and walked toward Blythe House.

The renegade wind subsided. A faint whisper of it shifted from the north, rustling what remained of dead oak leaves along the tree line on either side of the path. To his right, The Hudson River, partially frozen, did not gleam silver the length of the ice as it would most moonlit nights in winter. Even as the weak glow brightened to near dawn luminosity as he continued to climb the rocky path, the ice remained an insipid color of spent fire ash.

Deeply steeped tops of the stone cottage's roof came into view. Covered in snow, he could not confirm what Rockingham had warned. If the roof had indeed fallen into desperate disrepair, he could not be sure. He paused at the place where beneath the snow at his feet, large slate had been placed many years before by workers who had gathered them from the riverbanks. They had designed a steep walkway of fifteen steps that lead to the cottage's arched front door, but none were visible. He idly wondered how Meredith had managed them during the winter snows. Along the front of the house ran a picket fence, and joined in the center, a canopy of Hawthorn trees had been trained into an archway that stopped a few feet from the door. The stone walls of the house did not appear to be in partial ruin as he had been told, and he wondered why Rockingham had more than a few times suggested that the only correct answer would be to demolish it all to the ground.

The narrow front door, only slightly weather beaten, boasted an eyebrow top of six narrow glass panels, and through them, a soft light spread across his face and shoulders. He raised his hand to knock, but before he could, the door slowly opened. Meredith, standing in the tiny room beyond, one hand on the door and the other dangling at her side, reached and patted Philip's head. She smiled.

"Martin. I half expected you." She smiled again and stepped back so he could enter.

"I apologize for such a late arrival, Meredith, but I …"

"Yes, I presumed. And it seems your dog had a similar notion, yes?"

He found it necessary to bend his head down as he entered, lest he bang it on the low doorway. "Hmm. It seems tonight all my animals have deserted me. Even my mare refused to climb the hill despite my urging. Something spooked her." He walked past her, carefully, although he was not sure why he felt compelled to step lightly around her. The smell of jasmine wafted about him as he stooped and patted Philip's head. The dog wagged slowly and took his place near the fire as though he had done it a hundred times before. "He seems quite at home."

She shut the door and motioned for him to sit near the fire. Two red wing-backed chairs mirrored each other on each side of the stone fireplace. She sat to his right, and only then did he place his hat and gloves to the table between them, beside a book with a worn, grey cover. Sitting down, he gazed about the room, allowing his eyes to explore the little corners of the tidy space that long ago his mother had decorated with things his father could not tolerate but were treasures to her.

"You seem surprised, Martin."

"Yes?"

"Yes. Many of your mother's touches remain. She had a gentle eye...She filled this place with things some might call common. But I find it all so lovely and calming. But it doesn't matter what or why. Does it? Tell me, did your mare throw you?"

"No, no, she isn't want to do that sort of thing; no, she was, as I said, spooked by something. Perhaps the wind."

She hesitated and smiled before speaking. "Yes. The wind." The light from the fire accentuated her high cheekbones in soft pink. "And do tell me, are you simply escaping the confines of Waverly or have you come with an express purpose in mind, other than avoiding them all?" She leaned back and let her arms rest on the soft velvet of the chair's arms.

"I was escaping." He grinned. Her long, unbound hair fell in waves along the front of her simple blue dress. He liked that. "I did have a gift for you, but alas, my renegade horse has alighted home, and now I fear I've arrived not only uninvited but empty handed."

"Yes, yes, bad form, sir," she teased.

"Madam, do not taunt me so. Can you not observe my anxious condition and take pity on me?" He returned her smile.

"Ah, but sir, you do not strike me as a man that frightens easily, nor do you appear to be the sort to flee from adversity. Tell me. Why are you here tonight, Martin? Tell me true."

He paused, contemplating the ramifications of telling her the entirety of the truth he struggled with since first seeing her. Rather than go down a path he could not easily wander back from, he said, "I haven't been in this house for many years. In the interim, I have been told it had nearly fallen down."

"Does it appear so to you?"

"No. In fact, it is rather charming—even the glass within the panes gleam. Have you worked some magic here?" He crossed his large legs one over the other and pressed his hands together before placing them to his lap.

"Magic? What an interesting word...The magic we perceive is merely what we are led to believe. Or what we wish to see. Do you not agree, Martin?"

"I'm not certain what you mean by that, Meredith, but I simply wished to compliment you on the state of the house and its interiors. It is much like you. Warm. Without airs."

"I consider myself duly acknowledged and complimented, and I thank you."

His eyes reluctantly drifted from her beautiful face and shifted to a table over her shoulder where a glass vase sat atop a frilly cloth. The vase held a single white rose surrounded by lavender. He stood, not believing his very eyes, and walked past her to the table.

"How?" he asked and touched a petal of the rose.

She went to stand beside him. "*Magic*," she whispered.

He turned quickly toward her, wanting to see her expression, but before he could make sense of what she had said, jest or serious in nature, a thunderous bashing sound met their ears. "What in heaven's…"

"A ship." She turned her eyes toward the windows that looked out over the great river.

He ran to the door and pulled it open, not closing it as he made for the side of the cottage where he could view the river through the trees. The air was silent save for a faint murmur that arose from many feet below where unfrozen portions of river meandered around boulders. She stood at his side and listened.

"Meredith, I don't see anything. Do you?"

"It's too dark to see." She handed him a lantern, and he gratefully took it.

"I'll take my leave, Meredith, and thank you...for…" He strode off toward the bluffs above the river without finishing his sentence. One final look over his shoulder proved that his dog had no intention of following, and Meredith, in her plain blue dress that swept along the white crest of snow, looked all the more a bearer of strange magic than he could fully grasp.

"Be wary, Martin! Footfalls are perilous amid shadows!" she called out to him as the cottage slipped further away from his sight.

He made his way swiftly down the incline until he came to a clearing and stood atop a boulder to look down upon the river. From that high perch, he could at last make out the ill-defined mast of a ship, and along the shore, three men waded into the shallows of the icy waters.

"Hello there! Are all accounted for?" One man turned, scanning the tree line above until he saw Martin's silhouette and lantern against the sky.

"All but two, sir! We need assistance! My son! My son is trapped within!" he shouted, and pointed at the floundering vessel.

"Hold steady, man! I will make way!" The snow was difficult to walk upon as he struggled to reach the base of the hill where he might then turn back along the shore where the men stood. Tumbling down the last portion of rocky shore, he landed on the iced shallows of the river and stood, gathering himself. The lantern, not surviving the fall, lay shattered in pieces about his feet. Slipping and sometimes falling, he climbed rock and navigated the rugged shore without benefit of more than moonlight toward the men, until, out of breath, he stopped for a moment and peered down the shore.

The sound of flapping masts and rigs met his ears above the pounding of his blood, and he leaned over to place his hands upon his thighs to catch his breath. He counted the men on shore. Five. There were five now, and assured the two had escaped from what might have become an icy grave, he stood erect and walked toward them.

"Sir!" one man called, and walked toward him. "All is well, sir; my boy and his mate are freed. Thanks to the lady. But she…" He stopped and looked about himself as though bewilderment fetched his last wit. "She was here, and she waded to them, tossing them a rope and line. I did try to stop her sir, but she went straight away into the waters and returned none the worse for wear." The bearded man, quite old by Martin's estimation, and equally out of breath, suddenly thrust his hand out and grasped Martin by the arm. "She came from nowhere, sir, and I do not lie. Many sailors have their tales, but I am not among them, and now she is simply, well…*vanished*, sir. Gone like a pyff."

Martin turned his head to gaze along the ridges above and saw nothing but endless snow and weather-gnarled trees. Yes, he was well acquainted with rogue puffs of wind. "You shall all come to my home and warm yourselves. What is left of anything your ship carried will be retrieved tomorrow morn. Place the lantern on the rocks, sir, so no other ship meets a similar fate. Go there, to Waverly, sir, when you are done."

"Very kind of you to help ofersælics in need."

"All men of ships are friend to me. In that measure, you are not a stranger."

Of course the woman who had helped the sailors was not his Meredith. No. Even she, so lithe and sure of foot could not have clambered down the iced ledges and arrived at the wreck before he had. He walked away, occasionally looking over his shoulder back toward where he had come and thought perhaps the old man was simply overcome with grief at the very thought of losing his son to the river and had imagined the entire thing. He stopped, looked back the way he had come once more, as though he expected to find Meredith trailing close behind. Or perhaps, it was simply that he had wished it to be so.

The men from the sailboat were taken in as Martin had promised, and James tended to their needs alongside Miriam. Their clothing was dried near the fire. Each man was fed and given ample amounts of whiskey and sent to the two unoccupied rooms of the servant's quarters. He avoided any further contact with them, blaming it on his exhaustion, but his truth was clear. He did not want to hear more about the woman on The Hudson's shores, nor did he want to hear about wrecks or men nearly lost. He simply wanted to make certain that Isabella was properly bedded down. He then made straight for his bedchambers where he fell into his bed without undressing, the scent of jasmine lingering on his clothing, his dark hair. Her gentle blue eyes, strange and endearing, lingered in his mind as he fell into a fitful sleep.

He awoke sometime after ten that morning to find the men had already left. With the help of some able townsfolk, what had been spilt from the vessel had been secured and the men were driven to Saugerties where they boarded the ferry back to New York City. Curiosity tugged at him. He ate his breakfast in a hurry, refused Miriam's attempts at conversation that was intended to illicit information about his whereabouts the night before, and made straight for the barn. He stopped briefly to pat Isabella and chide her in his gentle way. Then he saddled Merlin, a black mare that was mostly ridden by the old or very young due to her gentleness and rather sluggish ways. He set off at a slow walk toward the shore where the ship floundered.

Near the wreck, he dismounted and examined the shoreline where the sailboat laid on her side. The grand sail mast pointed toward shore, its top resting on the jagged rocks. The hull, clearly beyond repair, bore a large hole where the brackish water lapped in and out. Ice had taken over the keel, and torn sails that had washed ashore rolled amidst the froth and seaweed, mingled together in a frozen stew. A lone seagull perched atop the bow and called out toward the river, its white wings thrusting out with each cry. The wind kicked up hard from the west toward him, and he buried his head into his long coat's collar against it.

He examined footprints left where men had worked hard to gather what could be salvaged from the wreck and then had loaded it onto carts to haul away. The prints led in circles, save for the tracks left by horses and carts. Not one solitary print led toward the wreck from any direction, save for the townsmen's and his own, and all led to and from Waverly or away in the direction he had come to the wreck the night before. Tilting his head toward the high bluffs above him and the twisted tree limbs along its top, he was more certain than before that Meredith could not have scaled the cliffs.

Who was the woman? No, he thought, as he climbed atop the mare again to head for home, the old sailor had simply been seized by his harrowing experience and had imagined the entire thing. Even as he had briefly contemplated speaking to the rescued sailors the night before, he had just as quickly pushed the notion away. Some things were not meant to be known. Some things were better left to the recesses of memory where they would soon be shoved aside and forgotten.

From high above she watched as Martin rode slowly away, his great black coat's bottoms tugged by wind and the motion of his horse. His head ducked down beneath his collar denied her a last much wanted look of his handsome face. The briny waters below, growing more still within the ice with each passing moment, splintered light across his black hair, and she watched until the horse passed by the cove where the path would lead him toward Waverly and away from her.

She turned and walked back toward the cottage, having nowhere else she might be understood, and paused beneath the arched doorway before entering, wishing she was some other that might see a tomorrow of womanly meaning with Martin Waverly. But it could not be.

All of them are gone?" Martin sat down at the table in the kitchen and looked toward James, who had brought him more unwelcomed news.

"All but me and Miriam. And Stephen. The rest of the servants have left your employ, citing their fear of this place and who might be next."

James pushed a mug of broth across the table toward Martin. "Drink it, Martin. You're looking rather peevish. Miriam does make a fine broth."

"I don't mean to hurt the woman's feelings, James, but we cannot survive on her broth." He pushed it away and rubbed his face. "Do they all feel this place to be so precariously uninviting that they could not have given fair notice?"

"They are fearful, and I can't say I blame them. But Miriam has called on her sister that she might come and help the household until we find more willing to work here. Even her sister is not inclined to be of help. Sadly, word is spreading across the town and to outreaching villages that Waverly is not a place to visit, much less find employment. Even the word of the sailors has reached New York by now, and while you might hope they brought good news of this household's assistance after the wreck, they are also inclined to report it occurred on Waverly property. Complete with spirit rescues."

"The river is no one's property, but I do suspect that it will make no difference to those who need a bit of gossip. Or a good ghost tale."

"Alas, sir, we must simply plow ahead and hope for spring to come early this year."

"It portends a particularly long winter, James, and we are in the midst of dissatisfaction and mystery and foul brews. Even now can you not hear the thrashing of wind up in the eaves? We are miles from spring." A loud thud struck upon the front doors, and both men, feeling the weight of anxiety and their nerves ever on guard for too many days on end, both leapt to their feet. "Uninvited arrive."

"I'll see to it, Martin." James scurried off toward the foyer and answered the door.

"Good afternoon." A properly dressed young woman with auburn hair and a wide smile dropped her one large cloth suitcase near her feet and thrust her hand out to James. "My name is Emily Walker, and I have come answering your household's search for a cook."

"A cook? From where have you heard we were in need of one? Oh, pardon me, miss, do come in." He reached for her bag and was surprised at its weight. She had handled it so easily.

"Thank you, sir. I presume you are James? Mrs. Cooper's great niece told me you were in need. I just arrived from Boston and hoped to be acceptable to you."

"Come meet Martin, miss. Master Martin Waverly. You may sit in his library and wait. Here." He thrust open the double doors of the library and set her suitcase just inside the door. "I'll fetch him at once."

"Thank you, James."

"Ah, sir!" James said, stepping aside. "I was just about to bring you here to see a Miss Emily Walker who has come to inquire about cook's position." James gently shut the door so he could not be heard by the woman in the library. "She is a lovely creature, Martin," he whispered, "perfectly dressed and her hair done up the way the fancy ladies do in the city. Surprising, I'd say. See for yourself."

"Thank you, James." He opened the door and straight away spotted Emily standing near his desk. "Miss Walker? I am told you are here to apply for a cook's place in the estate?"

"Indeed I am, Mr. Waverly." She walked toward him, her hand out to greet him. She caught herself in that little misstep, since no lady would ever extend her hand to a man first, much less toward a prospective new employer. "Forgive me, sir," she said, withdrawing her hand and reverting to a slight bow and curtsey. She allowed her eyes to remain lowered as he approached.

"Please sit. There." He pointed toward the chair that sat at the opposite side of his desk. She hesitated, waiting for him to sit first. "Sit." She did as instructed and tidied her dark green dress about herself.

"I have references, Mr. Waverly. And I add, if I may, that I am an acquaintance of Mrs. Cooper's great niece." She reached into her black fur muff and withdrew an envelope, which she placed gently in front of him on the desk.

He slid it toward himself but did not open it. "I would like you to know that this house has had its share of misery. My workers save for a few have fled. While I do not expect a lot of those employed by me, I do expect a measure of honesty and good conduct. I must also add that I am a straightforward man, and so I must tell you that I find you to be most unexpected and a most unusual prospect."

"Why, may I ask?" She managed a careful smile that did not reach her eyes. "I am a hard worker, sir, and if you would simply open the envelope, you would see that to be true." She tilted her head toward the letter before him, but he continued to ignore it.

"You are well presented, Miss Walker. You do not look like any cook I have seen."

"Must I be a frightful mess to be employed here, sir, or must I be old and tired and…" Her voice rose nervously as she spoke.

He flipped his gaze toward her and smiled. "Miss. Walker, I did not mean to sound accusatory, but if you are an honest person, you could well imagine why I say what I do. So tell me now why you want this job, and please tell me truthfully if you can abide living in such a cold place with little help."

"I am a widow, Mr. Waverly. I have no means to support myself any longer and so took to cooking jobs as I could. I am skilled, sir, and I assure you that you will not go hungry with me in your employ." Her bottom lip trembled, and he sat back into his chair.

He did not quite believe all she said, but was in no position to argue it further. "I offer my sincere condolences, Madam Walker." At last he opened the envelope and read glowing reports of her abilities as well as her upstanding character, and refolding the paper, he smiled. "You must be advised that if you take this position, Madam, there will be many lonely days here. We have not entertained in many months since my father fell ill."

"I have heard that, Mr. Waverly, and if I may say something?" He nodded his head. "I, too, am outspoken, sir, and so will tell you that I am well acquainted with tales that surround this estate. Perhaps all you need is a bit of frivolity to drown out the gossip and add some life back into this estate?"

He smiled warmly at her. "Madam, it has been many years since we have experienced gaiety here. I will call on Miriam, our house manager, to see you to your room. It is not what I would wish to offer you, but in time, I hope to improve the quarters, if you can bear with it until spring."

"Thank you, sir!" She jumped up from her seat and extended her hand, before yanking it away. "Again, I forget myself. I am enthusiastic, sir, and I hope you can forgive that."

"Make your finest dinner for tomorrow evening, Madam, and all shall be forgotten." He left the room to find Miriam, who had been standing outside the door for what he presumed was the entire time, and laughed. "See to her, please, Miriam. You must stop lurking about that way. One might call you an eavesdropper." He walked past her to the sound of Miriam giggling under her breath.

It would have been rude had he asked her how her husband had died, and worse to comment on how she had afforded the lovely clothing she wore that day. But he knew that within an hour, he would have a full report from Miriam, who could never be accused of letting propriety stand in her way of a good tale or bit of gossip. Emily was a beautiful woman, and surely, he thought as he went out to the second parlor to sit near the fire, she could have found herself decent employment somewhere that would not threaten to ruin her fair and unblemished skin or spirit. But he was not in any position to deny anyone the job at that juncture, and the worst thing that could happen, he surmised, was that Madam Emily Walker would need to improve her skills. Wasn't that so?

W illham sat at the rickety desk and scribbled on a paper with a shaky hand. If they couldn't follow a simple plan, then what was he to do? He jotted down thoughts regarding his next course of action as the grisly deer stew simmered in a pot placed over the small woodstove behind him. The windows were clouded with grime and fogged so he could not get a fair view of the valley below but imagined he could see the tops of Waverly Estate in the distance from across the river.

The cabin he rented was in shabby condition, and the two rooms smelled of stale alcohol and cigar smoke. The former tenant, he frowned at recalling what was told to him, had died right there on that very bed. It was the man's bad fortune but his luck that he had stumbled on the place the night he had left the inn, and at pennies for a night, he would hardly find reason to refuse it. Without adequate funds to return to France for René's funeral, he was unable to procure money and assets that were hidden away within Rene's home. Nearly out of money, and he feared equally out of time, he had motivated them to step up the plan's pace to be done with it and return home to France where he might begin his life again, far richer.

"It's ready," she said and dumped the pungent stew into a bowl. She dropped it down on the desk and stabbed a fork into the grizzled meat. "Eat it, and don't complain. It's what you have. It's what I have."

Willham turned slowly in his chair and swiveled his head toward her. "You're an ignorant and ill-bred snipe, and I will be the happiest man on this Earth when we part ways."

"Shut your trap, old man. You may dislike me, but you need me. So best mind your manners and say thank you once in a while."

"Theresa, you make a man shudder. You are a most unfortunate looking girl with your dropsy eyes and thin hair, your skin like old bread. But with some money, you might fix yourself up a bit. Then maybe a man will find you tolerable."

"I have me a man, you old flapdoodle, which is more than I can say for you." She burst into hysterical laughter that was abruptly stopped with one hard slap across her face.

"You don't know what you are talking about, and it would serve you well not to comment on my...preferences. Go away, and eat that out of my sight, lest I toss you to the snow and leave you out of my preparations. And feed that wretch. We can't have her expiring before she serves her purpose."

Theresa rubbed her face where Willham's hand stung her cheek and turned around to face the woman who crouched in the corner.

"You ain't so pretty and fine are you, now, mistress? No you ain't." Theresa snickered and tossed a crust of bread at Hannah before turning her back on them, staring through the filth of the tiny window toward the river.

Willham sighed and stood. "Have you no decency, Theresa? Untie her hands so she can eat what she was given out of the generosity of my heart."

Theresa, without turning around, replied, "Let her lean over and feed from the ground like a dog. She ain't no better."

"There, there," Willham soothed as he walked toward Hannah, his hand extended. "Let me untie your hands so you can eat."

Hannah, who had not spoken a word in days, said, 'Thank you, sir. How very kind."

Bruised from Theresa's fists, Hannah's eyes were nearly swollen shut.

Her lips, once perfect and smooth, bore a long cut to her lower lip that neither Theresa nor Willham had bothered to wash. The blood, dark and crusted, flaked as she spoke. Her feet, bound by cutting cord and attached to a wood beam in the corner, had become bloated, and even if she were freed, she could not have walked upon them without experiencing agonizing pain. Her once glorious tresses lay limply on her shoulders and down her back. She grabbed the bread from Willham's hands, and at her first bite, she vomited the little she had in her stomach and tossed the bread across the floor, where it landed near Theresa's feet.

"Now I suppose I'll have to clean that up! Bitch!" Theresa, screaming, in two steps, strode up to Hannah and backhanded her across the face. "Willham, you better make this all worth my while. Out here in the middle of nowhere with you two good-for-nothings and the stench of this place! The stench! I tell you, I can't stand it another moment!"

"Then don't," Willham replied as he calmly sat back at the desk. "Get out of here and walk the six miles to town and then take the boat back to the other side of The Hudson. Collect your Daniel and be gone. You'll have nothing more from me, and I won't stop you."

Theresa hurled herself toward him and slapped her hands on the desk, causing him to flinch. "And what you expect me to do with that?" she screamed, jerking her head toward Hannah.

"Hmm? Oh. Her? Well, I will wait till her use is expended, and then I'll toss her in the river." He shrugged and turned back to his paper.

"When this wind stops, I *will* leave you here with that wretch and get back to Daniel. I don't need you. I don't." She pounded her fists onto the desk and spun around.

Willham shrugged again. "As you wish, Theresa," he retorted easily since he had not believed she would leave alone. "I'm tired. I think I shall drink the last of the wine and make myself of no further use this evening. Goodnight ladies," he said as he blew out the lantern on the desk. He walked over to the bed, closed the curtains around it, and drank heavily from the wine bottle.

His dismissive manner had only infuriated Theresa more than he could have imagined, and when he woke the next morning, she was gone, and she had taken a horse with her. "What shall I do with you now, lady?" he asked Hannah who did not attempt to rise from the filthy rags upon which she laid.

"Let me go," she said through her swollen lips. "Please let me go."

"There, there. That can't be. You see, if I do that, you will have me jailed, and that isn't intended. I'm sure you see my dilemma."

She struggled to pull herself up and with great effort managed it. "But I will go away. I will not return to Waverly. I will go back to Philadelphia to be with my family."

Willham laughed unpleasantly. "Madam, do you refer to the people you have forsaken and denied existed for all these years while putting on airs and pretending all your relations have died or moved to England? No, I don't think you have anywhere to go but back to Waverly. Your Philadelphia kin are paupers and thieves. Making yourself known to Garson in New York City while he was attending business was a stroke of luck for you. Wasn't it? I know all about you, Madam. I made it my business to discover all that needed discovering."

A terrible sob rose up from her throat, and she lay back down and wept the bitterest tears Willham had ever seen or heard.

"Please. I beg of you," she sobbed.

"Madam, I can't very well take you back in this state, and I have no means by which to right your appearance."

"Take me back, and we will blame Theresa. You can tell them all that you rescued me from her and that Daniel of hers. You shall be a hero, and I shall be freed."

Willham turned his back on her to consider what she had proffered without the distraction of having to look into her distorted face. "What assurances do you have to offer me that you will not back deal?" He turned toward her again.

Hannah smiled, causing her lip to open again and bleed. "I know where vast stores of jewelry are hidden within the very walls of Waverly. Gems my husband procured from his many travels and that were secreted aboard his ships."

"Indeed?"

"Truly."

"And if we go back and I find you have lied?"

"I have not lied. Do you think I do not know all Waverly's secrets? Do you think I was an idle Mistress of Waverly for all those years and knew nothing? Sir, tell me true. Have I struck you as the sort of woman that would not make it her business to know all there is to know? In that way alone, we are much alike."

"Hmm! Now, lady. You have convinced me with the last of that, since never before have I encountered a woman as corruptible and devious as you. But I need assurances. Tell me where they are hidden, and I shall find it out for myself, and if it is true, I will return and free you. I shall go along the tunnel to succeed in same. " He crossed his arms over his small chest and smiled maliciously.

"No. What assurances have I that you shall return once you have located the jewels?"

"Madam, need I remind you that you are the one tied in a corner of this terrible hovel, miles from a town, with no means to escape considering your present condition?"

She thought for a moment and wiped her face with the back of her arm. "Very well, then. Let us reach a compromise before I agree to any of this. Fetch me, by whatever means necessary, water to wash and a clean cloth."

"Easily done. My horse has same stowed for such an occasion. I will retrieve it and bring it back. You are a good bargainer, lady. You are not afraid to reveal the darker part of yourself at opportune moments. I respect that. I will hitch the old sway back to the cart, and we will return together in the morning. It is far too late to travel this day."

"In better weather, it would take 5 hours considering the terrain we crossed to come here. With this weather, I say we will be back to Waverly by midnight if we leave within the hour."

"Your factoring is most likely reliable, lady, but we must account for unforeseen events, such as a lame horse. You will die out there in your current state if we lose the horse."

"Die?" she laughed unpleasantly. "I have no intention of dying."

"Very well, then. If you die along the way, I shall leave you where you expire."

"We have arrived at a satisfactory deal, Willham. Now please go fetch me what you promised."

"And the lady manages a 'please.' Imagine!"

He stumbled out into the snow and entered the falling down stall where the remaining horse stood. Fumbling through the saddlebag, he withdrew the peyote, water, and clean cloth. *If*, he thought as he made his way back to the cabin, *she thinks to misbehave, I shall simply force more peyote into her vile mouth and be done with the fuss.* He shoved the drug into his pocket and flung the door open.

She was not where he had left her sitting, and he walked further into the room. "Where are you hiding, woman?"

The answer was supplied via a brutal stabbing of a fork into his neck.

He went down hard and yowled in pain as she stepped over him and made for the door.

"You barbarian! You stupid, stupid little troll!"

She dragged herself through the snow, and as she came to the horse, she reached for the reins but was grabbed from behind with a terrible yank back to the snow.

"This is appalling!" he screamed and grabbed her by the hair, forcing her toward the cart. "It could have been simply done, but no! You insist on this nonsense!" The rage he experienced leant him the force of a much larger man, and he hurled her into the cart, head first. She, kicking and screaming, could do no better than to delay Willham's intent. He lay across her and crammed the parcel of peyote into her howling mouth. Then he slammed her teeth together, forcing her to swallow. Assured she had ingested it down, he then yanked at her jaw again and pushed pills down her throat. In minutes, she was quiet, and he tossed a thin blanket over her stilled body.

Urging the horse forward through the wind and snow, he headed down the overgrown horse path.

ᴺᴵᴺᴱ

Rockingham handed Martin the last wood board and stood back as it was hammered into place.

"There. That's the last of it." Martin stood and brushed his hands against his pant legs. "No other entry in or out has been found, and if someone thinks to enter, they must do it via the front door."

"Seems such a pity that you had to get your hands on this. Seeing as you are master of this house." Rockingham took a few steps back as Martin slung a box to the top of his shoulder.

"I'm a man first, sir. Hand me that hammer will you?" Rockingham retrieved it from the floor and handed it to Martin.

"I'm only sorry that we have arrived at such a tumultuous time."

"Our new cook, Emily, is in the kitchen preparing what she promised is a feast. That's something we could all use."

"You're far too familiar with your workers, Martin, if you don't mind me saying. Isn't it better to step away and keep your distance with the new ones? And there is something not right about her."

"Why would that be?" Rockingham followed Martin from the dining room and into the foyer.

"As for her, she is not what she seems. Mark my words, Martin. And as for respect, they won't give it to you if you behave as a friend."

Martin stopped and laughed. "My good man, I don't need their respect. They aren't slaves. I just need them to do their jobs."

"Fear works wonders."

Martin, taken aback, frowned at Rockingham. "You sound like my father who was not respected—and was not admired. The only thing he succeeded in doing was make them all hate him, myself included." Martin continued through the foyer and out into the courtyard with Rockingham close behind.

"But he loved you. He just didn't show it very well; I can say it for sure. But he always wanted the best for you. Even while, perhaps, he resented you, jealous, even, over the love you had for your mother."

"No, he wanted me to be just like him. He wanted someone to do his bidding and be the sort to smile in a friend's face whilst concocting ways to stab them in the back—and get away with it."

"It's a harsh assessment, sir, a very harsh assessment indeed. But I must confess I have seen it first hand in ways I cannot ever tell you….To tell you true, I feel no loss at his passing. He was a hard man. A cruel man. But we all have something good within us, Martin, if we care to look."

Reaching the barn, Martin dropped the box of nails and plains to the ground. He turned toward Rockingham and rested a hand on the man's shoulder.

"It's a truth that needed telling for many years, and while it took his death to end his dominion over us all, we are free. He didn't treat you much better. Which reminds me...we must settle accounts, and you need to have a sum more appropriate than what he left you—to take back to New York City."

"I feel like a thief. There is no need to."

"Nonsense. You aren't stealing. You are being given something you should have long ago been granted. Enough of this. Let's go in and get dressed for dinner. Hmm?"

Martin did not wait for Rockingham to reply and instead strode off toward the house, leaving him behind.

The laughter coming from the hayloft caused Rockingham to tilt back on his heels. "Who is that up there?"

"It is Daniel," the young man said as he descended from the loft. He jumped down when he neared the bottom.

"What are you doing here? Have you lost your mind, boy?" Rockingham clutched at his chest.

"I've been here every day. Watching...and things. So he hasn't given you the money yet?"

"No. Tonight, I suppose."

Daniel brushed the hay from his pant legs and shoulders and leaned against the horse stall beside Isabella. He crossed his legs one over the other and grinned. "He doesn't know, does he, Rockingham?"

"About you? Of course not, you fool."

"No, about the missing portion of the will. The part that spells out what is to be left to you? Martin has always been the more charitable one, by far. We both knew he wouldn't let you go with a measly sum from the will. And by the sound of it, you have made away with three times as much, had you let it be known what was truly offered by the old man."

"He trusts me, and I doubt he has any expertise where last wills and testaments are concerned. I made it so he could not discover the alteration."

"Old man Waverly was a town idiot. Full of bluster and thinking us all far inferior. Isn't that a belly laugh?"

"Still you are not contented. Do you think Martin should be murdered? Yes, I suppose you do."

Daniel shrugged. "Who would miss him? He's become much like his father. A hermit. A *wealthy* hermit that doesn't know what to do with what he has. If I were him, I'd be gallivanting around the world, not holed up in this god-forsaken place chasing ghosts that don't exist. He owes me and my family. He owes us more than can be repaid, but I will take what you have, Rockingham, in exchange for not telling him about his mother, as agreed."

Rockingham lunged toward Daniel and grabbed his throat. "You will never tell Martin about his mother's death, never. Do you hear me, boy?"

Daniel brushed him easily away and laughed. "Or what, old man?"

"The only reason I am agreeing to take the money he offers is to shut you up. You must keep to our agreement, boy, and that is that!"

"Get off it, Rockingham. You can't tell me you think you don't deserve it. You were used and tossed away by old man Waverly for all the years you worked for and with him."

"It's true, all of it. But I have a fondness for his son, and nothing will stand in my way to ensure he is happy. If I am even partially to blame for any unhappiness he experiences, I shall never forgive myself."

"Did that lot care when my father died at sea for their sake? Did they send my mother anything at all? No they did not. And I doubt that fool Martin even remembers that I told him my father was one of the merchants on their ship. Me and mine were left destitute and tossed from our house. My sister became a whore in Boston to make money to send home to feed us, and you lecture me about what Martin deserves? Get off it, old man. And do as you were told, or I *will* tell him about his mother. You best believe it."

"I loved her. I didn't mean to—"

"Everyone loved her."

"No, I *loved* her."

"Drowning her was an odd way to prove it."

Daniel walked away, and Rockingham hung his head. The wound caused by his deed had never healed. Of course it could not! And Daniel had just gashed it open again.

It was not enough for Daniel that he had found the letters that he and Martin's mother had written to each other. Blythe House had been left as it was after Martin's mother died, and Rockingham had never considered she might have kept their delicate correspondence there, where they had often met through the years. But after their discovery, Daniel had gone so far as to arrive in New York City and rifle through his belongings until he found Rockingham's personal journals. Blackmail and bribery were logical, albeit cruel, next steps for the young man whose heart was set on retribution—his soul burning to pay back to the Waverly clan what he felt had been inflicted upon his family. If found out, it would all be over for Rockingham, and his young friend, Martin, would be shattered.

Rockingham wondered if there were more letters left to be found. Daniel claimed to have had more than a dozen in his possession, and to prove that fact, he often recited lines he knew he had written over the many years.

He walked from the barn and stood in the courtyard facing the path and hill beyond. In that moment, despite the whirling winds and threat of more snow, he began the slow and steady climb toward Blythe House.

❧ Are you certain that we should all sit here in the dining room together? It doesn't seem quite proper." Miriam fussed lightly with her hair and sat down without waiting for reassurance.

"Martin said so. Not ten minutes ago." James sat beside her and shifted uncomfortably in his chair. "It is surely a beautiful room, isn't it?" He looked around as though seeing it for the first time.

"Will Mr. Rockingham be along? Otherwise it will be just us and Stephen, and Emily, and of course, Martin."

"He hasn't returned yet, Miriam. I have not seen him in more than an hour. I do hope he has not forgotten."

Martin walked into the room and smiled. "I'm pleased we could all sit together this evening. But did I hear you say that Rockingham has not returned? I left him in the barn." He sat down, and the smile crept from his face. "Ah, I hope I didn't fluster him. We had a discussion that—Oh, well...I suppose it won't matter once he has eaten Emily's meal with us."

Stephen walked in, and with his hair combed straight back and his shoes newly polished, he looked very much like a gentleman, a fact that Miriam could not resist noting. "Ah you look every bit a gentleman, Stephen!" she said, glowingly.

"This dinner invitation is kind of you, sir, and I thank you. I'm not sure I have ever been invited to such a feast." Martin waved his hand, asking him to sit across from him. "Thank you, sir." He sat sheepishly down and looked to his right and left, noting that Miriam and James had also attempted to mark the unusual occasion with neatly applied dress.

Emily peered into the room and counted the guests. "Is Mr. Rockingham attending? Or have I misunderstood? Shall we wait longer, sir?"

"We will give him a few more minutes, Emily. Thank you. But please, do bring in the breads and fruits. And sit with us if you can for a while."

"Thank you, sir! Are you quite sure?"

"Indeed! What use is good food if we cannot occasionally enjoy it together? James, please light our candles. Let's make joyful use of this room. There is no point in sitting in the dark to spare a wick. And by the way, I have asked Pastor O'Mara to join us. He is quite alone these days." He shot a look toward James who did not flinch.

Perhaps he was testing the veracity of Meredith's tale about the pastor being her father. Perhaps he wondered if James did not know that his wife Caroline had given birth to a child of another man, but Martin had decided he was tired of the foolery and whispers, and the thought to bring them all together might ease his mind. Had he done the wrong thing? Was he becoming as conniving as he deemed many had been toward him? He was not sure. But there it was. All invited, excluding Meredith whom he did not want to see again until he could be sure about her.

He had blamed his father for the mysterious deaths that occurred while he was alive, yet murder was still a familiar specter that haunted the halls under his watch. The hidden tunnels and inexplicable piano playing in the middle of the night and a trusted and composed horse suddenly fearful because of a gust of wind were just a handful of disconcerting events that baffled his sleep and caused him too many hours of strain. Deaths of those around him? He could not abide it. Even Miriam had taken to giving him sideways glances when she thought he might not notice. Perhaps she suspected him of being responsible for Hannah's disappearance. Worse, maybe even for one or more of the deaths. He could not say for sure. But this he knew: his chaotic house would be placed back into order, or there would be no peace for any of them.

Pastor O'Mara arrived nearly forty-five minutes late, but no one said a word about it. He did not offer an explanation, but in short order, it was forgotten as the food was set before them.

Martin thought about all that had happened since his father's death, and as he made small talk with those around him, he barely paid mind to much of what was said. He watched, and thought, and pondered, hoping that those nearest to him would not be the ones at the root of it all. Worse, that one he sat with would be the next to fall.

"Sir? Are you quite alright?" James inquired, leaning slightly forward.

"Oh. I do apologize. My mind had strayed to other things."

"Yes?" Miriam said, leaning forward a little toward him, too.

"Yes. Business things. Again, I do apologize. So Pastor O'Mara, do tell us about how you are faring."

"Well," the pastor said, clearing his throat and placing his fork on the blue china reserved for special occasions. "To tell you in a straightforward way, sir, I would like to see you all attend services. It has been many weeks since a single one of you have worshipped with your brethren."

A temporary silence fell between them, and each shifted uncomfortably in their chairs, save for James, who smiled, and said, "My Caroline frequented your church, pastor. I suppose after she left us, I lost my desire to pray."

O'Mara, unblinkingly, stared at James who then averted his eyes. Another uncomfortable silence lowered amidst them, and Martin could not help but examine each of their expressions. Miriam shrugged and took another forkful of chicken. Emily did not look up and fixed her eyes on the food before her. James toyed with a loose thread on his napkin. Stephen, who had remained mostly silent during the meal, seemed to be watching them all as carefully as Martin.

Finally, O'Mara broke the uncomfortable silence. "We must never give up on prayer, sir. It is our only hope. For salvation and peace and…"

"Nonsense," James said, his face turning a shade of red. "Prayer did not save my Caroline and neither has it provided any of us peace."

No one moved save for Stephen who peered under his lashes toward Martin, who returned the look. One side of Stephen's mouth crooked up into a small grin. Martin, knowing the conversation would come to no good, sighed, and put down his fork.

"Perhaps, James," O'Mara proceeded carefully, "you are not praying for the correct things. I have seen Nurse Margaret, who even now, maintains this house has become Godless and beleaguered by all manner of evil—and as she states, restless souls. If this house is disturbed, it is haunted only by those who dwell within these walls and refuse to see the face of God—and that they prefer their wild fairy tales of ghosts and spooks rather than make atonement to The One True God. The evil that lurks here might as well be invited in for a tidy and long winter stay because such actions as exhibited within these walls invites the very things you all say exists! A simple prayer for salvation, sir—a rightly prayer begging forgiveness might lead to easing of the ache that plagues this house."

"Is that so? James asked. "And are you the decider of right and wrong prayer, pastor? Or is this between God and the one who prays?"

O'Mara shifted in his chair and cleared his throat. "I didn't intend to insult you or anyone at this fine table. I simply …"

"Yes? You have done a fine job of it, none the less." James stood and dropped his napkin to the table. "If you will excuse me, I…" His words were interrupted by the sound of the front door swinging open, followed by a wild gust of wind and a shout. The candles flickered, and Martin sprung to his feet.

"Help us! Help us!"

They all rushed from the table, save for the pastor who did not move from his chair.

"My God!" Miriam clutched Martin's arm.

"Lady Waverly needs assistance!" Willham, exhausted from the journey back to Waverly and the weight of carrying Hannah in from the cart through the snow, fell to the floor with Hannah beside him.

"My God!" Miriam screamed again and rushed toward Hannah.

At the dining table, Pastor O'Mara smirked and rose slowly from the chair. "Yes, now they call upon God. Of course they do."

"Stand man; stand if you can," James said as he attempted to lift Willham from the cold floor.

"I cannot, sir. I cannot." It was partly true.

Martin pushed past the others and lifted Hannah into his arms and brought her to the second parlor where he laid her on the settee nearest the fire. "Bring me water!" he called out. "Now!" He brushed her matted hair away from eyes that were swollen shut and said her name, ever so softly, but the only reply was a soft groan that sounded as though it had come from a wounded creature near death.

James and Stephen dragged Willham into the room and laid him near the fire.

"I found her," Willham cried. "She was wandering the road across the river, and as I had just left The France to see to Rene's return to—well, I was quite exhausted and did my best to bring her straight here. But alas she appears in poor condition...Someone, please, bring me water!"

"France?" Martin said, twisting his head toward the man who lay crumpled on the floor. "We have all been looking for you. And when did you learn of Rene's death?"

"Sir, everyone knew in town where I had taken a room. I left you in peace, as it seemed I was not quite welcome here anymore. The sloop called *The France*. Not the country."

"And did you not think to come here and ask what had happened? You relied on rumor?"

"Ask? For what reason? I saw Theresa who informed me of all the sordid details, and I was tasked with Rene's care to …"

"I have heard enough from you, Willham, and I would thank you for returning Hannah to us if I thought it had truly occurred as you stated. But I do not believe any of this and ask that as soon as you can travel in the morning, you depart this house." He turned his attention back to Hannah. "Stephen, call upon the doctor, please. Tell him he is needed here."

"It is already done, sir. I saw a boy along the way and told him to fetch the physician and bring him to Waverly," Willham said. "He galloped his pony away, and I suspect that the doctor will be here straight away." Willham groaned for effect and turned away from them to stare at the fire. A smile spread across his face, and then he closed his eyes. He had not seen any such boy along the way back to Waverly. But who could prove it was other than he had said?

Theresa had taken some of his peyote when she had spirited away, but he had retaken it, and his arrival was no longer threatened by Theresa or her threats. Not in the least. He had taken care of the bother after spying her lying beneath an old oak near the lane they traveled. Half-frozen to death as he had predicted she would be found and crying out for help, he delivered her from frostbitten misery with one evenly applied thump to the back of the head. A metal rod he had retrieved from the back of the cart did the simple deed. He kicked her down the embankment toward the river where he thought the tide would take her away. She was not nearly as clever as she had supposed. He was roused by someone handing him a cup of cold water, and he took it, drank heavily from it.

Hannah opened her eyes, and the first person she saw was Pastor O'Mara. From her very pith, a wild scream rose from her throat, and she thrashed her arms and legs about as one overcome with some horror that no one else could perceive. O'Mara placed his hands on her face, and the thrashing became a wild shake that seized her all over.

Willham wanted to smile but did not, lest he be discovered as the only one in the room who took delight in her seizure. He could thank the Indians he had met for the peyote and the hallucinations they delivered. Her fevered body was enough to toss her into a state from which he hoped she would never return.

Pastor O'Mara crouched beside Hannah and attempted to calm her with prayer, but failing at lending any comfort, he rose slowly and placed his hand upon Martin's back. "Martin, she is possessed."

Martin shrugged him away with a jerk of his shoulder, refusing to believe any of it. "The woman is frightened to her core, pastor. She has the fever. This is not the effort of a demon. This is an evil work fashioned by man." He shifted his gaze toward Willham who continued to lie prostrate on the floor, eyes closed. "You, pastor, not minutes ago, stated you did not believe this house or its occupants to be possessed of anything save for godlessness. Now you claim she is beleaguered by the supernatural. Can't you make up your mind?" he asked, above the wails.

"Had I not seen this for myself, I would agree, sir. But the touches of a man of God has caused her to flail about and screech like I have only seen one time before whilst visiting a friend who was pastor up north. Nothing saved the woman. If they had believed, we might have…"

"Shut up," Martin commanded.

Miriam fled from the room with Emily and James followed close behind. He shut the parlor door as he went.

Guttural sounds emanated from Hannah's mouth, and then she let loose a tirade of obscene utterances that the men in the room had not heard save for in a whorehouse or tavern filled with crusty sailors—or in Pastor O'Mara's case, from the lips of the woman of which he had told them.

"You must let me call for pastoral help, Martin!" O'Mara implored. "Why can you not see this is true when the woman is clearly..."

"Get. Out. *Now.*" Martin pointed toward the door and then reached for the candle that was lit upon the mantle to illuminate Hannah's battered face.

"You shall all regret your refusal to give assistance to this poor creature. You shall. You will see!" And with those words, he spun on his heels, flung the door open so forcefully that it bashed against the wall, and walked out.

"Stephen, stay with her. And keep an eye on that one," he said, jerking his head toward Willham.

Martin stalked off, candle in hand, toward the kitchen where he assumed the others had gathered. The front door slammed as the pastor exited, and Martin paused to catch his breath. As he entered the foyer from the parlor, he stopped cold and spun around.

A tinkling of piano keys played—once, twice, three times, and then fell silent. Martin walked slowly back toward the room.

Willham, unable to continue his charade, sat straight up, crawled into the corner, and covered his ears with his hands, his eyes, fixed on the piano. Hannah became very silent, but in the next moment, she placed her hands atop her head and yanked at her hair, tearing clumps of it by the roots until her fists were full of her dark tresses. A feral growl, ascending in volume, shifted into a high-pitched laugh that truly could not have come from anyone, unless they had gone mad.

Hannah hauled herself up, gripping the sides of the table for support and stared at the piano, struggling to speak. "'*The spirits of the dead who stood in life before thee are again in death around thee—and their will shall then overshadow thee: be still.*'" She paused, her face expressionless, and she fell hard to the floor once again.

Martin did not run to assist her. Instead, he stood with one hand on the door, and he gripped the candle with the other. "She quotes Poe," he whispered. "Have I gone mad with sickness of mind or can the dead make themselves known as I have ardently denied?"

The room went silent, save for the clock's soft ticking in the hall. The candle's flame burned brightly, moving left, right and left again. A gentle breath fell across his hand, and then the flame extinguished, pitching the room into shadow.

He dropped the candlestick to the floor at his feet, turned, and walked away.

"I cannot abide this place a moment more!" Miriam shouted as Martin walked toward her. "What is it?" she asked, seeing his strange appearance. Truly he had gone white as the snow, and he sat heavily down at the table.

"The piano played. I heard it. Stephen heard it, as did Willham." He stared at the hand, which had held the candle. "I held the candle. Here. In my hand, pushed forward into the shadows and saw nothing that played the keys. Doubting what I had heard, fearing for my sanity, I questioned the spirit's existence. And it's answer?" He looked from James to Miriam.

"The answer was the snuffing out of the flame delivered by the specter's breath. And yes, Miriam, I can hardly blame you for wanting to leave this place never to return, but lady, I beseech you to stay, for I fear it is you and James who stand between me and the abyss of madness. I can take no more."

Miriam sat beside him and patted his hand. "Perhaps, Martin, we should all leave this place and permit the ghosts to take it for themselves. Let us board the windows and doors and take from it only what is truly ours, and be done with it." Emily came from the darkened servant's hall and stood near him.

"No." James grasped Martin's shoulders and shook them. "Listen to me, Martin. You have not gone mad. Whether fairy or devil, or human hand, we will not be forced from this place. No, sir, we shall not. We will find the culprit and expel it by any and all means. We shall try persuasion, or if we must, by using force, until we are freed. And I tell you now, Martin, this place can be restored to what it had been. Better, I believe. But we need you to be here since what use is it to any of us if you are gone? You shall not retreat, sir, no you shall not! No matter the force of mischief that seeks to further punish us in our distress, it cannot take what it is not entitled to, nor can they manipulate us another moment hoping we will surrender to it. I did not like your father, but I must say that no Waverly man I have known through all these years ever once surrendered. Not to man, or woman, or sea, or fear. Nor shall you. Now get up from that seat, sir, and go back to the room. Tend to Hannah and haul that vile Willham away to a locked room. Come. *Now*."

"What say you, Emily?" Martin looked up at Emily who had come to stand beside them.

"I am not fearful of the unseen, sir. I stand with you." She jutted her chin up and smiled.

"And you, Miriam? Will you stay?"

"I do not want to stay sir, nor do I wish to leave you. So, I guess my loyalty tells me to stay."

"Then so it will be. But mind you, good souls. You stay at your own peril, for I do not know what may come next."

James smiled. "Do any of us?"

"Then, let's be strong in our will and brave of heart, since no path can be forged between us if we stand collectively. Yet...Emily, you owe nothing to this shamed house, or any of us herein. So if you cannot abide this, please say so, and no harm will come to your reputation and I will compensate you for—"

"I stay, sir. I stay."

"James, you and I will get Willham up the stairs, and we will secure him in my father's room. I found it open after being sure I had locked it. But have since taken to carrying the key here, with me." He patted his breast pocket. "If any of you know of another key to that room please say so now...Fine. Then it is to father's chambers with Willham. And Miriam, please go along with Emily and sit with Hannah until we return. Then we shall bring her to her old room together and tend to her there."

Let me out of here! I must not be left alone in these rooms!" Willham pounded his fists against the doors of Garson Waverly's room, but was met with silence from the other side. "This is not humane! I am he who brought the lady back to you. Still, you keep me here? Will the act continue to be punished? I hear you in the hallways! Whoever you are, let me out this instant! You cannot hold me captive!" He stopped, very suddenly, as something occurred to him, and he pressed his back against the door and slid down to the floor. The dome above him confronted him with a mingling of memory and poison—a threat to his very life.

From where he sat, he scanned the stark white of the walls that held him within the former master's chambers. Adorning the walls and shelves around him hung artifacts secured from Garson's many trips abroad—most of which, he had no doubt, had been taken at contemptibly low cost from unsuspecting sellers or outright from his merchant sailors' plundering. The old man's cane, which once was used as part of a gentleman's attire, later, had become a mere stick of necessity as his gait failed and he could not walk without it. It leaned against what Willham deciphered was the man's favorite chair because its arms were slightly worn at the edges. It faced the river, a table near it with a book open to some page in the middle, never quite finished. His top hat, viewed from

Willham's perspective from the floor, appeared dusty and as though a mouse had gnawed on a rim. It sat atop a dressing table in front of an ornate mirror rimmed in pure gold. He could have made use of what it concealed. If only…

He stared out toward the windows that looked to The Hudson River beyond, thinking. *What was it she said about this room? What...what?* he asked himself, rubbing his bald head with both hands. His eyes strayed up to the immense dome of the ceiling that he himself had put into place. Despite it all, it remained beautiful—albeit deadly. He surveyed the recessed cabinet that held many books where the last of it met with the only part of the chambers that did not boast thick crown molding. Slowly he slid his spine back up against the door and stood. He was far too intent on a recollection to notice that it ached.

He pressed his ear against the door, listening, but heard nothing more than Martin's voice as he descended the stair to the left and the howl of a gathering winter storm that somehow seemed intent upon bursting through the many windows. Walking quietly toward them in tiny steps, he stood and stared into the veil of snow that whirled across the fields, obliterating any sight of The Hudson beyond. Something caught his attention as he scanned the spaces below, and he pressed his face to the frigid glass to spy it.

"No, no, no, no, this cannot be," he said softly to himself, squeezing his eyes shut, rubbing them hard, and then looking again as though his eyes or mind or both were playing some manner of trick on him. "Oh my god. He has returned…"

There was no time to waste. He twirled around and made for the cabinet and opened its doors. Removing the many articles of clothing he saw hanging and neatly folded, he tossed them to the floor. The eight drawers slid easily away and he placed them as quietly as he could manage to the floor near his feet. The space entirely cleared, he walked inside of it and dismissed the fleeting notion that the finely padded interiors resembled a coffin. The space, wide enough for him to reach both arms out and high enough for a much taller person, smelled of old man's belongings and something less distinct.

He ran his hands along both sides of the interior, and his left hand touched a square block of wood that did not match the right side. He exited, turned toward the mantle, grabbed a candlestick from it, and lit it. Before returning to the cabinet, he turned toward the door, pressed his ear upon it again, and listened. Nothing! His good fortune.

Again inside the interior of the cabinet, he moved the candle until he saw the block of wood and tugged at it. Rotating it, the panel opened, and he stepped into the newly found passage, three feet taller than he and a few feet wider. The sides, which were fashioned from wood, bore lanterns affixed to the walls. Rats scurried away from the light and vanished between holes they had made in the walls. The smell was so foul within the confines that he could taste it on his lips. Fearful that his exit point would be discovered, he drug the former contents of the cabinet back in and lined the passage with the cabinet drawers. Satisfied, he closed himself within the cabinet and gently shut the doors. Not one to enjoy mystery and less inclined to venture through cold, dark places, he forced himself to go forward.

Rockingham lay face up on the snow near the door of the cottage that Martin had gifted him. Powerless to do more than hope he would breathe a moment longer, he prayed to God to be forgiven—to be strong enough to forgive himself. Above his head, the canopy of trees shielded him from downward falling snow, but it could do nothing to stop the side-winding sheaths of wind-whipped white that began to cover him.

"Why is it that my life has always been such when nearing what I desire? Am I accursed?" He slid his arm from the snow that had nearly covered it and touched his leg where a jagged bone protruded at the shin. Bringing his hand in front of his face, a crimson drop of blood fell to his brow. He wiped it away and called out again as he had for the better part of two hours. But exhausted and falling in and out of a dream-like state that alternated between wakefulness and near-death sleep, his voice was thin and broken by a single sob he could not contain. Just as he closed his eyes to give in to a bitter death, a voice spoke near his head.

"Sir. Let me help you."

TEN

" No, Stephen, no one will ride out in this storm. Not tonight," Martin said as he sat in the kitchen. "There is no point in risking your life."

His voice was emphatic, but Stephen persisted.

"But we cannot leave her this way. What if she were to die in her room tonight? I could not forgive myself. I must get the doctor. Miriam cannot do this alone anymore."

"Nor would I forgive myself if you risked it all. Please do as I say, Stephen. You are of greater use here tonight. But I will go have a look about the grounds and see if there is any sign of Rockingham. Anything could have happened to him, and he did not appear well."

"How long will you be gone, sir, before I need to look for you?"

Martin smiled weakly. "If I am gone for more than an hour, consider me missing, but do not search for me. It may be that I simply have had enough and refuse to come back." Stephen smirked, understanding the sarcasm. "I shall walk it, since riding a horse in this storm gives me pause." He rose and walked toward the front doors.

Stephen rubbed his hands against his dirty pant legs and sighed. As he heard Martin shut the front doors, he spun around to see Emily push open the side door and struggle with an arm full of wood. "Why didn't you ask me to do this?" Stephen asked, taking the wood from her and depositing it near the fire. "This isn't your job. It's mine." He brushed her off and sat her into a chair near the fire. "Are you quite alright?"

"Yes, I'm fine, just fine." She pressed her hands to her red cheeks and smiled. "I noted that you were engaged with Master Martin and didn't want to intrude. Just now, I saw him walk away down the drive, his head down. Does he always do this sort of thing? Leave in a hurry like the wind?"

"Indeed he does, lady. Always for others but not for him, I fear." He sat beside her and smiled. "We haven't had a chance to talk, Emily. But I have wanted to since your arrival. Talk, I mean." He smiled again, feeling unsure if it was wise to know more about her considering she appeared to be a private sort of lass, and the house was not a favored place in recent days to strike up a conversation with a lovely woman such as she was.

"Yes?" She smiled and stood to stir something in a pot near to him over the fire. "I've tried to simply go about my business. I cannot afford a misstep in word or deed that could jeopardize my position here. And nerves are frayed. Distrust abounds within these walls. Perhaps it has simply been better to remain silent." Her black dress clung tightly to the obvious curves she possessed, and whether by design or simply an accidental lapse of judgment, one white button of her dress, undone, exposed lovely arcs of flesh where her breasts began. He tried not to look.

"You will find Martin to be long on patience and short on temper, Emily. There is no finer man in this county and I dare say beyond."

"Is that so? And you, sir, what manner of man are you?" She stopped stirring and turned to meet his eyes.

"Me? Oh, I don't know." He averted his eyes so she could not place blame on him for staring at the white skin of her delicate throat or breasts. He caught himself thinking about her with embarrassing frequency when he was hard at work in the stable—the green of her large eyes fringed with dark lashes, the smell of her—earthy and sometimes like fresh rose petals. "I would like to think I am much like Martin, in some ways. But I confess I have little patience. If it were me as master of this house, I would toss out all interlopers and dismiss us all. But one day I will go to university and study medicine. Martin promised to help me." He laughed, and ventured a look into her face. "Maybe…"

"Well, Stephen, it says a lot about you that you have stayed on when, by all evidence, you do not have to do it."

"Why is that?"

"Why? You're obviously intelligent." She tilted her head and smiled with one side of her pink lips. She saw his eyes become glassy with an all too familiar gaze, and asked, "Have you worked alone in the stables all along?"

He stopped staring and looked at his calloused hands—his nails an unfortunate gathering place for muck. "Daniel. He once worked with me, but he left when one of the staff was fired. They were thick. In love the girl said, but I don't know much about that. Daniel kept to himself and spent his time doing...whatever it was he did. Honestly, he didn't do much. I don't think he was lazy. He just seemed always so...preoccupied. All I know is that he had an eye for Theresa—the girl that was let go—and he said very little. It would have been better if we could have been friends."

"Do you need a friend, Stephen?" She took one-step closer, and he stood. Her sweet breath touched his face. He shifted his eyes up from where they had again fallen to her breasts, and he stared into her eyes.

"I do," he whispered.

"Then we shall be the best of friends, you and I, won't we?" She reached across the very short distance between them and touched her hands to his face, but he suddenly pushed her away.

"Who is that?" he asked.

"Where?" She looked into his face and turned her head toward the way he looked.

"I could have sworn I saw someone near the window. Right there. Looking in on us!" He ran for the side door that led to the courtyard and then out into the snow, with Emily close behind. The wind, wild and unyielding, stung his face and beat at his chest. Following footprints left in the snow, which were quickly becoming obliterated by gusts that turned the courtyard into a whirlwind of white, he made for the barn.

"Stephen!" Emily called out to him as she ran behind. "Come back inside!"

Whether he did not hear or ignored her, he was a moment later at the barn doors. He stopped once, just for a moment, as though listening, and in that next moment, the doors swung wide, and Isabella, followed by the black mare Merlin, and then the steed Arabia that had been gifted by Garson to James, bolted out from the barn. They went as though being chased and nearly ran headlong into Stephen as they jolted away into the snowstorm and out of his sight.

"Blasted!" Stephen, one foot in the barn and one out, in that instant, could not decide what he should do. He ran into the barn and grabbed tethers from the wall, swung himself up on the brown gelding that was too wild to be trusted, and went straight away at a gallop in the direction the horses had gone. "Close the doors!" he yelled over his back.

Emily walked into the barn and saw Daniel standing near the very rear stall with his back against the wood and one foot on a bale of hay. She turned slowly around and with great effort closed the barn doors against the wind and snow.

"You imbecile," he growled, suddenly walking toward her in long, angry strides. When he came to an abrupt stop at the tips of her shoes, he yanked her by the hair and tossed her to the ground. "I asked a simple thing of you. I asked you to keep Stephen out of the barn for just a half hour. But you couldn't do that, could you? No." Using his boot applied to her shoulder, he knocked Emily onto her back, but she quickly sat back up.

"I'm the imbecile? Had you called on me sooner, I would have had all this straightened for us! But now you have me cuddling up to the stable boy, who I must say smells of manure and wet hay—and cooking for dimwitted servants!" She took a fistful of dirt and hurled it in his direction, but he just laughed.

"Oh, yes, the fine Boston lady. The whore complains she has food and shelter and promise of riches she could not have earned spreading her legs for the riff raff along Endicott Street." She lurched herself up with hands prepared to give as she was given, but Daniel grasped her wrists together with one large hand. "Do not think to strike me, sister. You were convenient to call upon; that is all, and I can just as easily make you, shall we say...less convenient in an instant."

"You! I alone cared for mother and our younger siblings when father was killed. It was I who sent her money and was forced to bear the life I did for *you*!"

"Yes, yes, Emily, martyrdom has always been your strong suit. Now get out of here before someone discovers me. Blast you." He hurled her away toward the doors.

"You cannot set this barn afire, Daniel. You cannot."

"Why is that? All I need is a short diversion. It will bring us so close to collecting what should be mine—ours."

"That is not a diversion; it is something worse than that. At least free the rest of the horses. Do the humane thing, for once in your life. I suspect the others were freed only to cause Stephen to ride after them. You are a despicable person, brother. Rotten. Savage. Cruel." She walked back toward the stalls where five more horses were bedded in, but he stopped her.

"You're wasting time." He reached into his pocket and withdrew matches. "Go away and hide in some dusty corner of the house, Emily, if you don't want to be witness. Go ahead. Run away. Run!" he shouted, and strode to the back of the barn where he retrieved a bottle filled with liquid.

"No!" she screamed and ran toward him, grabbing above his head where he held the oil and matches. But he just laughed.

Meredith." Martin stood at her door, and by the looks of him, he had not come for a friendly visit.

"Martin! Please, come in!" She stepped aside, and he ducked to enter.

"I've come again unannounced, empty handed, and weary. Can you forgive me? I just need...I need to sit with you, I think."

"Ah, Martin...Of course, please sit by the fire, and I'll fetch you a brandy." He sat heavily down and closed his eyes, listening to the sound of the fire and the rhythmic breaths of his dog that had rather become hers. He heard the gentle tinkle of glasses as she filled them and then her voice as he opened his eyes again. "Here," she said gently, handing him a glass. "You look worse for wear, and I'm glad you came to me." She sat at his feet and placed her head slowly, gently, down onto his knee.

"I've come for tea and sympathy, lady. And after tonight, you surely will think the less of me, but you are somehow my refuge—and less of a stranger than those I call friend." He sipped from his glass and then placed it down beside himself on the table near a book she had been reading. The cover bore bright renderings of plants he recognized having seen in the woods and that he had once stopped to admire. Did he dare touch her?

Would it ask something or would it answer? He shut his eyes again and laid his hand upon her hair, gently stroking it. It was velvet to his touch.

"We all need a place to go...But tell me, why have you been wandering on this night of all nights?" She did not move.

"I've been out looking for our solicitor, Mr. Rockingham, who has departed without word. I fear he found some manner of trouble on this stormy night, but alas, I have looked all over these properties and have not found a single sign that he has passed this way." He lifted the glass again, and as it reached his lips, he realized that it smelled of her—the scent of jasmine had not come from a flower as he had supposed the last time he visited her, but rather, it came from her person, her hair, her skin, her clothing. Perhaps somewhere more secret. "I don't suppose I can hope that you have seen any sign of him?"

She hesitated ever so slightly and shifted to her knees before him. Looking into his face, she appeared to contemplate her words before speaking. "If I could send him to you, Martin, I would. But he is not here."

"As I presumed, Meredith, but I needed to ask." He reached out and brushed the top of her head with the back of his hand and waited for some sign that she might find it disagreeable. But she did not.

"Come with me." She took his hand and stood.

"Where?"

"Just to here, not out there." Gently she led him to a room behind the kitchen, and as he realized it was her bedroom, he stopped under the doorway.

"Meredith, I—"

"No, I want you to sleep. Alone. I want you to truly feel restful and without care. Whatever ails that house will wait, and surely you cannot rescue everyone from themselves." She pulled the white coverlet back and held his hand until he sat down on her bed, and then let go.

"But—"

"Shh...no one will know but you and I, as it should be. So sleep, Martin, just sleep."

"But where will you be, Meredith?"

She smiled warmly as he lay down and placed his head on her pillow. She stroked his head. "Where I am. Sleep." She pulled his boots off and laid them beside the bed and then left the room like a soft breeze. He fought to keep his eyes wide so that he might look around her little room with the cherry blossom curtains and photographs on her dresser; the candles within lovely blue glass holders; a dark green dress lying carefully across an old wood chair. But it was no use. He fell asleep, and within that slumber, he dreamt of nothing. Nothing. Blissful nothing.

Some minutes just after dawn, he woke, not with a start or jolt upright as one might when rousing in a strange place, but slowly, as after a long and restful sleep. The light filtered through the curtains, and a small mirror on her dresser reflected a warm peach-colored glow. He sat up and pulled one of his boots on, wondering what it was they could talk about after he had behaved as he did the night before. Would it be awkward, or would it be natural like it had been each time he had seen her? It wouldn't matter. Meredith was his. She had to be. That was a fact. His only fact. The only thing he was sure of.

He stopped as he was about to pull on the second boot because he heard her voice—although not to whom she spoke. Listening, he leaned forward and waited. Her voice, always delicate, was even sweeter and softer than before, and he wondered who else might have come unannounced. Did they also come empty handed like a foolish schoolboy? Not detecting another voice, just her lovely tone, he stood and opened the door that led to a small kitchen where copper pots and assorted kitchen utensils hung from a round carousel made of wood from the ceiling. A small arched window shone muted light onto a white sill that bore many violet plants of yellow, purple, and gold.

At the doorway to the living room he stopped and peered in, making certain that his body stayed well within the room, lest he make himself known. But no one else was there.

She sat near the fire in the chair he had previously occupied, and in the corner, Phillip slept on a bright red blanket, a beef bone near his head. He could see only the back of her head, as she again spoke. "I realize this, but truly, I think he'll—" She stopped, suddenly, and stood. "Good morning, Martin. You look much better today after your rest. Would you like some tea?"

He said nothing at first. How could he? She wanted to talk about sleep and tea when what he really wanted to discuss was far more intriguing. He glanced at the chair opposite from where she had sat, and no—no one was there. No one at all.

"I feel much better thank you. To whom were you speaking?"

"Tea? I have some delicious bread you might like. I made it myself just yesterday before you came." She moved toward him and the kitchen, but he put his hand gently out and stopped her.

"Meredith. To whom were you speaking?" She gazed up into his face and did not answer. "To yourself? The dog?"

"If you like, I can bring you some eggs to the table, but—"

"Meredith. Please. I have had far too many mysteries, and I do not have want of even one more."

"I...sometimes speak to those who have departed." She looked away from his face.

He glanced over her shoulder to the living room again. "You speak to them? You communicate or...just speak?"

"Oh, Martin, please. Just let me pass, and I will make us both something to eat." She slipped under his arm, and he let her pass. He followed her into the kitchen. "I made jam. Berry is all I have, but it's good. Would you like some?" she asked with her back toward him.

"No thank you."

"I made it myself. I'd like to consider myself a good cook, and I suppose if I had company I'd improve. But—"

"Does it bring you comfort to speak to the dead, Meredith?" She slowly placed the spoon she held back onto the table and faced him.

"Will you sit?" She pointed at the chair nearest to him. The moment was not unlike far too many he had experienced over the years when his feet said go, but his mind, too full of curiosity and, maybe, in her case want, could not agree. He sat down and waited. "I do find comfort in speaking with them, yes." She sat down, too, and for the first time since they had met, she refused to meet his eyes. Instead, she folded her long fingers together and stared down at them.

"But, you just said 'with them'. Are you saying, lady, that they speak in turn? To you?" He had a mighty hope that she would say no.

"Yes. Martin, yes. And with all you have seen and all you have been through, I expect you to leave this moment and never return. But know this; I am not mad, and I am not a fool, and to discover this caused me to think, in fact, that I was quite mad. Quite! But I am not mad, nor am I under some spell, and being a woman of science, I can dispute it and dismiss it out of hand, but some things cannot be denied, Martin. Some things are true, despite every wish we conjure to make events or circumstance what we want them to be. This is my fact, my dear man, and this is something you can believe or not. But I tell you this because it is true. I tell you this now, believing that you shall go, and I will never be blessed to see you again."

At last, she looked up into his face, and the problem he had long wrestled with was solved. But he believed her to be correct. He could not see her again. How could he? She believed what she believed, as simply as that, and there clearly was no way around it. Yet he was compelled to continue.

"Who spoke with you today, Meredith?" he asked softly, his sore heart beating hard in his chest.

"I spoke with my sister."

"Amelia?"

"Yes."

He stood slowly and bowed his head down. "Please give her my regards, lady." He turned around and headed for the door. Part of him wished she would beg him to stay—take back all the things she had told him and confess it was a terribly ill-gotten joke, but she did not, and he continued for the door until he put his hand to the knob and turned it, when she appeared at his side and touched his arm.

"She said, 'find your way out, Martin.' It *is* a harsh tone. But I don't think she meant for you to leave here. Sometimes the words are not succinct. Sometimes they just come and go, and I can't make sense of them."

He swung around so swiftly that he nearly knocked her over and grabbed her by the arms. "Woman! What reason do you have to torture me? Have I done you some harm that I did not intend? Do you hate me so much that you need to say this to me?"

She shook her head back and forth, causing her hair to fall into her face. "But I, I—I simply told you what she said, Martin. I have no reason to hurt you. Why would I want to do that?" Her eyes were wide and teary, and he gripped her arms tighter.

"What else has she said? Tell me!"

"She said, she said—tell him...tell him... 'Go where you must, and go with joy toward all things.'" She began to cry, and he let her.

"No one knows these things. Save for the dead." He pushed her away and walked back into the room. "My father told me that when he locked me in the root cellar when he was displeased with me. And the last words? Claire told them to me in a note, and no one could have seen it because she hid it for me in a secret place we shared. And when I was done reading it all those years ago, I folded it into very tiny pieces and ripped it up. But not before I read it many times to memorize it. Lady...Lady." He sunk into the chair and put his head into his hands.

"Who is Claire?" she asked, not moving from the place she stood.

"My governess...I want to leave you. I want to stay. But what am I to do with this confounded stream of illogical talk? "

"I don't know. I never have. I still do not. But they talk to me just the same, and there is no choice but to let them have their way in it. You see..." she began, and walked toward him to kneel at his side, "I have come to believe that they just want to be recognized. They want to be heard, or perhaps they think we need to listen, I don't know. But when it first happened to me some years ago while visiting here, I came to realize over time that the more we deny them, the angrier they become, and they are frustrated at their inability to be understood as they wish to be. They do wicked things, mischievous things...So I listen, Martin. I listen, for their sake as well as mine, since there is something terrible and fierce about them if they are denied."

"Tell me. Have you had words between you and my father? Since his death?"

"No," she answered swiftly. "I never have had that happen."

"And who else, Meredith? Who else have you spoken with?" He looked into her damp face, refusing the urge to touch her cheeks and wipe the tears away.

"Amelia. Mostly Amelia."

"Mostly?"

She bowed her head down and took a deep breath. "With my mother Caroline, on occasion, but it has become less and less over time. My adoptive mother, rarely, and one terrible man. I first saw him one night in your courtyard."

"Who?"

"Rene Bonhomme."

He squinted up his eyes and shook his head. "What do you know of him?"

"Martin, I have so little to tell, it seems only harmful if I repeat—"

"Tell me."

"The night I came to see you after I had left you on the path, the night of your father's funeral, I heard him speaking with Hannah. It sounded as though they had been lovers; dare I say that? And he was angry that she had been left nothing in the will. He struck her, and she left. Then that little man came through the shadow and spoke to Rene. They, too, had some manner of disagreement about the estate and where their alliances lay. I could not go closer or I would be found out, so I left when they parted ways and thought better of visiting you that night."

"And now?"

"And now he comes to the house but does not come in. He stands at the door, sometimes knocking three times, not more. He is a terrible specter that seems to be waiting for someone or something, but I know not which. One night, I went out to ask him why he continues to haunt my gardens, and he said, 'You shall let me in, lady. You shall one night let me in.' His voice is unpleasant like a growl from an injured wolf and as though it comes from far away. He has cruel eyes, and his smile is like a cat's. I do not trust him. I do not want to see him again. But I do not know how to make him depart and stay away."

"If this is all true, then tell me how do you stay here alone? Are you not afraid?"

"Sometimes I am quite fearful, yes. But to leave here means I cannot be near to you."

"Lady, if I find you have lied to me, I will not spare my hand to you, though never before have I struck a woman. I will be mightily tempted to beat you for your lies. Do you understand me?"

She nodded her head.

"Very well. Then we will leave today. I have fallen in love with you, Meredith, and I see no way clear of it save to prove you right or wrong, and until that time, there will be no peace for me. I cannot leave you here alone if you told the truth. So this is my trouble, my quandary. Pack your things, Meredith. You are coming home with me."

It was not the way he had imagined his love would be proclaimed. But nothing in his life ever went true to plan.

Willham sat amongst the discarded remnants of Waverly's former masters. From his perch high above the walls of Waverly Estate, he looked out over The Hudson River and rolling hills on the other side. The snow had stopped, and the storm left tattered green limbs lie strewn across the fields, and what he presumed were bits of the roof that had been torn from the rafters. The sky glowed pink, casting that early morning into a dreamscape, into which he wished he could escape.

The widow's walk was no more than a 20-foot circle that boasted windows along the entire room. The ceiling, higher than the space was wide, jutted up in severe angles that came to a point at top. Around him sat a pile of old trunks, some with missing hardware and others in pristine condition, save for the dust that covered everything he saw. Webs, intertwined with grey dust between disregarded artifacts, caused his skin to crawl, and the smell of mold and slowly degrading wood made him want to choke. With nowhere to sit and still finding himself too exhausted to stand, he shifted items around that he could move to make himself more comfortable. There was no telling how long he would be forced to inhabit the widow's walk, so he did his best to make it feel like something less than a prison.

It had taken him three minutes to traverse the tunnel from Garson's room to where he stood in the widows walk. If his absence had already been detected, there would be no way to know. The passageway had ended at what seemed to be a dead end, but upon further inspection, he realized that he was simply standing in a space between two walls, both with escape routes and with latches easily moved aside. The left led to the third floor sitting room, which would have led straight to the widows walk stairs, and the right, to an unused room. Avoiding the first, he went right, only to find that the room had, in fact, been recently used despite his initial impression.

The room was vacant save for a few broken down chairs and closed off fireplace. A blanket, crumpled in the corner, was not filled with dust as was the rest of the room. A goblet made of thin glass sat beside it, and it still held a mouthful worth of wine at the bottom. The floor near the fireplace was the only area that did not sport heavy dust. If anyone were to go to the widows walk, they would have entered via the sitting room, which he had avoided. But he recalled having heard Hannah speaking to Rene about a more ambiguous route to the loft area. Within a cloak closet, he found the back wall moved easily away, and he entered it to find that he was at the first step of twelve that would ascend in a narrow spiral to the widows walk above.

The eaves around and below him seemed to speak—whispers and faint utterances that, if he were not so faint of heart, might have become decipherable words, but no, he could not entertain the urge to translate. He had heard the stories of things lurking within the arches, but pushing aside what he had deemed to be the unintelligent prater of servants, he had paid little attention. Yet, having been made a subject of the ghostly apparition's unwanted attentions, he was no longer sure at all. He could not dwell on the unseen because surely his very life would depend on fending off the living that would see him harmed for his many transgressions.

Leaning on a window that faced directly east across the river, he pondered his next move. The glass, no doubt needing immediate need for repair, pulled from a rotting wood frame and was then suspended only by the top and one side. He stepped back, took a deep breath of the icy air that filtered in, and made a note that he must not tempt the decaying structure's worth with any more careless movement.

From a safe distance, he looked again across the fields and saw Martin walking along with a woman. He held his great black coat about her. He could not see her face concealed against his chest but spied her long wheat-colored hair flagging out. Martin held his arms about her, and Philip, whom most believed had alighted for good, walked to his side. Tugged by river wind, Martin's black coat tails whipped out behind them as they walked slowly down the hill toward the mansion. He watched them continue at that slow pace until suddenly they stopped. Led by Phillip, they ran toward the courtyard.

Willham moved to his right to view them from one glass pane and then the next and the next as they ran toward the courtyard until the treetops interrupted his view. So usual was it for one manner of mystery or backward circumstance to visit Waverly and its inhabitants that he scarcely paid the sudden run toward the house much mind at all. Never had he seen so much chaos and foolish goings-on confined in a single space! He found relief in reminding himself that once free of the place and his treasures, he would be the happiest man alive to get as far away from them all as possible.

Wishing he had stowed something to eat within his pockets before leaving Garson's room, he was forced to listen to the grumbling sounds of his stomach. But in his absence, the cake and tea they had left would be better served in Miriam's gut than his. He smiled, imagining her as she crammed his uneaten food into her fat mouth, just as he had seen her do with meals left half eaten on other's trays. She would look right and left and behind, making certain no one would see before gorging herself on what remained. She never once failed to binge on half-eaten food before taking the plates away. He wished he could see the look on her face when she began to see things that were not there. He wished he could have been a fly on the wall when they saw her go mad. Ah, yes. But such, he thought as he looked for a suitable place to sit, was her portion of cost to be paid for serving her up as part of the plan. Had she not been a glutton, none if it would occur, he reasoned. What happened to her would come to pass because of her own foul habit.

He sat on a trunk and listened to the babble of the wind voices until he felt himself doze. The scent of burning wood caused him to long for a warm flame because he felt dreadfully cold. Shivering, he bent partway down, his arms about himself, and allowed his weary body a small nap. Soon, he fell into a deep sleep and dreamed of Rene. His dark hair was reddened with blood that flowed from his fine head; his eyes, pitch like charcoal; his hands, gnarled, his face contorted. He regretted that his old friend who was the source of all hope and decider of their possible future together had chosen the wrong side. Hannah's side. The terrible visions of Rene's mangled body had been just one scene incorporated from true events; things he saw with his own eyes; words he heard but refused proper answer to; the scent of death; his love's pleas for mercy and request for more time. All were answered with Daniel's help—but not in Rene's favor. Still, despite the horror of what he had allowed replaying in his nightmare, Willham did not wish to wake. For on awakening, Willham would have lost Rene anew.

He could not have known that beyond his sight line, past the court yard and through a line of trees and hedgerow, the barn was ablaze. And Stephen, having managed to capture the runaway horses, could do nothing more but stand helplessly beside Martin and watch the structure burn to the ground.

The freed horses pulled and yanked at their tethers, the sight of the fire more than they could tolerate at that close of a distance. Stephen stepped near to each of them, delivering comforting pats of reassurance, but he did not succeed in calming them.

"How did this happen?" Martin asked and watched as Meredith took hold of Emily and hugged her closely. She was a stranger to them yet immediate friend—a comfortable fit as she was to him from the first moment he saw her.

"I don't know. It took all I had to free the remaining horses." He paused a moment to retie a tether on Isabella. His hands were blistered in spots, his clothes dark with soot. But he did not mention it, and if Martin had noticed, he would not have let on how badly they pained him. "But, now that I think of it," he continued, "I saw Emily when I returned. She was standing at the barn doors trying to snuff the flames out. Maybe she saw more than I."

The fire was white hot and singed the tree limbs nearest the barn. A few of the smaller trees had gone up in flame when the wind blew licks of fire too close to them. The snow, deep as it was, melted many feet away from the inferno.

"Where is Miriam? And James?" Martin asked. "I see his horse is missing."

"Miriam was with Hannah, last I knew. And James rode for Saugerties to fetch Doctor Matthews. Seeing how he never came along during the night." He shot a knowing look that Martin did not miss.

"James rode alone? That is not wise."

"He was a good rider in his day, and he and the horse are a perfect set. I would not worry for James, sir."

"And has anyone checked on that blackguard, Willham?"

"I do not know."

"Thank you, Stephen, for your swift thinking and of course for saving our stabled horses. Truly, you have raised yourself above your status in the stable—our former stable, I should say. We must find new quarters for them...I think the house is safe," Martin added, and taking a look over his shoulder, reassured that the wind had changed direction and blew away from it, he sighed deeply. "And you had left no flame lit within? Nothing? Please tell me the truth. There will be no serious repercussions."

"I am quite certain. Before I came in to speak with you last night and knowing the wind had picked up, I checked three times to be sure. You left to look for Rockingham. Emily came to the back door straight after that, and I helped her with wood. I thought I saw someone looking into the windows, and I went right away out to find them. Tracks lead here. The horses bolted out of the barn, and luckily, they had not gone far. I returned to see the barn on fire. I secured the remaining horses and various necessities. With Emily's help. We could do nothing but watch it burn. It was engulfed, sir. I am sorry." Stephen was tempted to ask Martin where he had been all night into the morning, but he refrained. He ventured a look toward Meredith, who continued to console Emily, who did not appear close to being soothed. Yet Meredith's presence gave him the answer he sought.

Martin looked toward Emily. "It is doubtful that anything useful will emerge from her. I suppose it can wait until tomorrow."

"Excuse me, Martin." Meredith came to his side and touched his arm. It was not something that Stephen missed, and he smiled.

"Ah, Meredith, this is Stephen, our stable worker. And reason that our horses were saved."

"I am pleased to make your acquaintance, Miss Meredith." Stephen bowed his head slightly and smiled.

"You are a hero to Waverly, sir," Meredith responded, bowing her head in turn, and she gave a small curtsey.

Stephen, embarrassed by a lady of her position and association showing him open respect, was taken aback. "Miss Meredith, please!" He took a step back and lowered his eyes.

"Stephen, you earned praise offered. All things are repaid. All things. Good or bad. And sir, you are to be wealthy." She smiled, offered her hand, and he took it, but only after seeing Martin nod his head.

"Miss Meredith, you have managed to bring a happier heart than could have been expected, considering all things this day and before. I must go and tend to the horses and find them a suitable place out of the elements." He smiled at her.

Martin could not have agreed more. Only Meredith could have brought the gift of hope amidst the ashes. Martin smiled down at her, and led her toward the house.

Willham examined the particles of the dream as though watching from outside of himself.

There was a patch of red. A shiny knife handle. A bit of tattered rose-colored dress. A shriek, a very loud shriek, possessed an echo if he listened for it. The whispers of wind through the broken window of the widow's walk spoke in sentences against his hope that they might not. Beneath him, the floor moved in sideways heaves as though unseen hands jerked him left and right and left again, the position of his head lagging behind the motion of his savaged body. The worst of it came clearly to him as his face elongated and his tongue detected fractured teeth, jagged and painful along his gums. The entities spun around him in unnatural motion, veering up and then down, behind him, all the while screaming, save for one. The last, just laughed and laughed.

He wanted to speak, but he could not. If he could have, he would have asked why the laughing man had spoiled the plan and delivered him too large a dose of his own bad medicine. He knew what it was. He knew he just had to ride it out and wait for the effects to wear off, but he was unsure if he would ever be right in his mind again.

Daniel sat back and examined his handiwork. If not for his youth and physical fortitude, it would not have gone as planned.

Hannah, at his feet, gagged and silenced with opium stolen from a hidden drawer within Garson Waverly's bedroom desk kept the disgusting woman from speaking. She had weeks before led him to it herself. The irony! He smiled.

The house had many secrets, but he had worked hard at stockpiling allies and persuaded them to join his campaign of retribution with never a single intention of paying them what was promised in exchange for their assistance. He had made clever use of them all, and now? He had it the way he wanted it. Almost. He was so close; he could feel the smooth gems in his work-roughened hands when he closed his eyes; smell the money he would count out on the Waverly's magnificent table. He would purchase a suitable headstone for his mother and for his brother and sister. Had they been able to afford medical care, they would still have been alive that day. Their deaths were on the head of any surviving Waverly. Garson or Martin could have prevented it, and even that witch Hannah could have cared to make it right. But they did not bother. The death of his father was less than an afterthought; the man had been a replaceable commodity that was soon forgotten.

Miriam, equally sedated, lay sprawled out in a position in the left corner. Perhaps he had forced her to consume more than her body could bear. Spittle amassed at the corners of her mouth, and her eyes, fixed on the great nothing of drug-induced trance, looked wide and dumb. But his favorite plaything was most decidedly Willham, who sat with his back against the wall under a window to his right. Ah yes, he was the most convenient of all.

All that was left to deal with was Martin and James. The latter of which, would be the easiest. It would take no more than one burly shoulder applied to the man's back to send him falling to the bottom of the stairs where he would expire of a broken neck or bleeding or his old heart would give out. How he ended James he did not care, as long as it was his finish. There was of course, Theresa, but he had not seen her in some days. He snorted, thinking about how easily he could have murdered her. It wouldn't have taken much—an easy rope knot around her neck and then a kick off one of the many roof tops that could be simply accessed via any number of windows. But he thought she might have lost her nerve and taken off to haunt another. It didn't matter to him in the least. Her disappearance simply saved him added effort. She was the loosest link of all, he thought, as he re-secured the ropes that tied Willham's hands together behind his back.

But Martin? At first look, it seemed his death would not be necessary, when Daniel had thought he would be content with what he could pillage from the estate and then be gone. No, it would not suffice. Could gems and some money ever compensate him for the loss of his father, or the death of his family members that he felt were directly related to the loss of his father? No, certainly it could not! Had Garson Waverly cared to tend properly to the merchant ship his father sailed, the accident that killed him would not have occurred. Had the Waverly clan cared to compensate his mother for the death of his father who had slaved many years for them, she and his siblings, save for Emily, would not have died. The realization called for a broader plan. How else, then, might he gather more riches? Rockingham was surely dead. He was no longer needed when his sister arrived. He had seen to that when he broke the old man's leg with a sledgehammer. Leaving him to die of exposure in the storm was the simplest of all tricks. Rene, dead, too. Ah, it was all sorting out perfectly to plan!

He rose and walked toward Hannah, who, exhausted and drugged, looked like a rag doll ready to be deposited into the trash. To his eye, she appeared half-dead. He didn't care. He despised her the most. He spit on her and placed his dirty boot on her back. She did not move, and it elicited a laugh that rose up from his belly. Looking toward Miriam, he felt the slightest sense of remorse. She had been kind to him and had cared for him as well or better than his own mother had. But she had a particular irksome penchant for meddling in the business of others. She had discovered him within the very walls of the estate that day as he tried to make his way into the old sitting room where he would then proceed to the widows walk. He had preferred the passageway through Garson's old room but found the door locked. He was left with no other option but to include her in his little gathering. Regrettably, she had sealed her own fate.

Willham roused and moaned.

"Shut up." Daniel kicked at him and landed a boot to his chest.

"You could have done them in neatly, one at a time. Why this? Why? Why me?" He groaned. "You pretended to bring me food to sustain me through our trials, yet you wish only to sustain yourself by harming me with my own trade!"

"I want you all here because no one comes to this place. Not anymore. Storing you all away until I can dispose of each of you keeps Martin and the rest of them out of my way."

"You are a despicable boy." Willham leaned over and retched. His stomach yielded nothing but a bitter taste of bile to his tongue.

Daniel laughed. "Do you think I don't realize what you were planning? To take it all from me?" Willham did not answer. "I am simply removing bothersome pieces of what could have been a perfect plan." He went to Hannah, ripped some cloth from the bottom of her soiled dress, and shoved it into Willham's mouth.

Rising, he looked toward the river where the sun sank low behind the hills. He wondered if the properties on the other side might also be his when he became a rich man. Surely, he could find a willing seller. He would help his filthy sister do what she did best—secure yet another man whilst using her well-learned womanly charms and marry Martin. Only then would the Master of Waverly Estate be done away with. *Perfect, perfect*, he said to himself and sat down for a little nap. Of course, he thought as he closed his eyes, Stephen might be kept on to see to the new stable he would build, which would someday house the finest breeding stock east of the Mississippi.

But he did not know that one person could dangerously compromise the perfect sketch he drew in his mind.

At that moment, she was securely folded within the arms of Martin Waverly.

Rockingham was vaguely aware of something or someone sitting near his head. He knew only that he was indoors and out of the snow. Words formed in his head. *Thank you. Where am I? Who are you?* But not a syllable was spoken. A faint sound, something similar to the turn of a page, signaled he was not alone.

He found it odd that his hearing was mostly intact, and he could smell the scent of a candle burning nearby. He detected the sound of a breeze gently flapping across the rooftop above him, and he felt the terrible ache of his injured leg and the woody pain of his frozen fingers, but he could not open his eyes, and he could not command his arms or legs to move. So he laid there, oddly undisturbed by the inscrutability of his situation. Perhaps he was simply surprised that he was alive. Perhaps his mind was baffled by the pain that would not subside. Whatever it was, he shut down the notion as soon as it reared up that he was, just maybe, not alive at all, but dead. Very dead. He needed more time. But, he thought idly, isn't that what most dying people crave? One more this, one more that; one more kiss from a lover; one more god-forsaken chance to get it all right.

"There is not much that I can do for you, sir, considering our distinct conditions," she said. "But I will make it known you are alive. Here, in the cottage."

Ah!' he thought. *I am alive, and help will arrive.*

She said nothing else. He neither heard a door shut nor felt her move away but had, within a moment of her speaking, felt convinced she had left. If he had tried to explain the feeling he had at her departure, he would have been unable to. It was a sense of relief and fear tied tightly together. If he had more closely examined it, neither emotion would have been distinct enough to name. But yes, he was alive, and that was the thing of it. He wasn't sure he cared at all.

❦ I dare not disturb them, Meredith." Martin stroked her hair as she sat beside him in the second parlor and looked across the piano toward the frozen garden. "Let's leave it for now."

"It is terribly quiet." She pressed closer to his chest.

"Let's assume that Miriam has Hannah well in hand, and Willham has accepted there is no way out for him. Not yet."

"Still...Should you check on them?"

"Let's wait for Doctor Matthews to arrive before we stir the hornet's nest again."

"I hope that James has arrived to town. Safely."

"You care for these people who you do not know. Not really. Why?"

"Because they are part of you."

He stopped brushing his hand across her head and leaned back to look into her face, examining something he could not distinguish behind her pale eyes. She gazed back at his and smiled. "Even if you are quite mad, I should tell you now that I intend to marry you, Meredith. And I intend for you to agree."

One side of her mouth slowly crooked up into a small smile that reached her eyes. "Even if I am mad?"

"I will have you even if you are a mad woman, since the absence of you, even for a night, would cause me to…"

"Unless you decide to change your mind?"

He laughed. "Waverly men do not change their minds as easily as The Catskill Mountains' weather falters from sun to clouds, lady. We consider. We ponder. We factor all perspectives, and only then, do we state intentions. Even if it appears ill-advised, we continue along."

"Is that the best way to make decisions about your life, Martin? Chasing after ill-advised wishes? Whims?"

He thought about her question for a long moment and then smiled. "No." He laughed. "And lady, you are far from a whim...Some things cannot be known. The future is an indiscernible affair; it is comprised of many multitudes of moments leading ever forward to the indistinct. Shrinking away from a desire for fear of the unknowable shuts a door that will remain closed forever. I would rather open a door I feel compelled to unlock than face the idea that I will never know what might have been. That is the thing of it, Meredith. We mourn most for chances we did not take."

"Then when do you intend to marry me, sir, so that I may fully express what would otherwise be inexpressible as I sit so near to you?"

His eyes went wide, and then he laughed. "You are an entirely indecent woman, Meredith!" He stood and took her hand, pulling her up. He dragged her to his chest and pressed her head into it. His arms, wrapping around her, completely engulfed her, and he could feel her heart beating fiercely. He held her tighter. "But we need to discuss one thing that has troubled me."

"Just one?" she asked, smiling against his chest. He pulled her gently away and stared down into her eyes.

"Should the pastor marry us? Beginning our life together that way, having your father marry us, when he does not know that you are his child?" She grinned. "This is serious, Meredith; please do not trifle with my concern."

"Perhaps we should tell him."

Martin pressed her against his body again and said, "Perhaps. Perhaps."

"Let's allow for a little time. Sort the disorder here, first."

"I think I hear a carriage. Let's pray that James and Doctor Matthews have arrived."

"Yes. I have wanted to speak to you about the doctor. He is the only other soul alive that knows my mother was Caroline and the pastor, my father. Perhaps we should seek his advice?"

"On what?"

"On whether or not we should speak to pastor—I mean, my father—about our impending marriage—and that I am his daughter. To discover if he will let it all be known."

"Let's wait and think on that. Come on." He grabbed her hand and led her to the doors and courtyard beyond.

Wake up, blast you!" Willham spit the rag from his bleeding mouth and attempted to wake Miriam and Hannah. He had little success, save for a few moans from Miriam and incoherent babbling from Hannah. "Wake the hell up!"

Miriam's eyes fluttered, and her head bobbed once, twice, before reaching for her face. "What is this?" she asked, struggling to keep her eyes open.

"That mad man, Daniel. He has taken us three captive, and he intends to kill us one by one. You need to wake up, Miriam, and get me untied. Get yourself together, madam, lest we die!" Willham lay down and rolled toward Miriam until his back faced her. "Untie me, damn it!"

"I cannot." Miriam's head rolled to one side, and she closed her eyes again.

"Hannah! Wake up! This instant! Do you want to die?" She did not stir. Frantically looking from one to the other, he thought for a moment that if he could just scream loudly enough, someone from within the house might hear

154

him and free them. He would sort out the problems that would arise afterward. But he did not know where Daniel had gone to, and so he rolled back to where he had been and felt for the first time in many, many years, he might actually cry.

Maybe, he thought, he could slow Daniel down if he managed to use his legs to push some of the trunks in front of the door? Maybe it would give him time to untie himself. Maybe it would provide adequate moments for Miriam to wake up and help him. He pushed the trunks toward the door, and as he did, he became aware of a voice from below in the courtyard. Martin. He struggled to his feet and went near the broken window to look out over the hills. He could not see the courtyard through the trees, but he was certain that he heard a carriage and the sound of Martin's voice. Had he been discovered missing yet? He hoped.

Emily, fetch Doctor Matthew's things for him, and bring them straight away to Mrs. Waverly's room." Martin and Meredith stood at the carriage and watched as James and the doctor exited.

"Yes, sir." She took the bags and ran with them for the door.

"Martin, I would have been here yesterday had I known I was so in need. James has told me that Mr. Willham Montrose had sent a boy to me, but nothing of that sort occurred."

"As I suspected. Please hurry, doctor. She has been silent today, but I am troubled by her condition, which, I must tell you, the pastor believes a matter of spirit possession, not medicine."

Matthews rolled his eyes. "Witchcraft worshippers wearing the cloth. Let's go. I will tend to her."

James untied his horse from the rear of the carriage and stood in the courtyard, staring at the smoldering remains of the barn. "All such a pity."

"Stephen is stalling the horses at one of the cottages as we speak. Tie your beast to the post, James, and come in. He will surely see to it presently." Martin did not like the wearied look about James, and he patted him gently on the back. "Thank you for the ride out, James. Thank you, sincerely."

The doctor stood in the foyer beside Emily and sighed. "I have left a bag in the carriage. I will be a moment to retrieve it." Without waiting for a reply, he turned and walked back out the doors.

Emily's eyes slipped down to the sight of Martin's hand lightly clasping Meredith's in his. Meredith noticed, and she waited as the younger woman's eyes slid slowly to hers. Emily forced a smile that sent a message of sorts. It read that Emily was not pleased.

"Fetch us something to drink, please, Emily. You can leave the bags here for now. Tea and some cakes, if you would," Martin said and turned away toward the stairs with Meredith in tow.

"Yes, sir, right away." She walked slowly off toward the kitchen and looked once over her shoulder toward Meredith who had not taken her eyes from the girl.

"She has interest in you, Martin," Meredith said as they climbed the stairs.

"Who?" He pulled her up two steps and stopped.

"Emily," Meredith replied.

Martin turned his head around toward the kitchen. "Is this so? How do you know?"

"I just do," she said, flatly.

"Witchery?" He half smiled.

"Yes, Martin, the Feminine sort."

He laughed, and they walked further up the stairs. "Jealous, my dear?" he smirked.

"Of course I am."

"You are not."

She shrugged. "I am not."

Reaching the second landing, they stopped, and Martin took a deep breath. "I am wholly anticipating more anxiety, even with the doctor's arrival. I dare offer that the doctor will do no good for the situation considering Matthews has once before said he could do nothing for her."

The horses whinnied. It was not the way they would sound when greeting each other or expressing their delight at seeing Stephen's approach. No, it was an anxiety-filled concert of three worried horses that caused Meredith and Martin to walk back down the stairs and toward the doors.

They stood together at the top step, hand in hand, and Meredith gasped. She turned her face away and buried it behind his shoulder. "No!" she screamed, as the carriage horses sped from right to left in front of them across the courtyard, hauling the doctor's carriage along, fully engulfed in flames from within.

Martin, stunned, watched as the doctor's body heaved from side to side against the confines. Blood-curdling screams emanating from the carriage caused Martin's breath to catch in his lungs. The sounds were guttural, shrieking utterances, that clenched at Martin's heart, his ears, and he could do nothing for a moment but fight the reality of what he saw.

Led by the terrified horses, the carriage flew away over the courtyard as the flames licked the wheels, setting them afire. At top speed, diagonally across the hill, the carriage, then aflame, jolted from side to side. He found himself running full out after it, but there was little he could do.

The carriage came to a steep embankment, and flagging hard once and then twice left and right, it flipped to its side, dragging the horses over with it. In one horrifying bash and crash of wood and metal and horseflesh, the doctor's screams silenced. The only sound that remained was one horse who cried out in pain.

Stephen rode down the hill from its crest and arrived at the horrific scene a moment before Martin. He jumped from the horse and stood some yards from the mangled carriage, surveying what was left. "I'll fetch the rifle, sir," he said, and leapt onto the horse's back, riding fast through the snow toward the mansion.

The fire, still flicking from the carriage, choked Martin's throat closed, but he rushed near as he dared to the wreck and saw Doctor Matthew's contorted figure, black as coal. What remained of his torso, still smoldering, pressed against the door, his arms up, and frozen in place. He turned and walked through the dense black smoke to kneel beside the horse that had survived. But it was clear she was in desperate pain. The bay mare cried out. "You are a fine mare." He patted her bloodied neck and spoke soothingly to her. "This life is not meant for so much sorrow." But the moment he spoke the words, he was gripped with a sense that they were lies. Perhaps life was just something to endure between ever-brief seconds of joy followed closely behind by pain and confusion and regret. His face, wet with something he did not immediately identify, turned hot with the flames and abhorrence for what had been done. He looked toward Meredith who arrived at his side.

"Martin." She laid a gentle hand to his shoulder.

"Go back to the house, Meredith. This is not something for a lady to see." He yanked his shoulder away and continued to gently stroke the horse's neck and face. He was not certain if he had wanted to prevent her from experiencing the sight of his tears or the wreck about them.

Meredith looked toward the rubble of carriage and to the charred remains of Doctor Matthew's corpse and then to the second horse that was clearly dead— its neck twisted unnaturally to the left, one eye bashed from its socket, and its mouth open wide. Blood marred the otherwise pristine mantle of snow. Instead of retreating, she knelt down into the ash-laden snow beside Martin and placed her hand to his back. "I go where you go. My place is where ever you are." He said nothing to her and rose as Stephen returned with the rifle.

"I'll do it, sir," Stephen said, his voice filled with ache. "Take the lady into the house, sir." He placed his hand to Martin's shoulder. "I will do it, sir," he repeated, but more emphatically than the first.

"No," Martin said firmly and reached to take the rifle from Stephen's hands. "It's for me to do."

"No, sir. Please," Stephen argued and pulled the gun away from Martin's reach. It came within an inch of Meredith's hands. She could not abide the dispute that arose for her sake alone at the cost of the horse's continued pain. In one motion, she pulled the gun from Stephen's hands, positioned it against her small shoulder, aimed, pulled the trigger, and ended the mare's agony.

Stephen flinched. Martin recoiled at the sound. She laid the rifle to the bloodied snow, turned, and slowly walked away.

Eleven

arberry stood near the wreck and scratched his head. From the corner of his eye he watched as Martin, standing alone in the snow some yards away, stared across the fields with an empty gaze. Barberry flung his hands up and shook his head. He inhaled deeply before turning toward Martin.

"I'm tired of riding out here, Mr. Waverly. Sick of it, actually."

Martin snickered. "Yes, I can imagine you are." He continued to look over the hill at the immense roll of whitened snow, preferring to rest his eyes on the clean perfection of it than what laid about the hill near to him. Barberry leaned closer to what remained of the carriage and charred remains of the doctor within. Martin turned toward him and said, "I offer a similar statement of fact. I am tired of having to call you to this place."

"Your servant Miriam is gone yet again after having reappeared." Bayberry turned toward him and continued to enumerate. It was a habit that Martin found infuriating, especially since the man seemed intent on stating the obvious. "Mrs. Waverly is also gone, after being delivered by Mr. Montrose, who is also gone, after having disappeared to reappear again. Mr. Rockingham, who left for places unknown, has yet to return. Because I cannot know when the four disappeared this time, I am adding them to the list of those who may have done this despicable thing. James, and your stable hand that now has no stable to tend, Miss Meredith, and, well, you. Oh and let us not forget Emily."

"When will this wreck be cleared away, Mr. Barberry?" Martin asked, ignoring the man's lengthy list.

"Today. His widow has been informed."

"Will you assist me in finding these people, sir?" Martin clenched his fists against his thighs. Barberry tilted his head, noticing.

"Of course...If I were you, Mr. Waverly, I would be wishing that this entire estate burned down right along with the stables. Good day, sir."

Martin walked away toward the house but not before allowing Barberry ample time to leave the courtyard and estate. The scent of used up fire and the doctor's remains clung to his nostrils, his hair, his black coat, and above his head, eight or so buzzards looped around and around in ever lowering circles. The two dead horses and the doctor's corpse signaled victuals awaited their pointed beaks and cruel claws. But Martin walked away anyway and refused his inclination to look back again.

Daniel crept slowly up the back stairs that led to the passageway ending at the abandoned sitting room. He stopped to listen to the sounds of the house, and at the door, he paused once more before entering.

As had been agreed, the package left for him sat behind an old chair. Lifting it, he did not stop to examine the contents but continued toward the widow's walk and his captives above. His clothes smelled of oil, and his hands, bloodied from his scramble along the thorny vines exiting the root cellar, burned. The root cellar was the last entrance and exit into the house that had not been discovered, and he had been forced to use it. Located at the very rear of the house, it connected to a cloak closet at the end of one of the halls closest to the kitchen. He detested the root cellar, and on the occasions he was asked to enter it to retrieve some manner of food, he was forced to summon all his will to do as asked. It was a dark place filled with unseen corners and infested with large spiders and rats. The place had become so foul that Martin had ordered it to be left unused. But of course, Daniel had heard stories of why Martin had really ordered it sealed after the death of Garson.

Arriving at the narrow door to the widow's walk, he pushed it and became immediately aware that someone had placed objects to bar his reentrance. But it was easy enough for him to enter after shoving hard at the door with his shoulders until the things moved away. It did not amuse him. He entered, shoved the trunks to the furthest parts of the space, and sat down on one of them.

"I see one or more of you have been up to mischief." Willham, the only one sitting upright, said nothing and looked away. "Very well then. I was going to feed you, but alas, your bad conduct has changed my mind. I would rather have been kind to you, sir, but you have made that impossible, lest you assume I have gone all weak and mushy hearted, and you think to take advantage of that."

"I am hungry, Daniel. Can you not spare an old man a small morsel of food?" Willham asked.

Daniel opened the bag and withdrew some sugary cakes, a small jug of water, roasted chicken, and bread. He set it aside, ignoring Willham's pleas and read the note that Emily had written. *'Martin is to marry a woman by the name of Meredith. I do not know when. She is within the house.'* Daniel crumbled the paper and deposited it back into the bag. "Does he now," he said, smirking.

"Does who what?" Willham asked, eyeing the food near Daniel's feet.

"I suppose it won't do any harm to tell you, since you will soon be dead, but Martin is going to be married." He reached down and tossed Willham a dry crust from the bread.

Willham scrambled for it and bent his head down to eat it from the floor. Chewing, he said, "Who is the woman?"

Daniel scowled at the sight of the other man spewing crumbs and said, "You disgust me."

"What would you have me to do? My hands are tied behind my back. Who is the woman?"

"What do you care?" Daniel swallowed large mouthfuls of the chicken and then gulps of the water.

"An idle curiosity."

"Then just shut up before I gag you again." He wiped his mouth with the back of his sleeve.

"I saw the carriage afire. Right through these very windows to the fields below. Do you know about this terrible thing?"

"Indeed I do," Daniel responded, chewing loudly.

"Pray tell, sir, and may I have some water?"

Daniel got up and positioned the jug over Willham's face. "Open up or waste it." Willham was allowed a brief drink of water, and Daniel sat back down.

"Thank you, Daniel. Now what of the carriage?"

"The only tool I had to stop the doctor from entering and finding the three of you gone had to be used. If they found you all missing, it would not have been an opportune time, and no time would allow me to secure the jewels. It would not have given me the chance to go back 'round the property to the root cellar and reenter here. I risked discovery."

"So you set the carriage afire? With the doctor within?"

"Indeed I did." Daniel belched and continued to chew as though he had just related something uninteresting. "I hit him on the head hoping to make it easier for us both, but he woke as he began to burn."

"You are matter of fact about this. How barbaric!" Daniel looked slowly toward Willham and smiled wickedly. It sent a chill along Willham's already cold back. "*You* are!"

"Imagine, just for a moment, Willham, what I will do to you?" He went back to eating and contemplating the contents of Emily's note.

"Hannah is near death, I think."

"Okay."

"Do you understand? Hannah is near death, I think, and we…"

"I am not stupid. I heard you. And I do not care. You have done your share of ill, I remind you. Throw no stones at me."

"I cannot argue that, but people are beneficial assets. Are they not?" Daniel tossed a chicken bone down and lunged for Willham's throat with his bleeding hands.

"My father was considered an asset by the very people I plot and plan against. An expendable asset that was of use when alive and then utterly forgotten when dead, due to their own negligence. As for these two women? They are not assets; they are tools that earned their place tied in this room, sir. I ask that you refrain from speaking to me further, or I will be tempted to end you right here and now, and it surely will not be a suitable time or place for that." He shoved Willham away and growled like a dog before choosing another part of chicken.

The doctor was not wealthy, Martin. I am sad to know she has nothing to sustain her. At least their children are grown." James sat at the kitchen table and bent his head down to the table and onto his arms.

"I have sent my condolences to the widow and will pay for the funeral and her needs. I do not know what else to do." Martin set his hand across Meredith's.

"I could call on her, but being a stranger to her, I think it would not be helpful. Is there anything I can do?" Meredith leaned toward Martin, who shook his head.

"Nothing. But thank you, Meredith. Our immediate concern is that we have lost Hannah and Miriam yet again. And Mr. Rockingham. As for the loathsome Mr. Montrose, I care only because I sense he holds the key to this entire ugly affair."

Outside, Emily stood near the courtyard, looking toward the carriage wreck as the large vultures with great red heads swooped down and landed upon it. She winced and walked back into the house via the front doors. She made straight for the kitchen, and seeing the three sitting there, she hovered near the door.

"What is it?" Martin asked her, seeing her hang back with an expression that spoiled the look of her pretty face.

"The vultures, sir. At the carriage."

"Blast it." Martin rose and grabbed for the rifle that had yet to be returned to the gun closet, lying at the end of the table. "Vile creatures. I hoped to ignore it but…" he strode away and out the front doors.

The vultures, wholly intent on their meal, picked at the horses' faces and mouths, grabbing away chunks of fur and flesh. Tilting their heads back, they swallowed hard to gulp the bloodied tissue down before one turned its attention toward the carriage itself and the doctor within. Martin walked slowly toward the dozen vultures that had gathered, and as he raised his arms up to fire, Stephen appeared at his side.

Stephen said nothing but continued to walk closer and closer until he was nearly ten feet away before pausing. The vultures stopped eating but seemed intent on remaining, despite the intrusion. He raised his long rifle up and fired once into the air. All but one vulture took flight. A single shot to the bird atop the carriage struck the creature and it fell to the snow, its long and wide wings flapping furiously against the ground.

"They remain." Martin pointed toward the others flying overhead. "I will stay." He sat down and laid his gun across his lap. The vulture on the ground stopped moving. Its wings spread out in awkward positions; its head tilted toward the men who sat and waited, looked just as contemptible dead as it had alive. A bit of horseflesh hung from its beak.

"Nasty creatures," Stephen, remarked and settled his weapon down.

"They need to eat, too, but not here and not today." Martin rose to one knee and took aim at a vulture that descended, and he pulled the trigger. The bird began a death spiral down, and as it fell, feathers twisted and spun about its body. An unpleasant thump signaled it had landed to the other side of the carriage.

"Ten left." Stephen, taking aim at one, pulled the trigger, and the next bird fell as the other, but it did not die right off. It lay twisting this way and that against the cold earth until Stephen walked to it and stomped on its throat. He knocked his boots against each other to dislodge bloodied feathers from the soles. He sat back down beside Martin.

"Nine." They said nothing for a long while, until the birds regrouped and began their death circles again. "They aren't very bright."

Martin snorted. "Or maybe just very hungry. Greed produces waste." He took another shot, and the next fell.

"Eight," Stephen counted. "Sir, I was thinking." He stopped before continuing to aim for the next, missing. "Blast...I was wondering, sir, if it is quite safe for Miss Meredith to be here. Although I do believe you know what is best for the lady, I felt I needed to ask." He took a knee, and his next shot succeeded. "Seven."

"I will not let her out of my sight."

"She is out of your sight now, sir."

"James is my proxy when not there. And Emily." Martin took a shot and felled the sixth bird.

"That one. I'm not quite sure about her. I confess I took a fancy to her, sir, but she was rather...how shall I say it? Overly eager to make my intimate acquaintance."

Martin chuckled. "Is this the worst thing that has happened to you, Stephen?" Martin fired his weapon, and the next bird fell to the earth.

"Five. No. But I saw how she looked at you. I think she has motives less innocent than first spied."

"Meredith said that." Martin shrugged. "She is quite lovely, but I agree. Something is not right about her, and we best watch."

"I suppose we will have to burn these creatures or others will show up."

"Yes, I have seen them cannibalize each other. Nasty animals. Rather like humans in their way aren't they? Any manner of thing is acceptable as long as they are satiated." Martin fired, and the next bird fell and hit the carriage with a thump. "Four."

"Why are we counting them down?" Stephen smiled, despite himself. He felled another. "Three."

Martin shrugged. "Because we can…. Two."

"You're a good man, sir. It's a privilege…One."

"I am being punished. For something."

"God doesn't punish."

"I was not speaking of God." Martin grimaced before reloading his gun. "One more dead, another arrives. It must be the dumbest of the bunch. Filling in their ranks."

"God doesn't need you to speak of him in order for him to exist. He just does." Both men stood and simultaneously fired their weapons at the last bird.

"None left," Martin said. "I think we both hit it."

"I'll pile them together and burn them."

"Thank you, Stephen."

"Sir. Before you go. I need to ask something of you. I am twenty-three. It is getting late for me to make something of myself. I would like to enter the university at Boston this spring. As we discussed."

"All will be paid. Make your plans. But I ask something in turn. You must find me a suitable replacement. The sooner the better." He patted Stephen on the back and turned away toward the house.

"You three are suffocating me with the stench you emit." Daniel slapped his hands across his nose and sat down. "Truly."

"Let us go." Miriam wobbled as she rose from where she had laid on the floor and sat upright. "I don't care what you have done, boy, but this cannot go on."

"Right you are, dear Miriam." Daniel eyed them, making a decision.

"I choose you." He pointed toward Hannah who had finally awoken, and she stared straight into his eyes. "Do I cut your tongue out so you cannot speak? Or do I find a more permanent solution? I cannot bear another night in this room as it is." Hannah closed her eyes again.

Willham edged closer to Daniel and used his most practice voice as he spoke. "As I see it, it is best to rid her from the lot and be done with it. She is nothing but a useless link. If I were kind, though I surely am not, I would say let her die on her own accord. But why permit her to continue?"

Daniel looked at Willham and smirked. "Is that your opinion, sir?"

"It is. What use is she now? None. She is a liability. Pure and plain like that."

"And what use are you to *me*, Willham? Do say, and tell it now before I lose the last wick of patience I have for you."

"It is simple, Daniel," he said as he edged even closer. "I know where all the hidden jewels are because she told me herself." He jerked his head toward Hannah. He seemed rather sure of it, even smug, and it made Daniel smile unpleasantly.

"Where? I know of one place. But having checked the location, it was emptied. Yet you might know of another?"

"Why should I tell you? This is not reasonable, and I know well you will kill me as soon as you find them. Let me go. This place has expended its last use, and any money gained or jewels claimed by me at this juncture are not worth dying for."

Daniel turned away from them and stood to stare out at the place where the day before the carriage had sat. What remained were bloody patches of snow and a black film of ash across the snow. He was right, Daniel thought, and pressed his face to one of the windowpanes. And not only was he correct in his statement, but he was also the least likely of them to talk. Desperation creates the most dangerous of enemies, but Willham was not the desperate sort. "Very well. This is how we will manage our situation. You and I will leave tonight through the tunnel and passageway, and you will lead me to the jewels. If I find them as you say I shall, then you will be free. But I will deny every bit of what has happened here and before if you betray your oath to me. And afterward, I will kill you. Horribly. Slowly. I promise you that, Willham. I promise you."

"What of me?" Miriam wanted to cry, but she was so in need of water that no tears could be summoned.

"You? Hmm. I am sorry, Miriam, but you will be used as another diversion. I assume you pray, madam. I suggest you start now to plead for a speedy death."

"But what have I done to you, save for finding you out? Why not take all you can and then leave us? There is nothing here for you, Daniel. Nothing."

"But Miriam, you don't seem to understand. I don't want some of it. I have gone so far now that I want it all. All of it. Every rail and fence and stone; every penny, every horse; every chair, and every split piece of wood. Surely God will punish me in the hereafter. So I will enjoy what life is left to me wholly and completely because in hell, there will be no such happiness for me."

"You assume you will not be punished here on Earth. While you live?"

"I have no intention of being caught before I secure what I earned. What I deserve."

"Punishments are sometimes slow to coming and linger to make the life you lead not worth the living. Not all penalties are served by an Earthly judge; not all retribution will announce its coming. You are not exempt from that." Daniel shrugged. "Have you become so corrupt of heart and mind that you will take pleasure in life despite the unspeakable things you have done and intend to do still?"

"Well, my dear Miriam. Yes, I suppose I have. There comes a point when a person has gone too far, and there is no way back from that place."

"There is always a path back, Daniel."

"That is a lie told by preachers to sooth their flock and feed their pockets. It is a fairy tale repeated by those who need to avoid the truth."

"Do you see them?" Martin sat beside her and slid a cup of hot tea toward her.

"Sometimes. In a way. I suppose you can say that." She took the tea and sipped from the cup, letting her eyes stray from Martin's face to the piano that had not sounded in some days. The fire cracked over a log and the room smelled of her skin. Jasmine and warmth. "Mostly I feel them," she whispered. "Sometimes I can sense them coming into a room and they make themselves known by brushing against my arm."

"Like a touch?"

"No. Like a breeze."

"And when they speak, do they sound as you and I do?" He leaned forward.

"Yes. But it is as though they are speaking through a closed window. Through many panes of heavy glass. Muffled, like that."

"You stare at the piano. Do you see something there? It has long haunted this room. The tinkling of keys."

"Martin, are you certain that they are not haunted by you? Wishing to be near but unable to bridge the space between here and there?"

"I did not consider that, but then I have always refused the notion that the sound was caused by anything ethereal. Rather, I wanted to believe that it was some malfunction of key or human by nature."

"I, too, felt that way at first, but when I stopped denying its truth, I was no longer haunted. Except..."

"Yes, my dear?" He leaned in and touched her face. "How I love to see you in this soft fire light with your hair unbound, your eyes soft from the candles; your skin glowing, and ever so warm." She leaned her face into his palm and closed her eyes. "But you are a most surprising creature. Putting the mare down as you did."

"Do you think I would live so alone or when working out in the fields and meadows, the mountains, and not know how to use a weapon? Do you find greater value in women who prefer to use their charms rather than their God-given brains?"

"I suppose not. But it takes a certain kind of person to do it. Woman or man. And still...you are most confounding to everything I have known."

"Is this bad?"

"No, Meredith. No. You are what I needed and did not know it.... The fire is faded. I'll bring in some wood. With so few left to see to this sort of thing, I'm afraid I must interrupt our talk."

She watched him walk away, and when he was out of the room, she let go of the sigh she had held onto, for fear he would hear it and ask why. She was grateful that he did not notice she hadn't answered his question about the piano. For in the corner near it, standing by the windows, Amelia stood.

"Go. Go away, Amelia," she whispered and then looked anxiously toward the doorway where Martin had passed through. "Now is not the time." She waved her hand gently in the direction of the apparition as Martin returned. She feigned another motion of her hand and straightened her lavender dress.

"What are you doing?" He laughed lightly.

"It is rather warm in here. I would love to stand a while outdoors on the walk near the garden and breathe the night air if you are inclined."

"I thought it very chilly, quite suddenly, and so fetched this wood, but as you wish." He extended his hand to her and pulled her gently up.

Stopping near the piano, he pulled her close to his body, and a humming sound crossed from his wide chest along his throat. She reached to touch where it met his chin, and she smiled. But Amelia did not seem to share her delight. She placed her vaporous hands across her eyes. A quick sob emerged, and she dissolved much like a feather of candle smoke disappears into the dark. A shift of air caused Martin to pull her away, and he stared into her eyes.

"Did you feel it?" she asked.

"Yes. Is it...them?"

"It is Amelia, come to see what we are doing, and seeing me here in your arms, she seemed not to like it. She has gone."

He stepped away and looked about himself, first to the piano and then toward the windows that led to the garden. "Why does she protest?"

"She always loved you, Martin. She thought of herself as your defender when she lived. But I think she is jealous of what we have. Of what the living can provide and take."

"Do you call them back when they leave?"

"I have never had cause."

"Call her back, Meredith. I want to see for myself. If I dare."

"No, Martin. I do not think it wise to meddle in the affairs of Waverly spirits. They do as they wish, and I do not ask much of them. They make themselves known to those they choose...I fear only their wrath, but thus far, they are slow to anger....Save for that horrid Rene Bonhomme, whom

I fear and dread, and have asked as you know, to leave me in peace."

"Ah, you have me believing all these stories. I am sorry, my love. I am troubled by it all. Not knowing which way to think of it…Or if I should think of it at all. As you told me again about Rene, I was seized with a sense that I must do battle for you. But not knowing if this is a true thing, I think I could go mad with the idea entirely."

"Battles can either be won or lost. Do you suppose either can be if you simply stand down?"

"If this spirit plague is real, lady, perhaps someday I will have no choice. I have never felt myself in a neutral position when in your presence. Having glimpsed them myself, I still struggle, not knowing if I invent it or it is real."

"Let's go outside. Just for a few moments, shall we?"

He led her by the hand to the garden where they stood beneath the great umbrella of sleeping wisteria vine. Above, the stars shone brightly as only winter stars can. In the distance, a solitary coyote called out—its howl, desperately lonely and searching for something akin to what he held in his arms.

Meredith drew in a deep breath and held it.

"What is it? Are you afraid?" he asked.

"No. Not of the coyote. They speak. I cannot hear...I do not know this voice. It is new to me."

He looked about himself and then to her face. "Do you—"

"Shhh…be still." She hung her head down and listened, and he waited. "I think she says...*Rockingham*." Her eyes darted up to his, and they did not break away. "Rockingham is in the second cottage. The one nearest the cliff by the old maple tree. Off in the woods."

"Lady, if this is found to be true, I will spend the rest of my days proving my sorrow over ever doubting you." He pulled her by the hand and went off to the kitchen where he left her seated and then down the servant's hall to gather Stephen. A few moments later he returned and told her to come with them, not letting on to Stephen why he thought she be better to walk with them than stay behind.

"Hasn't that cottage been searched? I was there, sheltering and feeding the horses just this evening. No one was about. How do you know he is there?" Stephen pulled his long coat on and waited.

"Did you enter the cottage?" Martin asked, helping Meredith pull her coat on. He ignored Stephen's last question and walked toward the door.

"No, I saw no reason to. But hadn't Barberry gone inside?"

"I do not know. Let's go."

R ockingham heard their voices before he saw them. The indistinct babble of more than a dozen surrounded him. He did not count them but somehow knew their numbers. Yes they were voices, yes, he was certain. But he could not make out a word of what they said. It was rather like the sounds within a large hall during a posh ball when musicians play their instruments and many speak above the serenade of strings and bows. Cacophony of word and music meld together in one large mangled hum. There was a woman who laughed. It was a pleasant sound that somehow reassured him even though he could not tell whether she even knew he was there. Above her voice, a man chimed in and then another asked a question. Somewhere in their midst, a child spoke to what he felt must have been its mother. She answered something, and the child responded in turn.

Forcing his eyes open, he saw them at last—a mysterious group of incandescent persons or beings wandering around near him but behaving as if he was not there. Was he? He could distinguish man from woman and child, and differentiate old from young. Some wore gowns, and some donned working clothes. Some were rather portly and some thin as nails. He willed himself to focus, urged his limbs to do his bidding, to stand, to sit, to call out, but it was wasteful time spent. Suspended between the multiplicities of here, there, then, now, and past, he could not bridge the divide.

He heard one of the male beings shush the others, and they all fell very silent. A door opened, and then someone or something came near to him. She laid her hand to his head. It was a warm hand, and though she was not nearly as radiant as the others about her, she was no less bright.

Grateful to be seen at last, he waited to know what might come next. He was sure she was a woman, yes. Hands lifted him. He heard a familiar voice. Martin spoke near his head. "You're going to be alright, old man. You're going to be alright," he said.

He could not be satisfied that any of it was real. Not Martin, not the woman, not those that seemed to float nearby. That was the thing of it. The quirk of thought and consciousness versus reality perplexed him.

There was another man. He was becoming quite certain that he and Martin were really there with him, joined in his altered reality. And the woman, she was there, too. They were more distinct than the others, and the men appeared oblivious to those who surrounded them as they carried him from the cottage. But one woman was more like them and seemed to know they were there about her. She said something to one of them, and he was sure it said something in return.

"My dear love," one of the luminous beings said as he was led away from the rest, "it is close to your time, but you must not die here. Not before you can tell Martin what he needs to know. Go away in peace, with joy, and ease, and know that I watch over you for all time..." Her voice caused him to speak. He had never allowed the sweetness of it to leave his dreams, even after so many years.

"My darling Anne. My sweet, sweet darling Annie. Why must I leave here? Why?"

Martin jerked his head to look into Rockingham's face and then to Meredith. She smiled.

Daniel and Willham crept silently along the moisture-sodden walls of the passageway that led to the master bedroom chambers. The lanterns had dimmed as they walked, and the going had become harder with each step.

"You better be telling me the truth, you weird little man." Daniel shoved him with his arm, urging him forward.

"Be quiet, boy. We have no idea who is about this night, and it will make our destination impossible to reach if we are found out."

"Just go on." Daniel shoved him again.

"Blast it all. If you continue to push at me, I shall fall over, and then what?"

Daniel grumbled something and then said, "Just make sure you do as you said you would. I am not in the humor to make any new deals with you." Willham was certain that Daniel did not intend to keep the last one they had made, so the assertion made him laugh.

They reached the end of the long passage and stopped to listen. Hearing nothing, Daniel pushed Willham aside and slid the false door open to peer inside the room. It was very dark, and so he held a lantern above his head and slowly proceeded to walk in.

"There, behind that mirror near the dressing table," Willham whispered. "Take it gently down and see for yourself what lies behind." Daniel placed the lantern on the table, reached to grab the sides of the mirror, and ever so gently took it from its hook on the wall. "See? I told you."

"I see nothing but a wall and hook." Daniel turned in an angry move toward Willham, who instinctually ducked away. "Are you sure this is the place?"

"Untie my hands. Do it, we have no time to waste." Reluctantly, Daniel did as Willham demanded. "Move aside and I will show you." Willham, much shorter than Daniel, lifted a chair and placed it beneath the space where the mirror had hung and climbed atop it. He wedged his fingernails beneath barely visible crack-like protuberances that ran along the wall and then got down from the chair. "Now you go up. Just pull it ever so gently, and a part of the wall will release. Be careful now; it is rather heavy. And behind that you will see a squared out space. Reach within it. Careful, now." He got off the chair and stood behind it as Daniel climbed up.

Willham reached to his right side and ran his hand along the desk, searching, his eyes never leaving Daniel. Something long and smooth moved beneath his fingers. He slid it from the desk and secreted it into his back pocket.

"I have it. I have it! Here, take the wood slat." Willham received it and placed it near the chair as Daniel pushed up to the balls of his feet and reached in. "You are correct. I feel something. Something...like a parcel. A velvet parcel. Two, there are two." He could do nothing to conceal his delight.

They heard the sound of the front door opening and slamming shut, followed by the shrill exclamations of Emily's voice from two flights down the stairs.

"Hurry, hurry!" Willham breathed out in a husky whisper. "So close now! We should not have our plan spoiled by your slow pace." He eyed the distance between the passageway and the door that would lead out and opted for the former. His hands jutted out and with all the strength he could muster, he tilted the chair back then quickly side to side. As Daniel flung his arms out desperately attempting to catch his balance, Willham gave him a final push, and Daniel tumbled to the floor.

"Bastard!" Daniel spit, clenching his teeth. Still clutching the velvet pouches in his hand, he growled. "You shall pay!" He floundered momentarily on his back but then stopped as he saw something spiteful pass across Willham's face.

"No, boy. *You* shall." With one measured move, Willham reached into his back pocket, withdrew the pointed letter-opener bearing the initials GW, and thrust it into Daniel's shoulder as the younger man moved to sit up.

Daniel yowled and dropped the pouches, which Willham immediately retrieved. He made straight for the door and yanked it, but it was locked again! He turned toward the passageway and bolted past Daniel who had regained himself enough to stand, and as Willham ran for the passage, closing the false wall behind, he disappeared into the darkness like one of the many rats that made it their home. He heard Martin's voice, a scuffle, and then the sound of Stephen yelling.

Hurriedly making his way along, he came to the end and went left to exit through the upstairs old parlor door. Bolting down the steps, a few times falling, he made it to the bottom of the stair at last, and turning the corner, he stopped and looked left and right before proceeding toward the dining room and doors beyond. Yanking the front doors open, he ran headlong down the steps and then under the arches where the first blast of clean air took his nearly spent breath away, but nothing could stop him. He ran the entire length of the drive and then paused beneath the last row of hemlock to catch his breath. Dipping his head down and pressing his hands against his knees, he was overcome with a sense of freedom that he had become entirely deprived of for too many days, and, he dare thought, years.

He patted the pouches within his pocket, smiled, moved to the narrow lane beyond, and made away into the very cold night.

❦ Scoundrel!" Stephen yelled into Daniel's face. "Thief!" Stephen yanked the letter opener from Daniel's shoulder and tossed it aside.

Daniel, held fast by the two men, squirmed and kicked, attempting to free himself from their grasp. "I have done nothing! Follow Willham, detain him! Not me! He has burgled the jewels, gentlemen, and I had merely tried to stop him! Go quickly!"

But Martin was not buying any of it, and he thrust Daniel to the ground, applying a boot that held him in place. "I am finished being lied to. Get up." He bent down and grabbed Daniel by the shoulders, then thrust him to the wall. Stepping toward him, fists clenched, he fought the urge to bash Daniel in the face. "I have a multitude of questions for you, you repulsive man, but I shall save them. For now. Save for this. Where is Hannah? Where is Miriam? And you best spill it out, boy, lest I kill you with my bear hands!"

"I know not! How could I? I have been away since you dismissed Theresa. I came to look for her. I miss her so terribly! Finding no one here to let me in, I came to search for myself. Then I found Willham lurking about. That is all I know. Fault me for wandering your house, sir; fault me not for looking for the one I love! Now let me go!"

"*Liar*," Stephen, sneered. "Lies. I can think of many ways to find her, and had you waited a short while, you might have knocked upon the door to inquire. But you took it on yourself to trespass. You gave up your position here when you left without a word. And since you have been gone, too much has happened for it to be a coincidence of timing."

"You're a fool. All of you! Fools! While you cast blame on me for things I cannot know occurred, you allow Willham, who is the real culprit, to make away with your possessions. But as you wish." Daniel jerked out of Martin's hands and righted his clothing.

"You are lying to me. I can see that. What you say does not add up. Stephen, help me with him. We will tie him and call upon Barberry, yet again."

As they gripped his arms tightly and hauled him away, he looked over his shoulder at Meredith who had stood silently at the door. "You...I know you. Are you not the one who plays upon the piano late at night?" He smirked and allowed them to tug him away. "If not for me you would not know who has sought to bring fear to this house. Listen to me! I know what I am saying. You would not know if not for me! I tell you true! That woman is the culprit!" he exclaimed as they walked down the hall and nearly carried him down the stairs.

Emily stood at the bottom of the stairs and bit her lip. She wrung her white apron between her hands and stepped away as they came to the bottom of the step. She waited only to know if Daniel would give away her secret. Looking at her from the corner of his eye, one side of his mouth jerked up into a grin.

"Let's bring him to my library." Martin yanked Daniel in the direction of it and kicked open its door. "Set him there. On the floor in the corner." He let go, and Stephen hurled him down. "Get the rope. It's in the corner cabinet near the kitchen door. Hurry or you might find him dead if you tarry." Martin loomed over Daniel, and his fists, still tightly drawn together into hard knots, wanted nothing more than to beat the truth from the man. His dark hair, long and hanging in his face, did nothing to conceal that he was indeed prepared to end the man if need be. James walked slowly in and sat heavily down into a chair nearby, temporarily giving Daniel reprieve.

"I would ride out again, to fetch Barberry, but I confess I do not know if I have one more ride in me to spare." James wiped his face with a cloth and leaned back. "As for this young man needing a doctor, there is none, of course, save for Doctor Billingsworth, who is some miles away in the next town."

"He can bleed his last drop for all I care." Martin shoved him roughly with his boot.

"But you wouldn't want me to spoil this lovely Oriental rug no doubt gained through your father's dubious trades, would you?" Daniel asked.

"Remark on his practices all you wish, Daniel. You cannot incite me or cause worry over a dead man's reputation that I cared nothing for—or for the rug you are bleeding across. I care nothing for possessions. Nothing."

"You are rather stingy with your money for that to be true."

"Stingy?" James leaned forward and frowned. "This man is not a miser. He simply is not."

"Yes, yes, the beyond reproach Mr. Martin Waverly who knew of my father's death, caused by his family's greed, and then did nothing to repay my family for the loss."

"Angry, Daniel? At me? My family? Is that what all of the trouble has been about? Money?"

"No, you fool," Daniel sneered and grabbed his bleeding shoulder. "I am angry and have been about the unnecessary deaths of those I held dear. If not for your family's greed, they might still be alive."

"If you needed compensation, then it was my father's to know and not I. If not, why didn't you simply ask for assistance? From me?" Daniel had no reply.

James leaned back again, sighing. "Funny thing about it, isn't it, Daniel? Even you cannot say why you did not do the easiest thing. Hate is such a vile fixation. Blinding, isn't it, to those who are weak?"

"I have no idea what you are talking about. Just because I detest the lot of you, it doesn't mean I have done anything to any of you. Shut up old man. Shut your mouth."

Stephen, coming up behind them, grabbed Martin's arm as he swung it up to beat Daniel, who cowered at the sight. "Stop sir, stop." He grabbed Daniel by the shirt, hauled him upright, and steadied him. "Let me." He punched him in the face, causing Daniel to reel backward; his head smacked on the bookcases, and then he crumpled to the ground. "I've wanted to do that for a long time," he said, handing the ropes to Martin.

Meredith stepped forward. "Enough of this," she said, standing in front of Daniel with her arms spread out. "Enough. Unless you wish to be like him."

Martin, still seething, turned the unconscious man to his chest, and tied his legs and arms together. "He can't get out of this," he said, breathing heavily.

"I will ride out for Barberry and then Doctor Billingsworth. The weather is clear, and I should reach each within an hour if I ride hard."

"Go carefully, Stephen." Martin grabbed his shoulders and tugged. "Take Isabella…She is the most reliable. There are few who can claim a better friend than you."

"I am useless, simply useless." James closed his eyes as Stephen departed.

"Nonsense." Martin sat down near to him and patted his knee. "Meredith, please tend to Mr. Rockingham and take Emily with you."

Emily, who had witnessed it all from just outside the entrance, took a step back. "And stop lurking about in doorways, madam. Go on; get moving."

"Brutal. They were brutal to that man." Emily walked up the steps up toward Rockingham, but Meredith clenched the woman's apron strings and prevented her from proceeding. "What is it? Do you not agree?"

"It does not matter what I think, and I dare say it matters less what you think," Meredith said in a sharp tone.

"They seemed to think otherwise. You have made a comfortable place for yourself here, have you not? So quickly, too—swooping in and taking possession of Martin and acting as though you are the keeper of kindness and reason in this house." She yanked her apron out of Meredith's hand and continued up the stairs ahead of her.

"If you find it objectionable to be here, no one could blame you. But if you are to stay, perhaps you might consider keeping your opinions to yourself and just do your job."

Emily, not liking the tone of the conversation, turned swiftly around toward Meredith. "Ask your lovely Mr. Waverly about his intentions toward me, miss. Ask him about the day in his library when he...we had just met."

"Keep moving, Emily," Meredith said evenly and pressed her hand onto the younger woman's back.

"What is the trouble? Many masters take, however should I say it...*privileges*...with the servants. Why should *our* Martin be any different?"

"You trifle with the wrong woman, Emily. Move."

"As you wish. But you shall see," Emily said almost merrily.

Daniel's accusation that Meredith had been behind the unexplained playing of piano keys had not been missed by Martin. Although she had proven that she knew where Rockingham could be found, did it mean that a spirit had truly told her what they all needed to know? Was there any chance that she was playing a terrible and dangerous game with him? He did not wish to believe it could be true, yet doubts lingered. Perhaps, he thought as he checked Daniel's tethers, he was simply exhausted and unable to make the simplest estimation of all.

"He's rousing, Martin. For a moment I thought he might not. Stephen did not hold back." James picked up a glass of water he had retrieved for Martin and handed it to him.

"Thank you. Yes, I think there was more animosity between them than I realized. Can you sit with this one for a while? I want to check on Rockingham."

"Certainly. It does not appear he can go anywhere."

Martin walked slowly up the stairs and stopped once he arrived outside the door of Rockingham's room. He took a deep breath, exhaled, and ventured in.

"He is sleeping, I think, Martin." Meredith rose to greet him and slid her arm around his. "He said something about Daniel, but I could not make out the entirety of what he said."

"It was the ravings of a desperately sick man, sir. That is all. I did not hear him speak Daniel's name." Emily rose from where she had positioned herself beside the man's bed and walked toward them. "Will the doctor come?" She wrung her hands together and tilted her head toward Rockingham.

"He did say the name Daniel, Martin. I am quite certain of it," Meredith interjected. "Quite certain."

"Lady Meredith, I think you are mistaken. Who could make sense of what he said? Not I, and I dare say, not you. Odd, is it not? You knew where he could be found. And now you point your finger toward Daniel who was simply here searching for his love." Her lips smiled, but the expression did not cross her eyes.

Meredith frowned. "I say for certain he said the name, Martin. Have you had anything to eat? Can I make something for you?"

"Why must you all do this to me? Dismiss me when I am making perfectly good sense? I am simply trying to help! And Miss Meredith does nothing but try to make a disagreement from every little word I say! Perhaps the truth torments her."

Martin sighed and sat down. "Emily, I saw her myself comforting you when the barn burned to the ground. She has been accurate in her assessments of all things. Let it be. Do not argue with her. You are stepping far from your place in this house. Now go fetch us something to eat, and please do it now. Please." He turned his attention away from the women and buried his head into his hands, closing his eyes.

"Always at your request, sir, I will be a moment." Emily walked briskly away, partially closing the door as she walked into the hallway.

"He said Daniel. It concerns me she would argue it since he said it a number of times, and it was the clearest word he spoke."

"Is that so…" He took his hands from his face and stared at her. "I suppose we cannot know until he opens his eyes again. I pray he will do just that. We can trust the doctor arrives sooner than later. Stephen is seeing it through. We can only hope it is quick work."

"Do you believe anything that girl says? Do you think I know something and have not told you?"

Emily leaned her head against the wall outside the room and smiled. Not all of her ideas were good ones, but if nothing else, she was distinctly adept at providing distractions. She did not wait to hear Martin reply to Meredith. She trotted down the stairs. Once near the library, she peered in. James sat in the chair sleeping, and Daniel, who had awoken, sat straight up and smiled. She pressed her fingers to her lips, crept in, and untied his legs and hands. "Wait until they see you as they pass by, brother. Be patient. Wait and watch." Untied, he left the ropes loosened about his limbs and closed his eyes.

"Hannah and Miriam remain in the widows walk," he whispered. "There is the drug in my pocket. Take it and use it wisely, but use it!" She grabbed into his pocket, withdrew the little container and parcel, and ran to the second parlor, straight for the piano, and when there, she banged at the keys before running out straight to the kitchen. She positioned herself near the rear door with her back turned to the room. It only took a moment. Martin's voice, followed by James,' reached her ears.

"The confounded piano!" James exclaimed, and then she heard Martin's voice speaking to Meredith.

She waited for the moment when she heard James walk into the foyer before letting go of a blood-curdling scream. Martin arrived first, and as she saw him come toward her from the corner of her eye, she slumped to the floor and writhed there as he picked her up and sat her on a chair near the table.

"What is it? Have you seen something?" he asked, pulling her face around to meet his eyes. "Or is it the piano that has scared you?"

"At the door! I saw a face at the door. A strange and most ghastly figure. It was with large teeth and bright red hair! Oh lord!" She whimpered and fell straight to the floor again.

"See to it, please, James," Martin asked and lifted her once again. "Emily, are you certain? Perhaps—"

"I am quite sure, and it came as I turned from hearing the piano keys struck. Oh, sir, I am terribly sorry, but I am frightened! Frightened for my life!"

"There is nothing out there. Perhaps you were just fearful of the piano playing and thought you saw something or someone?" James sat beside her and patted her hand.

"Oh, James. I am quite certain. I am so fortunate to have such able men about me during these terrible times!"

Meredith, who stood in the corner of the kitchen squinted her eyes at the girl and tilted her head. Something was not right, of course, but she had the sense that Emily was into things that she should not be. Meredith walked nearer to more-closely examine the girl's expression. "Would you like me to make you a tea, dear?" she asked Emily, smiling. "All will be well. We have had a series of dreadful things happen, and it is normal to feel so—ill at ease."

"Tea would be lovely, if you don't mind, lady."

"Very well, then, tea it shall be." She smiled weakly. "Martin, perhaps someone should check on Daniel?" When he looked to her face, she twisted her mouth up to one side, and he did not miss the cue. Emily, making a move to get up as Martin sprung for the door, was sat back down by Meredith's firm hand. "Now, now. No need to rush away and follow the men. Sit here, Emily, and drink your tea." She grabbed a cup and dropped it on the table. It fell to its side and then rolled along the wood until Emily jutted her hand out and stopped it. She looked to Meredith. Their eyes met. Meredith smiled.

Martin, having discovered that Daniel was missing along with the ropes he had been tethered with, slammed his fist to the wall, and whirled toward James. "Find another set of ropes and tie that blasted girl up. I am done being treated like an idiot!" He went out the door, grabbing his coat as he went, and ran straight to the last horse that James had left outside in case of such an emergency. He mounted it and rode off, as James walked back into the kitchen.

"How is your tea, Emily?" he asked slowly, and caught the expression in Meredith's eyes. Emily moved to rise, but Meredith pushed her back down.

"Now tell me, dear girl, why did you do that?" Meredith asked, and laid her hand across Emily's shoulders. "Why did you untie the lad? Why help him against Martin's obvious demand to keep him tied?"

"I was afraid. That is why I screamed so! I made no move to Daniel. He may be wicked, but I am not like him. I did nothing to free him!"

"Oh, it is nonsense, all nonsense. But if I am proven wrong, you will receive many apologies from me." She watched as James walked up slowly from behind Emily and handed one set of cord to Meredith.

"What is this?" Emily asked, her voice rising.

"A little hope, in the fashion of cord, that you will be prevented from causing more problems."

Emily let go of a shriek that rivaled the one she had feigned moments before and thrust her arms and legs about, attempting to avoid what was to happen.

"Oh, stop it, girl," Meredith snorted as she succeeded in grabbing Emily's' arms together. "If you fight me more, I will be tempted to give you what Stephen delivered to Daniel. Now just stop it. Do you understand me?" Her voice was not unkind but rather soft and yet insistent, and the distinction between the two made James laugh aloud.

"I wouldn't toy with Meredith, my dear, if I were you." He handed Meredith the other cording and sat down beside Emily. "So tell us, dear. What is Daniel to you? A lover? A romantic interest? Something else perhaps?"

Emily struggled briefly with the cording and finding that she was not going anywhere, smiled at James.

"Sir, you get it all wrong. I saw something and I was afraid. Terribly afraid, but now I think perhaps I am more afraid of Meredith than anyone in this house!"

Meredith, amused at the girl's persistence, laughed lightly and sat down beside her. "There is no one here left that might untie you. But you are a wily creature, aren't you? I think I need an assurance that you will not flee if we turn our backs on you." She got up again and walked to the hearth where she had seen a chain used for hoisting the black kettle above the flame. She removed it from its anchoring and then set to attaching it to the table. "Do find me a hammer, will you, James, please?"

He retrieved it in a moment from shelving near them and handed it to her. She circled one end of the chain around the heavy oak table leg and then wrapped it around Emily's calf. Then she repeated the process in reverse and stood to admire her handy work.

"What am I?!" Emily shouted, yanking against the chain. "A dog!?"

Meredith stepped back and smiled. "I don't know, Emily. Are you?" It elicited more howls of protestation from Emily, but Meredith shrugged. "You sound like one. Howling that way. But go ahead, girl. Do your best. No one cares, and no one can hear you...I'm going to sit with Rockingham for a moment." She turned on her heels and walked away to the sound of the woman screaming obscenities.

James flinched. But despite all the terribleness of it, of the day, the weeks preceding, he sat down and indulged himself with a riotous belly laugh. Nothing was particularly funny, but the irony of it all was comic, in it's unavoidable, hard to miss, sardonic way.

TWELVE

Willham stood near a thicket at the shore of The Hudson River, intent on boarding a ferry that would take him down to New York City. Keeping out of sight, he lingered in the shadows, waiting for the ferryman to call the handful of passengers aboard.

What would have been a two-hour walk to the ferry landing was shortened by more than an hour. Along his way, he saw an empty horse-drawn ice wagon and begged a ride to the landing. It was a risky sojourn, considering it was done in broad day light, and he was certain they would seek him, but no time seemed any better than the next to leave.

Seeing the ferry's approach and stealing some hasty looks around, he stepped further back into the protective covering of the evergreens and thorny bramble, withdrew the two parcels holding his much fought for loot, and smiled. He simply could not wait another moment to examine his newly acquired riches. He untied a black string that closed the first from around the smooth velvet and took a deep breath. Dumping the contents into his palm, he stared, considered, and then dropped it to the ground before untying the next. Just as the first, bits of splintered rock and slate fell into his palm. Unwilling to believe what he saw, he knelt down into the snow and touched the crushed stone at his feet.

"No. No." They were the only words he could summon, and he said them aloud. "How can this be?" he asked, digging his fingers into the snow to examine each. "How?" A quick, hard slap to the back of his head was the reply.

"Idiot."

Willham grasped the back of his head and turned around. "Oh."

"Oh? Is that all you can think to say?" Stephen grabbed him by the back of the neck and led him away toward Barberry who had readied a special place for him in the back of his police wagon.

"So this is the scalawag, is it?" Barberry climbed down from the wagon, tossed his cigar to the ground, and laughed. "Despite numerous accounts of your physical description, I did not imagine you to be quite as small or insignificant. I dare say, an unfortunate sight, indeed. What is that in your hand?"

"Nothing. Parcels. Nothing."

"Hmm. I see. Hand them over to me, Stephen...I see they must have contained something of import or at least this little man thought they had...Why else did you run off with them and now share your squirrel-like look of utter desperation? Has someone switched out your acorns, sir? Yes, we saw you. I should say I am quite amused."

"I'm a free man in a free country, and I come and go as I choose. I have done nothing wrong here, sir. I cannot be detained. The ferry is boarding."

"Yes, I see that it is. Pity you will not be on it, you strange, little creature. Perhaps I am utterly wrong and you are an innocent man. We shall see. This nice officer, Webster Stern, will take you with him to our comfortable jail where he will ask you all about your grand adventures in our town. Go on. That's a man." He shoved Willham toward Stern who took him by the scruff of his neck to the waiting cart. "Tie his hands, Stern. I hear this is a cagey one."

"I'm glad I figured that one right. Even if Daniel was lying about him, I didn't see harm in waiting for a few minutes to watch for him if he thought to leave by ferry. He is a creature of habit and fond of that confounded vessel."

"Indeed...If you thought to become a police officer, we could use the help."

"Me? Oh no, sir, I am bound for medical school in the spring!"

"Well, as you know, we also need a new medical doctor. Perhaps when you complete your studies you will consider returning to us."

"I have thought of it. I very well may."

"Good man. Climb aboard your horse, and let's be on our way to Waverly. The doctor will be there when we arrive, and I hope to get a word in with Mr. Rockingham. If it is as bad as you surmise, we have no time to waste. I must speak to him."

They waited for another moment as Willham was less than gingerly forced to board the cart. As Stern drove them away, Willham's voice could be heard raising loud objections, all of which were ignored. Stern showed no sign that he was even slightly moved by Willham's claims of innocence. A former slate mineworker, Stern lived up to this name. He was brawny and tall with hands that resembled giant clubs, and his features had taken on the appearance of the stone he had worked for many years. No, William Montrose was not going to flee. The cart turned down the next street, headed to the jail.

Even as they mounted their horses and turned in the other direction, Willham's voice could be heard above the ferry's horn as it departed the banks of The Hudson. Stephen could not help but imagine how the sounding of horn's blast must have stung the little man to the core. The thought pleased him.

Doctor Billingsworth sat beside Rockingham and patted his hand. He was far younger than Doctor Matthews had been, and his bedside manner was a vast improvement over the elder man's brisk attitude. He was short, with long salt and pepper hair that framed his inquisitive blue eyes. A studious calm clung to him, and Martin felt secure that whatever the doctor said, it would be precise, correct, and delivered with composed words. He was grateful for that.

The doctor tapped Rockingham's hand very gently and stood. "I will come back shortly, sir. Just lay still and rest." He motioned for Martin to stand with him in the hall.

"Will he be alright?"

"No, Mr. Waverly. I think not. The fractured leg has gone cold, and the alternative to letting him die of it would be to amputate his limb." Martin took in a deep breath, and the doctor reached out to touch his arm. "But that is not the worst of it, I fear. Whatever, whomever, dealt that gash to the back of his head has struck a mortal blow. I fear he bleeds within his brain, and there is nothing I can do without the proper equipment that would ease the blood out and away."

"Then tell me where to get such equipment! I will secure it by whatever means!"

"No, he is too weak for it. He would not survive. He has lost blood, he is in shock, and he has frostbite of one hand and part of his foot. His heart is not at ease, and his lungs are filling with fluid. He is going to die, Mr. Waverly. I sincerely wish there was more I could do. Any additional treatment will simply prolong your friend's pain, and he will end the same, whether it is in an hour or two, or the morning. I am deeply sorry, sir. But perhaps now is the time to say farewell."

Martin hung his head and nodded. "I realize you have to get back, and I thank you for riding out here. I shall compensate you accordingly."

"I have my father back home. He is retired from our profession and can take care of things if you wish me to stay at least for the night. He had already assumed I might stay here, and he understands."

"Thank you, doctor. Thank you. I will have...someone.... make a room readied for you."

"I have heard you are without most of your staff, and so any corner with a blanket will do. May I go to your kitchen and find myself some coffee?"

"Of course you should! You are a blessing to this house. I will join you there shortly." The doctor turned away and gently placed his hand to Martin's arm.

"Martin."

"I'm here." Martin walked to sit beside Rockingham and touched his hand. "What can I do for you?"

"Nothing. I know I am dying, son. But before I go, I need to talk with you about some things." His lungs rattled, and the breaths they expelled were coarse and shallow. Martin leaned closer. "I need to."

"There is no need, sir, but if you need me to see to things for you, after...tell me what you need, what is required, and I will do it."

"Firstly, Daniel is the one who did this to me. He thought to leave me dying in the snow. You're a good lad. You always were." He forced a smile that pained him to share. "All my affairs are in order. You will find my will and so forth in my office. The key to the drawer where it is all contained is in my luggage. There." His moved his arm slowly toward the corner. "I will tell you things that will cause you to wish my death had come sooner."

"What are you going on about? This is nonsense."

"No, I have never lied to you out of malice. Never. But my lies came in the form of many omissions, and each has taken their toll on us all. Please, Martin, before I cannot tell it, let me speak now. Before it is too late."

Martin nodded, and Rockingham forced a deep breath in and out.

"You have long suspected your father of killing your mother. You didn't need to say it in words, but I knew." He took another painful breath and gasped for a better breath of air before continuing. "But it was not your father who caused her drowning."

"Sir, you protect him even now. We all know she was an excellent swimmer. She could not have drowned in the lake. He was last seen with her there, and it was calm that day. She was quite well."

"I have not been protecting him, Martin. I die with the knowledge that I did not attempt to correct your wayward beliefs. I sought only to protect myself and your mother's honor as well as your vision of her. Much to my ever-lasting shame. I killed your mother, Martin. Please. I beg of you to forgive me, for it was not done out of wickedness. Or accident. It was intentionally committed to spare her more pain."

"What are you saying? What…" Martin sat back and closed his eyes. "You must try to find it within you to explain this to me."

"Your father found out that…Martin, I must make a short way through the events or I shall not complete the telling…Forgive me for that, too, if you can."

"Go on." Martin buried his head into his hands.

"Anne—your mother and I had frequently written to each other through all the many years, even before your father and she met. Once my letters were read, she secreted them in Blythe House where she would escape the mansion and your father. But on one occasion, she failed to do so and left a letter within a box on a shelf within her dressing closet, intending to see to it later that evening. Your father discovered it and learned that it was possible that he was not your father. But he never knew who was, despite years of trying to figure it out."

Martin dropped his hands away from his face and stared into Rockingham's partially open eyes.

"I am your father, Martin."

"This is madness. A fever. You must not continue. You must not." Martin stood and walked to the windows to stare out at the deepening night.

"Your father—Garson suspected me, I think, of having interest in your mother while he courted her. That is true. He employed me, I think, to keep watch over his suspicions. To the day he died, he suspected, but he kept his enemies quite close. That is most likely why he left me nothing in his will. I was the one who drew it up, and I think it delighted him to know he had hurt me." He took a shallow breath and then another, before his body became wracked with a shudder that forced him to stop for a moment.

Martin moved back beside him and sat down. "You must not continue...Rest."

"No," Rockingham said, composing himself. "I cannot die with these many lies blackening me. I fear I have too frequently tried His patience...One morning, it was a lovely July day, a Sunday...She and your—Garson—engaged in a terrible argument. It was so horrendous that he struck her many times. Many." He gasped at the recollection and coughed again. "I saw it and tried to stop it, but she fled on horseback. Bloodied, she was, and crying. Garson raced after her, and I, without horse, just a carriage that was not hitched, could do nothing but pray aloud that no further harm would come to her. He came back perhaps ten minutes later while the stable hand was readying a horse for me to make chase. He said nothing to me. I rode out the way they had gone." He stopped again, grabbed his throat, and fought to sit up.

"Let me," Martin said gently and placed three pillows atop each other before settling Rockingham back down.

"I found her," he continued, his voice becoming nothing more than a whisper. "She lay by the lake. Her lovely long hair blossomed about her head. Her arms and legs spread out. Her face, unrecognizable, bloodied. Beaten. Red welts rose along her arms and legs that looked to have been delivered by a riding crop. Her teeth, dismantled, some had fallen to her hair. Her lips, bearing gashes, and from her mouth great streams of blood flowed."

"Stop it! I can hear no more!" Martin gripped the sides of his head and closed his eyes. But Rockingham continued.

"She was near death. Her throat had been split by something, and dark blood flowed out. I dare not imagine what had done it. She said through the blood that crowded her once beautiful throat, *'Please, my love, please. I cannot die from his hand. Not his.'* I begged her to wait, that I would summon for the doctor, but she used the last of her strength to reach and touch my face. *'Please, I beg of you, let him not have his final say in this.'* And as her beautiful eyes shut, I took her hand from my face, kissed it, and carried her a few yards to the lake. She was in terrible pain—the kind that there is no returning from, and I carried her into the water and laid her body down."

"Did she suffer? Did she fight? I must know." Martin grabbed for the man's hand and squeezed.

"No. She smiled. She said, *'My love, feel no guilt. Watch over our son.'* And then she was gone." He drew in a breath, and when he released, it was in the form of a desperate sob.

"Tell me," Martin asked, seeing that he could not wait to inquire, "Why did they assume she had drowned if she was so badly broken?"

"When she did not return, Garson went to look for her. He saw her submerged and retrieved her. He thought that she had wandered into the lake. Not wanting anyone to see the state of her body, he ordered a casket, ordered three of his slaves to lower her into it, and refused to allow another to see her within it. He claimed that it grieved him to glimpse her face such as it was having been in the water for so long. No one pressed him."

"What of the slaves? Had they no care?" Martin asked, and Rockingham's eyes slipped up to Martin's.

"They were sent away. So Garson said. But some days later I saw three distinct areas on the grounds near the river. Do you understand?"

Martin nodded. He closed his eyes and pushed his fingers into them before speaking. "I understand so much now. I understand. And if there is doubt, ease it now. I forgive you. I forgive you." He laid his hand to Rockingham's chest and watched as his expression eased.

"I ask something of you. I know I have no right to it."

"What do you require?" Martin leaned in very near to his mouth so he could hear what the man whispered.

"Just once, Martin. Once before I go to see Anne, please...call me father."

Martin's voice, choked with emotion, and he whispered back to Rockingham. "I respected and admired you. I always cared for you and loved you. Father, you can be at peace."

D aniel had not gotten very far. He didn't have to.
While Martin had ridden down the lane, Daniel simply entered the root cellar and went back through the tunnel, re-entered the house, crept past the kitchen where Emily sat chained, and made straight for the widow's walk again.

He sat near the window so that the fresh air would waft about his head. The stench of the room had become too much for him to bear. He glanced at the women who lie facing each other sleeping. What to do next? Emily, having been accused of freeing him, and Willham gone, he reassessed the entire plan that seemed to unravel, no matter how he tried to prevent it. He concluded he could only flee.

He had seen Rockingham being carried into the house. The doctor arrived an hour or so later. Was the man alive to tell them what he had done? Or had the doctor arrived to tend to some other? He reached for the water jug and took a deep swallow, set it down, and laid on the floor to sleep.

Miriam opened her eyes to see a small smile spread across Hannah's mouth, and it exposed her broken, bloodied teeth. Miriam winked. And waited.

You knew? But how?" Martin waited for her response and turned his attention away from her toward the river. A January thaw was usual, but that particular one was especially sudden. He listened to the ice creak and crack as it shoved against the rocky shore.

"Because I have the letters." He turned toward her, waiting. "I found them in the attic space when I came back here after Garson died. And then the other night, I saw Daniel mulling about outside. Of course, I opened the door to ask what it was he wanted, not knowing at the time that Daniel was he. He told me that he and his lady friend had left things behind during one of their trysts, and he apologized most profusely for having entered. He said he did not know the house was again occupied. I had an uneasy feeling about him and asked what it was that he needed to retrieve. But he mentioned things that I knew not to be there and so I thought of the letters I had found. After he left, I opened them."

"Were they addressed?"

"Just with initials, and none resembling those of any I knew. But once opened, I realized the initials were mere subterfuge and their names were clearly written within." She turned to look at the river with him. The air, warmer than in weeks, softly played in her hair. She brushed it from her eyes and waited.

"And when you realized this, why didn't you tell me straight away?" His voice rung with annoyance, and he wrapped his arms about his chest.

"I thought it best for you to sleep that night. Could I have tolerated inflicting more harm to you than had already been done? I decided to wait. But then all the dreadful things happened one after the other, and no time was right."

"Meredith…" he turned toward her at last and looked down into her face, which she reluctantly turned up toward his, fearful that whatever he needed to say would not be subtle or what she wished to hear. "I told you what Rock—my true father said about Garson—his treatment of my mother particularly on her last day. Does your opinion of him change now that you see what the rest of us have known?"

"Yes. I just didn't see any of it. He was always so kind to me, as I have said many times. But there is dark to any light, save that of God's…I suppose."

"God?" he snickered and went back to staring out at the river and sighed. "When he passes, I wish to bury him in the family plot. And see to it that Garson's body is exhumed. Even as he is far off at the edge of the cemetery, he does not belong on hallowed ground. He will be sent to the county grave site."

"The pauper's cemetery?"

"Do you disagree?" He frowned at her.

She nodded. "He was a vile man. He must be cast out."

"I want to sit with Rockingham...My God, I scarcely know what to call him...It will most likely be his last night."

"Shall I go with you?" She pressed her hand to his arm, but he moved it away.

"No. I want to be alone with him. It looks like rain. Let's go."

A tepid wind kicked up dead leaves that had been buried beneath the snow for many weeks and skittered along the graying snow as Martin and Meredith walked. Atop the hill behind them, with the river wind wild in her hair, Amelia looked down upon them and cried.

"That sound is ghastly," Martin said, taking her arm to pull her along. "Almost as bad as the wind through the roof's turrets."

"Yes," Meredith replied softly, looking over her shoulder. But she knew better than he, the origin of its moan.

W illham refused to answer more questions flung at him via Officer Stern. No, he had not killed anyone. No, he had not colluded with Daniel to thieve the Waverly family of a single dime. No, no, no to it all.

"But you tried, didn't you?" Stern sat behind the small one-drawer desk and thumped his fist onto it. His eyes, sharp like a falcon's, his hands thickly calloused with the work he had done, caused Willham to see that he clearly was not someone with which to toy. His jawbone seemed overly large for his otherwise thin face, and when he spoke it was apparent that he was equipped with a keen mind. And he was having none of what Willham dished out in monosyllabic portions.

"No." Willham sat erect in the wobbly chair at the police station, and his hands sat quietly on his lap, realizing that the surest way to be presumed guilty without a doubt was to act it.

"Not even tried? Is that what you are telling me? Lying will get you one thing."

"That is?"

"My wrath." Stern smiled, exposing nubby, white teeth. "We aren't all fancied out like you folks in France. We don't bother with the frills and highfaluting talk. No, sir, we surely do not. We say what we mean—and mean what we say. No doubt you noticed today." Willham smirked. "But I have a little gift for you, seeing how I'm the generous type." He crooked one finger toward someone who stood behind Willham, and he smiled. "Come on now, don't be shy. Say hello to your partner in crime."

Theresa shuffled forward and stopped when she arrived at Willham's side.

"Of course," he said tiredly, and hung his head down. "You have arrived to share more of your lies and vile talk. Do you know about this girl, Stern? Who she is and what she has done previous to and during, and yes after her employment at Waverly Estate?"

"Indeed I do. Indeed I do. She confessed. But being a street lurker has little to do with this. A man or woman's station in life doesn't mean they are automatically presumed more guilty or innocent just because of their vocation, or in your case, lack of one. Does it, Mr. Montrose?"

"I differ, sir! I most emphatically disagree!"

"The way I see it, you both are cut from the same cloth. Lock them up, Barnabas. I'm tired of looking at them both."

"You promised me something," Theresa said softly and pushed back her matted hair. Her face, swollen, her eyes mere slits; she took one step closer toward the desk.

"Ah, indeed I did. Seeing how your hands are untied and his are tethered, anything can happen in a blink. Can't it…"

Theresa took another step forward, and Willham turned his head toward her. "What do you want, alley lurker? And who do you think you are to look at me with that contemptible scorn smeared across your homely face? Who do you think you are!?"

"The woman you left for dead, you son of a bitch." She pulled her arm back, and before Willham could react, she slammed her fist into his face.

Don't waste more time, son. None of us can count our days forward. Marry the woman." Rockingham spoke with his eyes shut, and his face, grey, had lost many of its lines and deep crevices. Martin grabbed the man's hand. "If you love her."

"I do."

"Then do it. Today."

"Today? But why today? This is not fitting of—"

"A wedding amidst a death watch? It seems to be the most suitable time. I want to leave this Earth knowing you are quite alright. I want to die happy."

"Then I will ask the lady." He got up without saying another word and then paused at the doorway. The morning light flowed in small river-like ribbons across the bed. Illuminated in each, particles of dust filtered down along them. The room was filled with a golden radiance that turned the otherwise austere room into something heavenly. He turned back to see that Rockingham had turned his head to the side, and he nodded as though to someone nearby. Rockingham saw that he noticed and turned his eyes slowly toward Martin.

"We all stand in the doorway as spirits, Martin. Who can say from which hallway we shall enter or depart?"

"I do not know anymore, father. I just know that I am."

"Do you?"

"Sir, I do not know what came before, and I do not know what comes after, having not seen it with my own eyes. But yes, I know that I am."

"Aren't we all just spirits crossing from that mysterious before toward the after, waiting to be born into one or the other?" Rockingham turned back toward the empty chair and smiled.

Martin closed the door and sought out Meredith whom he found sitting in the second parlor near the fire.

"Has he passed, Martin?" She stood and walked toward him.

"No. But he told me to ask that you marry me today. I realize it's sudden, but he seems to feel it is the best time, even as he lay near death. I'm sorry, but perhaps he is right. He said we cannot count our days forward…"

"Then we shall not try, and go on faith."

Barberry, who sat unnoticed by Martin in the corner of the room, lowered a book he had been reading, and laid it gently to the table near him. Martin swung his head around. "I love a good wedding." He raised the book up again, and from behind it, he said, "I saw Pastor O'Mara arrive not five minutes ago, to pray over Rockingham before he departs. How fortuitous, is that?" He turned a page and sighed.

There was very little ceremony to the marriage vows. Pastor spoke, prayed, and spoke some more. In attendance within Rockingham's room were Stephen, the doctor, Barberry, and James. Customary words were exchanged. It was a solemn affair, all things considered, and rather than a celebration following the marriage, all but Barberry, who had hauled Emily away to jail, stayed near to Rockingham, and waited.

He died at six PM that evening, holding his son's hand, a smile upon his face.

Daniel slept for most the day. At seven PM, he woke, glanced at the women who he presumed were sleeping on the floor, and lit a small candle. Looking again toward them, he reached for the water and drank all of what remained. He grimaced and wiped his hand across his mouth.

"I need more water. It has gone foul," he said aloud to himself. He placed the candle near the window so that he could see the contents of the bag that had previously contained bread and cheese. "Empty. In the morning I will go for more. We will eat well, we three," he said to the air. "Indeed we will. Because this is your last night, ladies. Tomorrow I take care of the problem and end you." He sat back down and found that a small bit of bread had rolled from the bag. He snatched it up to eat it. Miriam smiled at Hannah.

In a few moments, he complained of being seized with some manner of faintness, and then his eyes took on the color of two dead marbles. Clutching at his chest, he swore something under his breath and then flung himself about the room like a man gone mad.

Taking the opportunity they had waited patiently for, the women rose and fled from the room. Having given Daniel a literal taste of his own medicine, they found the passageway and emerged in the old parlor.

"You are a smart old hag, aren't you," Hannah said flatly.

"Yes, indeed I am."

They walked down the stairs and straight into the foyer where James stood, his mouth open, his eyes wide as they could go.

"Daniel is in the widows walk. Where is Martin?" Miriam asked and went straight for the kitchen where she knew a pistol was hidden.

"But...how?" James asked, following behind her. "And—Miss Hannah? Miriam? You are in terrible disarray. Are you sick? What has happened? You're hurt!" He spun Miriam around and bore his fingers into her meaty arm.

"Not now! Where is Martin?" Miriam asked.

"At the Lady Meredith's cottage. It is their wedding night!"

"What?" Hannah shrieked and grabbed at her filthy hair.

Miriam took the pistol and headed out the door toward the barn. But coming to where it had been, she stopped, dropped her hands to her sides, and looked back over her shoulder at James who had come toward her. Over his shoulder, she saw the black crepe on the doors and front windows.

"James?" Baffled, she shook her head. "Tell me all now!"

"Madam! Is this the time? With the murderous man in the walk and perhaps loose in the house as we stand here?"

"Now!"

"Good god, woman! Have it your way. Rockingham has died. He is the true father of Martin. The barn fell to arson's hand. Willham and Theresa are jailed, as is Emily, who it turns out is Daniel's sister, as confessed to Barberry. Stephen is in his room. I will have him ride out to Martin and Meredith right away."

"Good god, this place has gone utterly mad!"

Hannah lingered in the doorway and stepped back inside as James made his way past her. Her eyes wandered toward the hill and Blythe House beyond where her eyes could see. Her life had been spared via Miriam's plan. But Martin, her last resort, was married, and she could do nothing about it. She turned away and walked back into the house as Stephen, side-stepping her as though she was not there, ran out to the courtyard and grabbed Miriam up in a bear hug. He jumped atop the bay horse closest to him and rode in a gallop to Blythe House. As he sped away without a coat on his back, wet snow flung out around and behind him— the moon, bright like noon on the hill swathed the crest with silver light.

Surely, Hannah thought as she stood at the bottom of the stairs and looked up, Waverly Estate was not large enough for her and Martin any longer. That truth was the simplest of others. The conspirators, who were at that moment jailed, would waste no time in pointing a collective accusatory finger straight at her. All was lost. All.

She walked slowly back up the stairs and headed to her room, where she brushed as many tangles from her hair as she could. Then she dropped the hairbrush, which had pulled clumps of dead hair from her crusted head, to the dresser table. Sitting down at the mirror, she touched her swollen face and leaned in, seeing for the first time that the damage done to her lips and eyes could not be entirely repaired. Gone were her bright eyes. Her once perfect teeth, shattered. As though still gripped by the drugs' evil, trance-like spell, she applied bright rose-colored rouge to her black and blue cheeks. She removed her filthy dress, dropped it where she stood, and pulled on a pale lilac one that lay across her chair. She walked from the room and up the next flight of stairs toward Daniel.

Here are the letters." Meredith leaned across him from the bed where they lay and placed envelops to his bare chest. "There are beautiful sentiments within, my love. It may soothe you to know that she was very much loved."

The sound of Stephen bashing his fists to the door stopped Martin before he could respond. He shoved the letters into his coat pocket and leapt from the bed. "Stay here," he said, as he quickly pulled his clothing on. But she was behind him in an instant.

Stephen spoke before the door was fully open, and in one breath said, "Daniel is in the widows walk. Miriam and Hannah did some manner of something, I know not what to him while captive, and you must come now!" He did not wait for Martin but ran back to the horse and galloped back down the long hill.

Martin, seeing Meredith already dressed and at his side, sighed. "This is how it will be? You don't listen!" He did not bother to sit in order to pull on his boots and coat. Turning toward her again, he saw she had done the same thing. "Woman, no! Stay here!"

"I am not your dog. I don't obey as you'd like. You're wasting time. Let's go!" She ran out the door and climbed aboard a mare and Martin onto Isabella's back, and both rode hard toward Waverly Mansion.

Despite her infuriating way, despite her ill-timed expression of same; regardless of what he might face when finally at the doors of Waverly, he watched as she sped the horse away ahead of him. He took those moments to admire her strength, her courage, and yes, her long wheat hair flowing out behind her, haloed in the moonlight.

Ghost dance," Hannah whispered as she stood in the doorway of the widow's walk. "Just as Willham described he had witnessed when with the Indians."

She watched as Daniel waved his arms out and let loose with incomprehensible words strung together as unbroken chords of sound. He seemed to dance with an invisible, disincorporated soul, as he laughed wildly one moment, and in the next, he cried out for someone to take his hand. She did not feel sympathy for him, and so she simply stood there and watched, wondering if she, too, had behaved in that way. He stopped, turned toward her, and stared, as if he experienced a moment of lucidity, but then his eyes said he was seeing her for the first time in his life.

"Lady," he said, and reached his hand out. "Why have you stopped dancing with me?" He continued to move toward her, but she did not step away.

Whatever was to come, she did not care. As he came near to her, she felt his heavy breaths on her face, and not wanting to look into his wild eyes, she turned her face to stare at the candle near the window for a moment before she closed her eyes. He brushed past her, and she waited for the next blow of evil to be done to her. But he did not touch her. He continued to entreat someone behind her for a dance.

She turned slowly around and opened her eyes. A sight caught her breath in her throat and held it there. "Who are you?" She asked it flatly, but her tone did not relay the emotion that overtook the last of what she thought she knew about the world and those in it. She took one small step back. It did not answer.

"Lady, why are you not dancing? Do I not please you?" Daniel said and bowed before her, making a grand sweeping motion with his uninjured arm. He twirled again, and with wild flourishes, he spun across the small room—his arms and legs thrusting out side to side, his eyes fixed on the specter across the room.

Hannah gasped as she watched the dirty grey apparition ease past her, either ignoring her presence or not caring she was there at all, and it went toward Daniel who bowed grandly once again. Still bowed down, his eyes to the floor, he extended his hand and offered it. Hannah eased herself into the corner and could not do more than watch.

The grey being took his hand, and toe to toe with Daniel, it allowed him to twirl her slowly around and around until the window stopped them. It was then that she lifted one hand toward his face, and he shut his eyes. Her pale green dress trailed long behind her. Her eyes of the same color turned toward Hannah. The apparition smiled. Turning back toward Daniel, it spun its long, wheat-colored hair about his neck, the motion revealing a dark red line that encompassed her throat, ear to ear. Once her hair was bound securely about his neck, she pressed her lips to his face, and he sighed. Only then did she tighten her hair around his throat. He didn't seem to care as she pulled it harder round and around again as Daniel's face became as grey as her own. Hannah had seen enough.

"Stop." Hannah walked slowly, carefully, toward them. Whether out of fear or curiosity or a momentary desire to do something for someone else without thought or hope of personal gain, she did not know.

"Leave me be, lady," it whispered in a voice as vaporous as her flesh. It turned its attention back to Daniel, but Hannah was not dissuaded from stopping it all.

"No. This is wrong. I know who you are. I know it by the rope scars on your throat. Your name is Amelia."

"Shh. Do not speak my name," she said, frowning, "or they will come and take me away."

"To where?"

"To the place I cannot go. To the place where all things like me must be, but I cannot leave Waverly without—" Hannah did not hear if Amelia said more, as Martin, followed by Stephen and then James, barreled through the door.

"Don't." Hannah held her hand up and stopped the men from going near to them.

"Ah. Martin." Amelia, not loosening her hold on Daniel, smiled.

"What manner of demon are you!?" Martin shouted, and it caused Amelia to frown. He went to move forward, but Stephen grabbed at his arm.

"I am not a demon, Martin. I am simply Amelia, engaged in a dance with Daniel, who has done you all harm. Why are you so cruel, sir? Why?" When she wailed, there was no doubt that the wind they had heard for so many years was not wind at all—but the terrible moans let loose by lonely, love sick, Amelia.

"Daughter." James walked closer and reached his hand out. "Go away from this place. Find peace with your own."

"Father." She turned away as if feeling shame.

"I never believed this could be, but here you are, my only daughter, my love, my child." He reached closer to her, and when she opened her mouth, a scream came forth from her bruised throat that duplicated the screech of a mortally wounded creature. Hannah pushed her hands against her ears to stop from hearing the ghastly sound and she shut her eyes.

From behind Martin, Meredith emerged and walked past him. He thrust his arm out to stop her, but she shrugged him away.

"Sister. Let Daniel go. There is nothing to be solved by this. Let him go." Daniel opened his eyes, spied those around him, and laughed as Amelia leaned him against the broken window. The light from the moon filtered through her body as dust along a stream of light. The stars, bright, serene, and without care, framed their bodies in a delicate wash of silver.

"Shall I tell the secrets, sister?" Amelia asked, smiling unpleasantly. "Leave me to this, or I shall tell it all."

"Mind yourself, sister; there is something that comes after, even as you refuse it tonight and have avoided it for so many nights before. Do not make this world worse for the telling of what you think to do here tonight. Do not make it impossible for all of us that remain to hold good memories of you. For if you continue, the mention of your name will make us unhappy, and we will speak ill of you. Come away from the window and let Daniel go."

She loosened her grip, ever so slightly, and wailed again in her shrieking way that set their bones to ice. Taking one step back, she lowered her head and appeared ready to release him. James rushed forward and grabbed Daniel, tugging violently at his arms, dragging him away. But she would have none of it and took Daniel to her again.

"No!" Amelia screamed and wrapped her arm about her father's neck. Though he could not feel her touch, he was captured in her grip, unable to move. He raised a hand as Martin lunged forward. "Stop." James shook his head. "It's alright, Martin; it's alright." Amelia tilted her head back and laughed.

"Always for Martin—In life, I loved him. All I did was because of him. For my Martin, who never loved me. Even in this cold place of shadows you call death, I love him still. I don't want to hurt father. I want *her*." She stared intently at Hannah who had done her best to remain unobserved. But in a wicked flash of speed and resolve that showed itself faster than their eyes could trace, Amelia went straight for Hannah. Tugging her back with her to Daniel's side, she smiled. "Always for Martin. All for Martin." She grabbed Hannah around the neck. Daniel, clinging to Amelia like a lovesick child fell backward out through the window, the glass shattering into multitudes of fragments glinted bright by the stars.

"No!" Martin screamed and made straight for the window. Leaning out, he looked down and saw their bodies crumpled together, blood already pooling across the snow beneath the star-blazoned sky, surrounded by the shattered glass.

What will you do with me?" she asked him as they sat beneath the old maple at the top of the hill, oblivious to the falling snow and wind.

"Whatever I wish, my dear, Hannah. Whatever I wish."

Rene's laughter, caught up in the wind, carried down to Waverly Estate and to the second parlor where it met Martin's and Meredith's ears. They looked into each other's eyes and did not say a word. There was no need to. They knew what it was. Martin shrugged and dipped his eyes back to the book on his lap, and Meredith resumed playing on the piano, which sounded no more unless under her hands.

EPiLOGUE

"What became of them all, Lilly?" Brynn leaned forward and strained to see the woman's face through the murk of the candlelit room.

"I shall tell you, since no story is worthwhile unless it is completed...Willham Montrose was never found guilty for his crimes, simply because he died one night while waiting for his trial. Some said his heart gave out, but others disagreed. Meredith had her own thoughts regarding it, and they were confirmed via Officer Stern's statements detailing how a strange, dark-haired man with a French accent suddenly appeared within the jail but departed when chased via a path unknown and wholly illogical. Willham was found dead within the hour.

Theresa was released to a tuberculosis hospital where she lived one more year before dying. Some say she still visits the halls of Waverly Estate, manifesting herself through chilling cries, calling out Daniel's name.

The Civil War came, and during the first year of it, James passed away, followed that same year by Miriam. Both were buried in the Waverly's burial grounds near to Rockingham, as family. Upon Rockingham's stone were inscribed the words, *'Love each other, for we know not from which door we shall emerge.'*

As for Martin and Meredith...they lived to see many trials of faith and love. Stephen became a physician, and as he had hoped, he returned to become the town's doctor. He married and had children of his own. His descendants still live nearby, and each of the following generations have become doctors, and they stay on here, too."

"And Emily? What about her?"

"Emily was convicted of various small crimes related to Waverly and was sent away to an indigent's house where she died at the age of fifty three. By her own hand, some say, but I cannot say if this is true or a lie."

"But I must know. What about Amelia? She seemed so sad, so lost…"

Lilly hesitated and lowered her head before speaking. "Amelia walks these very rooms. To this day, you can still sometimes hear her when she wishes to make herself known. But she is quieter now. She takes a more human form when it pleases her or she fears she might frighten off the little company that comes to this place. She is better behaved now that she has made peace with Martin's choice—and now that they are all dead. Yet she is still grieved. She passes her time wandering about the grounds, and sometimes, for no apparent reason, she remains silent for many years. But all this is really a cautionary tale, lady. You must not stay here if you are faint of heart. Rene and Hannah are not to be trusted, even in their death! And others walk these halls, miss….Others, I have not told you about."

"It's a ghastly story in most ways! But it's just a story. No more."

"Indeed, it is all ghastly. And I would know that best of all."

"Why is that? Is this a hobby of yours, tracking family history?"

She smiled and rose smoothly from the chair. "How? Because I, miss, am Amelia."

Made in the
USA
Columbia, SC